The Fall Of A Warrior

J. L. Cook

Editing, typesetting and publishing by UK Book Publishing
www.ukbookpublishing.com

ISBN: 978-1-914195-31-0

Dedicated to Betty Cook, I couldn't have done this without your support.

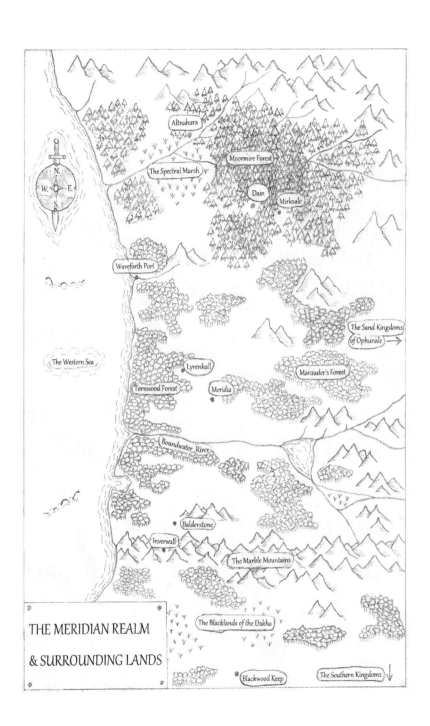

Prologue

I T FELT like an eternity as the ambassador from Meridia stared at the large doors ahead of him while he waited nervously for instructions. He remembered his family back home and with each passing second, wished he was with them. He was flanked either side by a guard, both of whom stared ahead, not acknowledging the northerner's presence. With his eyes transfixed on the door that would lead him to the great hall, Tomlor thought of the meeting that was to come.

He shuffled his feet and moved his tongue around his dry gums as he tried to remain calm. Swallowing loudly with the lack of saliva in his mouth, he fiddled slightly with the white cape that was draped over his narrow shoulders. Not being much of a fighter himself, he adjusted the respectable looking longsword strapped to his hip and tried his best to feel more confident. Attempting to puff out his chest with little to no success, Tomlor exhaled slowly under his breath. It had been the proudest day of his life when Queen Orellia had asked him to travel south and negotiate with Badrang, Lord of the Dakha. After the recent events, Tomlor was to make sure all the current treaties and agreements were to remain in place with the Blackland leader.

The envoy had done his utmost to memorise what he was going to say, but that had not stopped him from getting nervous. Tomlor knew Badrang had now united all of the Dakha tribes under his one banner. Although, he had still been shocked by the sheer number of soldiers stationed around Blackwood Keep. In recent months, Badrang had invaded and destroyed the Southern Kingdoms, but as far as Meridia was concerned, this had only been a matter of time. The Southern Kingdoms were a cruel people and had always been involved in needless wars with their raids and greedy expansion. It was only natural that the Dakha would eventually rise up and defend themselves.

It had been days since Tomlor's arrival at Blackwood Keep and he had been anxious ever since, but the Dakha had been considerate enough. He had been given comfortable quarters, rich foods and time enough to reflect on what he would say to Badrang. He was confident the Dakha Lord would understand the reasons to avoid war and how costly this could be to everyone involved. Tomlor reassured himself that the Meridians had always treated the Dakha Tribes with fairness, respect and prosperous trade. Tomlor knew Badrang was a valued friend and ally of the Meridian Realms.

As he continued to wait, Tomlor snuck a quick look at the guard on his left. The soldier was much shorter than the ambassador but looked vicious and carried a menacing looking spear. Foreign-looking symbols and emblems had been carved into the metal head of the weapon, making it look even more formidable. Tomlor looked at the skin of the Dakha soldier's arm, noticing the scars of battle etched all the way up to his shoulder. A light dusting of mud stuck to the clammy skin of the guard as he spat on the floor crudely. Just then, the soldier swiftly turned his head and stared back at the ambassador, an ugly smile painted on his dirty face. Tomlor was frightened by the confidence shown by the soldier, and quickly returned his gaze back to the door ahead.

While he waited, he tried to take his mind away from the current surroundings by counting the knots in the wooden door. He remembered what the Knightguards of Merdia had told him before he left the capital. He needed to succeed in this mission. Finally, the doors opened and he could leave the two guards at the entrance. Taking a deep breath and with one final adjustment of the sword on his hip, Tomlor marched inside with fake assertiveness. The great hall was lengthy and extravagantly grand. A long line of thick wooden columns supported a high ceiling, enveloped in darkness. There was a fire brazier at the base of each column, with the flames casting disfigured shadows on the walls around them. Half a dozen guards stood in the dimness along each partition, only slightly illuminated with each crackling of the brazier.

With his eyes set firmly ahead, Tomlor marched two dozen paces until he was standing at the base of a platform, upon which a great throne rested. The throne was made of the finest wood and rimmed with gold and other precious metals. Two large animal pelts were symmetrically draped across the backrest; one was a great bear and the other was a scarier looking animal with scales and horns that Tomlor did not recognise. Sitting on this extravagant throne sat Badrang, Warlord of the Dakha.

Badrang was not a big man by any means but he emanated power, and from where Tomlor stood he could sense the charismatic charm the warlord possessed. He was dressed in a dark-brown cloth tunic that was lined with red and gold thread. He had the deep-black hair of the Dakha, and sported a satanic beard that pointed downward from his chin. He smiled and looked friendly despite some of his grimmer features. With his casual poise, he waved his hand and invited the northern envoy to speak.

'I bring you word from Queen Orellia, beloved ruler of the Meridian Realm,' said Tomlor, as he nodded and bowed his head.

Slumping back comfortably on his throne, Badrang made another gesture with his hand for the sweating herald to continue. He looked happy enough and was content to let the Meridian ambassador speak.

'We respect and applaud your victory against the final city of the Southern Kingdoms. We hope that war is now behind your people and would like assurances that you will honour the existing treaties and trade agreements. Please kindly read this letter from my Queen. The seal is unbroken but I am told it includes a copy of the treaty.' Tomlor moved slowly but semi-assertively toward the seated warlord and handed him the scroll.

Badrang held out his hand gratefully. 'Thank you, this is greatly appreciated. Please help yourself to wine while I read these,' he said, and nodded towards the table on his left.

'Thank you,' replied Tomlor as he bowed again. He then shuffled out of the way and towards the candle-lit table. He poured himself a goblet of warm red wine and drank.

Meanwhile Badrang broke the seal of the scroll and began to read, his face showing no emotion as his eyes moved down the paper. Within minutes he had finished reading and beckoned Tomlor back to the throne.

The Dakha leader nodded at the ambassador before him. 'Firstly, Tomlor, I must apologise for keeping you waiting these last few days. As you can imagine I have been a very busy man recently. Secondly, I would like to thank you for the distance you have travelled to present this to me.' The black-haired warlord stood from his throne. 'Will you walk with me?'

'Certainly, my Lord.' Tomlor had not expected such a warm reception from the Dakha Lord. The recent stories in the Meridian Realm were that Badrang was losing his mind and cared only for routes to more power. Tomlor wondered who this soft-spoken, smiling leader was.

For the second time in the space of ten minutes, Tomlor began walking the length of the great hall, this time with powerful company. Badrang walked commandingly with his hands crossed behind his back, grasping his left wrist with this right palm.

'How long have you been in the service of Orellia?' asked Badrang.

Tomlor did not like to hear the name Orellia unless it followed the words Queen or Lady. 'Over fifteen years, my Lord.'

'It is good to see a loyal man. You are a dying breed. To take on such a mission, she must have a lot of faith in you, Tomlor.'

'Thank you, I will be sure to mention that to her when I return,' Tomlor replied jokingly; he had begun to feel more at ease with the Lord of the Dakha. He was not sure if he could attribute his relaxed nature to the mannerisms of Badrang or the warm wine coursing through his chest and softening his head.

'Ha-ha! That's the spirit. A leader needs to be reminded from time to time,' laughed Badrang.

Tomlor continued to be shocked by the informality of the southern warlord. His bare head was now bone dry, as if Badrang possessed the same qualities of a cool eastern wind.

Badrang continued to smile. 'When we first met, you congratulated me for my victory against the *final* city of the Southern Kingdoms.'

Tomlor could not help but notice the emphasis on the word "*final*" but did not interrupt.

Badrang continued. 'As you know, my lands have not had a leader for two centuries, and for those two hundred years, anarchy has reigned. The tribes would murder and steal from one another until the end of days. I put an end to this, but for distinct reasons.'

'My Lady was very pleased to hear the wars had ended.' Tomlor had been with the Queen when news was brought that the city of Kalmonsun, the last of the Southern Kingdoms, had been defeated by the Dakha Warlord.

Badrang nodded, again as if he had anticipated Tomlor's response. 'The Meridian Realms have always been good to us; this I cannot deny. You have never asked us for anything and left us to our business. We have honoured the agreements to date, and I have the utmost respect for *your* Queen. But she is not *my* Queen.' In one swift movement, from the back of his belt, Badrang produced a double-edged dagger and embedded the point deep into the middle of Tomlor's throat. He gazed sternly into the panicking eyes of the Meridian herald. 'This is my new offer to the Meridian Realm.'

Chapter 1

OFF THE western shores of the Meridian Realm a heavy fog persisted. The afternoon had not fulfilled the morning's promise. Beneath a dirty grey sky, layers of pale mist sat indifferent on a still sea. The slight swell of the water lapped against the starboard side of a large barnacle-encrusted ship.

A strong looking figure leaned over the barrier of the ship as it continued south. Two alert eyes staring out into the seemingly endless fog. After five days at sea the man had lost all patience for the slow progress. 'We will never catch them in this blasted fog,' he cursed with annoyance.

The Old Maid had seen too many winters and had outlived too many men. Built originally for cargo, she was not the first choice for the current mission. The group who had recently hired her had been desperate, and the Old Maid had been the only crew willing to take up the task.

'Be it the weather or the vessel, you will always find something to complain about, Roar,' replied a softer voice from behind.

Roar had never been a man to shy away from a war of words. He stepped back from the divide and turned to face his old comrade. 'While I'm at it, I haven't commented on this rabble of a crew *you* hired! The whole situation is awful. The Wolves of Glory were built for land, for mountains, for forests, not for the seas.'

The Wolves of Glory were a group of bounty-hunters who dedicated themselves to hunting the criminals of the Meridian

Realm. It had been ten years since their founding, and they had made a handsome amount of money during that time. Their group were wealthy; well armoured, well equipped and well paid. However, jobs were becoming scarce and the competition was growing fiercer amongst the other mercenary groups.

'How many times must we have this argument? To make this kind of money, you must spend this kind of money. We are paid killers, no denying that, and sometimes a hunter cannot choose his prey,' replied the other man.

'Rommel…' Roar replied, with his patience now wearing thin. 'That's all very well and good but this will all have been for nothing if we don't pick up our pace. We will have spent a small fortune hiring a run-down ship to catch nothing.'

'We will catch them!' snapped the usually calm Rommel.

'Sometimes the money just isn't worth the hassle. Our men do not suit being out here at sea. That said, most would rather be drinking ale back in Meridia the rest of their days,' replied the old Wolf, Roar.

Having no desire to ever expand the pack to this size, Roar thought to himself. He did not like half the men in the company and did not trust the other half. He had an uneasy feeling on the hired crew of the Old Maid – most of them had never seen combat, spending their whole lives at sea pulling lines and lifting freight. When the Wolves had arrived in the port of Waveforth to hire a vessel, the Old Maid was the only ship and crew willing to listen to offers. Others felt the mission was too dangerous. The Flaming Sails had raided and pillaged the west coast for years and were known the land and seas over as the most ruthless pirates the Realm had seen in centuries.

Since the closing of the southern trade routes a season back, work had been hard to come by for an old cargo boat like the Old Maid. An easily convinced Captain was a sweet sight for Roar and Rommel, who were beginning to feel The Flaming Sails were out of their reach. "You worry about the sailing and we will worry about the fighting" – was enough to persuade the coin-starved Skipper of the ancient ship.

The two middle-aged commanders stood on the deck staring at one another as the damp air surrounded them. Eventually Rommel turned his head to the side. 'You know we must pay the men. I could count on one hand the men that would stick around if we run out of coin. The group only know fighting. Where would they go? Of those who have left our group, how many have become the men we hunt?' Rommel paused and pressed his teeth together tightly. 'I cannot allow the same thing to happen again…'

Roar could see the distress in his comrade's eyes, and this softened him. 'I admit we have not managed things like we should have in the past, but you must remember, we hired these men knowing that as soon as the ale, women and gold run out, they will too.'

'We bought these men to save them from themselves. To serve a purpose. Yes, the nobles and knights of the Realm may not approve of our methods, but we bring evil men to justice. Most of our group would have ended up as criminals had it not…'

Rommel was interrupted by two other members of the Wolves. Both men were having an afternoon stroll across the deck. One of them was clearly trying to distract himself from sea-sickness with huge breaths of fresh air.

'Afternoon, Commanders,' he said, as he nodded at Rommel, plainly afraid to catch eyes with the gruffer Roar.

'Good afternoon,' replied Rommel in his smooth voice.

There was no response from Roar.

When the two men were out of earshot, Rommel continued. 'What happened to the Roar I met fifteen years ago? The man who wanted to be the best? The man who wanted to help the Realm? All I see now is a tired, cold and, dare I say, broken Roar.'

Anger flashed through Roar's eyes. 'Be careful what you say,

Rommel. You are the only man I would dare let speak to me like that. I won't allow it again. Do you understand?'

'I understand,' replied Rommel. He then went silent for a moment; he ran his fingers through his grey tinted beard. He pondered saying something he had wanted to say for the last three seasons. 'Let's make this our last run. After we take down these corsairs, we go it alone? Like the old days?'

'But what of the men?' asked Roar.

'If we ever had a man to replace us as leader, it is Torquil. He is strong, quick, charismatic and not a day over twenty. So, there is even room for improvement. You know yourself he doesn't share our weaknesses. He will do right by the group and the money will keep flowing for these men,' replied Rommel.

'Torquil? Granted the man is skilled with those two swords of his and he seems to have a good head on his shoulders, but can the man lead?' asked Roar.

Rommel laughed a little. 'I see a leader in him, yes. He reminds me of you.'

Roar supressed a laugh of his own and began massaging the back of his broad neck. Before he could say another word, The Old Maid jolted under a heavy thud and gave a large knee-shaking shudder, as if she had just run ashore. They were three miles out from land.

Chapter 2

A HEAVY SUN beat down on the capital city Meridia. The weather had been the only shining light on such dark times. War in the Realms had awoken after a long slumber. Within a single season, Badrang's forces had reached just south of the Marble Mountains, nature's natural border dividing the Meridian Realm from the Dakha to the South. In the red stone courtroom adjacent to White Castle, Sir Oakheart and the rest of the Queen's council listened as Wease, a local potion seller, persisted with his lies.

'I am no traitor,' Wease stuttered. 'I have lived in Meridia for almost three winters; this city is my home. Its occupants are my friends, my family!'

'Wease, you must explain why, when we searched your home, we found the following...' Sir Oakheart stretched open a scroll and began to list the incriminating items. 'One map detailing inner city defences, one map detailing the city's underground drainage systems, one map detailing caravan supply lines including times of arrivals and departures...'

Wease shifted uncomfortably in his seat.

'Two vials of waspbane poison, a banned substance. One chain of newly cut keys, and thirty gold coins within a leather duffle.' Oakheart peered up from the paper. 'Have I missed anything?'

'Sir, those items are not mine,' said Wease, before turning his eyes to Queen Orellia, sat in the stands on his left. 'My Lady, you must believe me.'

The Queen sat unmoved.

'Then what were they doing in your home? You have no family, few friends and those who admit to knowing you have stated they have never entered your premise.' As he spoke, Oakheart sat back in his seat. 'With all that has transpired in recent months, you must realise we have come to our conclusion. Let me ask you this, Wease, how long were you expected to last? Even if Badrang took Inverwall to the south and passed through the Marble Mountains, it would be months before you were of any use to him?'

Wease sat in silence, admitting defeat. His eyes were fixed upon the broad shoulders of Sir Oakheart. The Knightguard was over six foot, with a clean shaven, chiselled jaw. His brown hair neatly pulled back, with a few small strands dividing his forehead at the front.

The traitor sneered and with slanted eyes turned to the surrounding council. 'You will all be dead by this winter. My Lord Badrang will be here within a year; Inverwall will not hold. You all know this to be true!?'

Sir Oakheart stood before the murmurs developing within the council could breed even more. 'Guards, take this traitor to the cells. Wease, you will be hung at dawn.'

The Knightguard said no more as the former potion salesman was lifted by each arm and dragged from the room, cursing all Meridian life.

The rest of the council disbanded from the rows of wooden benches that were flanking the courtroom, with Queen Orellia being the last to stand. Sir Oakheart made his way round towards her, his white cape flowing behind him.

Beside the Queen, Sir Blake, another Knightguard, stood and nodded towards Sir Oakheart as he approached. 'Congratulations, Commander, today you brought punishment to a man who would have sought to damage these lands.' Sir Blake then bowed to the Queen. 'I must take my leave, My Lady, I will see you at the meeting tonight.'

Although the Queen had recently celebrated her fortieth birthday her beauty had not diminished. She held the poise and grace of a woman half her age and the wisdom of a woman double it. Her long blonde hair cascaded down her back to the top of her slender hips. 'Sir Oakheart, you have done this city a great service. It is good we have condemned such a traitor.'

'Today, we were lucky, My Lady.' Sir Oakheart bent his right arm to allow the queen to interlock her left and they began to walk. 'Of all the raids we have conducted these past few weeks, this is our first success, and I'm afraid there are plenty more rats in this farmhouse.' The Queen nodded as they reached the steps that would take them up to the west wing of White Castle. 'Badrang has not yet commenced his assault on Inverwall. We must take action to prevent our last defence to the south from falling.'

'What would *you* have me do, Oakheart? The rest of my council are too old or too weak to suggest action that does not line their own pockets. We have known each other since we were children; I trust you more than anyone in this world. What must I do?'

'The Inverwall garrison is unorganised. I know your relationship with Steward Rhaneth has been fragile at best, and I cannot see him suffering much loss before handing Badrang the victory. Inverwall is our shield, My Lady, but a shield is only as strong as the arm that carries it.'

'Oakheart, you know Inverwall will not hold. We do not have the forces to repel Badrang there.' As she spoke, the Queen's emotions were finally beginning to get the better of her.

Sir Oakheart was of the same opinion. Inverwall was set in the middle of two large unpassable mountains, stretching from the far east to the coast on the west. It was the only option for an army to travel into the Meridian Realms from the south. There were smaller passages, but with an army fifty thousand strong, it would take years. Over the past century Inverwall had expanded out of the pass and into the southern fields, becoming a city in place of the fort it once was. Farms, mills, traders, houses, women, children. Oakheart knew each of these were a knife to the belly of the defences. The fort itself would be easier to defend, its high walls stretching from one mountain cliff to another. Anyone invading from the south knew the only way through the Marble Mountains was through Inverwall.

'My Lady, I will go to Inverwall,' said Sir Oakheart. He watched as the Queen closed her eyes with silent pain. 'I will take charge of the city's defences and have the refugees sent north with a platoon of the local soldiers. I will take four of my Knightguard companions and two hundred of our Meridian defenders. If we leave tomorrow, we should have a few weeks to strengthen before Badrang hits.'

They were halfway up the stairway, when the Queen nodded. 'You are right and we can finalise these plans tonight with the council.'

'Thank you, My Lady.' Sir Oakheart released his Queen's arm, kissed her hand and descended back down the steps to the court.

Queen Orellia ascended the rest of the stairs alone, tears streaming from her face. 'My loyal advisor, my brave Knightguard...' she muttered under her breath. 'My darling Oakheart.'

Chapter 3

THE WHOLE deck shook violently, creating an earthquake-like effect for all those on-board. The vessel creaked and moaned until calmness eventually return and the deck steadied. No one knew what had happened and panic had instantaneously set in. What seemed like everyone aboard The Old Maid was now on the main deck making their way port-side to where some commotion was continuing.

'He fell overboard, Commander! Just after we had walked past you two, we made our way over here to have a smoke,' Geddes said as he felt his voice break with shock. 'I can't remember what came first, the noise or the shake, but he was overboard before I could grab him.'

'He must still be out there,' said Roar while ignoring the gathering crowd. He made his way towards the barrier and over the side. 'Halbert?' he shouted, before waiting for a reply that did not come. 'In Amundsen's name, will you lot keep quiet! If he is out there drowning, how will we hear him?' He called out again, this time louder. The water remained deathly still, taunting the old Wolf.

By the eighth, ninth, maybe even tenth shout, Roar turned back to his comrades. 'The boy must have drowned. He is lost.'

'He can't have drowned, Commander. Halbert was the strongest swimmer in our company,' said Geddes.

Rommel was quick to add, 'Not only that, the sea is as calm she can be.'

'Then what do you think has happened to him? He could have gone under the boat and been trapped? Maybe hit his head on the way down?' suggested Roar, not believing his own words as they were spoken. 'It seems the boy is gone anyway.' Roar then stepped down from the railing and stood face to face with a clearly upset Geddes. He almost wanted to give the younger Wolf a pat on the shoulder, but instead he stormed past towards the stairs.

With Roar making his way down below deck, Rommel resumed command of the Wolves of Glory. 'I want four groups of two. Take station at each quarter of the ship and call for Halbert at ten second intervals.' I want you to report down to us in fifteen minutes with any form of news.' Rommel was halfway towards the steps when he turned back to his men. 'And for the love of Azmara keep your wits about you.'

Sitting at a table on the second deck, Roar was sharpening his longsword with a whetstone. The steel was immaculate, casting a perfectly deformed reflection of its owner. He said nothing as his partner entered the room.

'What in the name of Sarpen caused that?' asked Rommel.

Roar did not break eye-contact with his sword as he replied. 'I don't know, but we must be over two miles out from land. So, you can rule out touching the bottom.'

'I don't think I need to ask you why you are sharpening that.' Rommel nodded towards the sword gripped in Roar's hands. 'Say we are facing some kind of sea monster, what do you think a longsword is going to do?'

'It will make me feel better. Always feel stronger with a bit of steel on the end of my arm. Plus, might not get another chance to sharpen her before we catch up with these corsairs.'

It was then, another loud thud came from the depths. Both men knew it came from underwater this time. The vessel tilted forward, knocking both of them to the hard deck. Wasting no time, they leapt to their feet and dashed towards the stairs.

By the time they reached the top, chaos was running wild. The Wolves of Glory were strong warriors on land, but at sea they panicked like frightened children. Relentless waves crashed into the side of the vessel as horror-filled screams echoed in the air.

The main mast of the ship began to creak, twist and eventually snap. The top three quarters came crashing down hard onto the top deck.

Avoiding the cascading timber, Rommel turned to Roar and shouted. 'We need to get off this ship, we can't fight this enemy.'

Roar nodded and scanned the surrounding area.

As Rommel tried to keep his balance, he turned and came face to face with young Torquil. 'Tell the men, we need to get as many floating objects as possible overboard; barrels, crates, doors, anything.' He pointed towards the east and continued shouting orders, cold water slapping him in the face. 'I want it all thrown over that side.'

Minutes went by; those who weren't on the floor were trying to keep stable. Those who could keep their balance were throwing timber over the port-side railing. Then it happened: a huge set of lizard-like claws landed heavily on the starboard side of the deck and began to pull. The grotesque nails dug into the wood, while the webbed claws gripped at the vessel.

'It's a Sea Scale!' someone from the front of the ship called out.

As the pressure built, the vessel began to lean towards the uninvited intruder from the deep. The creature tugged with monstrous strength and its horrifying moan resonated from the depths below the water.

'Everyone overboard! Now!' bellowed Rommel at the top of his voice.

Torquil grabbed the nearest man and threw him over the east side, then another and another, until there was no one else. He,

Roar and Rommel then leapt from the doomed ship just in time. The hull split down the middle, spilling out cargo and crew like guts from an opened carcass.

Seconds, maybe even minutes later, Rommel raised his head out of the sea. He felt the merciless water weight of his clothes wrap around him. Even naked he had never been a strong swimmer but between his heavy leather boots and the sword around his waist, he was going to drown. Rommel needed someone to help him.

Amongst the floating wreckage Torquil had found two half-filled barrels that were tied at the middle with a strongly weaved rope. 'Commander! I'm coming for you!' he shouted as he beat and kicked out at the water, making his way towards the back of his struggling leader. He then reached out and grabbed the shoulder and pulled his old Wolf back towards him. 'Here, grab the rope. It will stop you from going under.'

'Where is Rommel?' shouted Roar as his hands fumbled at the barrels.

Chapter 4

'I can't give you any more, sir,' pleaded a soft voice. In the far north, three days' travel from the city of Dain and on the outskirts of the village Mirkvale, a woodsman and his boy lived. It was a humble cottage flanked by a large woodworking shed, used mostly for storage. The cottage itself was moss-eaten and meagre, but it was homely in its own way.

The woodsman had never refused to pay his tax in the past, but with each passing visit the guards would increase their demands. He had never been a hunter and could never master the art of fishing. He needed the money for food and nothing else.

'I only have five bronze coins left,' he explained exasperatedly.

Although a large strong man, the woodsman had not acquired his physique from fighting. The only combat he had ever known was his daily wrestling matches with logs, planks and a saw blade. 'It's just me and the boy here. We need the money for food, it will be a struggle enough already. Please show us mercy. I promise I will make up for the overdue amount next year.'

'Oh really? And where is this boy?' the smaller of the two guards snarled. 'You know the rules, tree-man, if you can't pay, it's to the gallows with you!' he said as his hand crept towards the shortsword on his belt. 'These are the orders of Duke Delgath, Warden of Dain.'

'Please don't hurt him!' called out a young voice from behind a half-closed shed door. The voice ran from his hiding place towards his father and leapt into the safety of his opened arms. 'Please,

Father, just don't let them hurt you again.'

'Sirs, I beg you. We will die if you take this money,' pleaded the woodsman.

'Well...' the larger of the guards interrupted, his eyes now fixed on the boy. 'If you don't have the money, the Duke is always looking for new recruits!' He took a step forward.

Before he could get any closer two quick-fire whistles sounded from behind. Caught by surprise, the guards both turned and could see a lone figure standing in the middle of the dirt path. The man was tall, with shoulder-length brown hair. He was slender yet looked strong. Unkempt yet looked handsome. He wore a light brown leather jerkin over a cream-coloured laced shirt. On his back rested a sheathed longsword, under-which his dark green cape cascaded down to the top of his brown leather boots. He carried a walking staff that came up to just above his shoulder.

With a suave voice, the mysterious man spoke for the first time and confronted the larger of the two dumbstruck guards. 'Firstly, I would like you to step away from the two folk you seem to be harassing...'

The guards looked at one another, both speechless at the insolence shown by the stranger.

'Good, I seem to have your attention. Secondly, I would like you both to unbuckle your sword belts and toss them into that ditch over there.' As he spoke, the loner beckoned his staff towards a small stream on his right.

'Who do you think you are talking to!?' shouted the smaller guard, finally snapping out of his confusion. He turned to his comrade and spoke. 'Belrus, if the boy or his father moves, kill them both!' He then took a step towards the wanderer. 'Under the power granted to me as a member of the Duke's guard, I am placing you under arrest!'

The stranger stood unmoved with a smile, confidence radiating from his body language.

'Don't try to run, you are coming with us,' added the guard.

'What if I don't run but refuse to come along?' replied the stranger.

'Then we kill you,' said the guard bluntly.

'What if I don't let you do that either?' The wanderer then took up an obvious fighting stance with his staff set across his body, arms and legs slightly bent.

The first guard wasted no time; ripping his sword from its sheath, he ran towards his prey screaming maniacally.

In one simple movement the lone warrior parried the first clumsy blow and hooked the leg of the rushing guard. Taking a step back he watched as his opponent tumbled to the ground clumsily. The wanderer then regained his stance, his weight spread evenly between both legs, waiting for another attack.

The guard was up in seconds and charged again wildly. He swung his sword multiple times in a crude fashion. 'Stay still!' he shouted after the fourth unsuccessful swing of his sword.

The wanderer ducked, weaved, bobbed and stepped until the swings began to tire. His cape swept the dusty floor with his graceful footwork and movement. One well timed hit to the head was all it took to send the guard falling again; this time he would not be getting up.

After seeing his partner hit the floor, Belrus, the larger guard, drew his sword and entered the fray. He was stronger and surprisingly quicker than his other half. With one downward chop from his blade he split the wanderer's staff in two.

Swiftly moving back to avoid the blade's next strike, the young wanderer tossed the two broken halves of wood aside. He then shrugged his shoulders and readied himself for the next attack, but still did not reach for the sword strung across his back.

This angered Belrus. 'What are you doing, you fool! Go for your sword!'

'That thing?' replied the smiling stranger, tilting his head towards the pommel of the blade near his right ear. 'No need.'

An infuriated Belrus lunged forward, his two hands grasping the hilt of his sword. This was the only chance the wanderer needed. Firstly, he dodged the swipe with relative ease. Secondly, he grabbed at the handle of the guard's sword with his left hand. Finally, he created a fist with his right hand and dealt one heavy counterpunch.

Belrus staggered a moment and loosened the grip on his sword, he had lost. He felt the young stranger push him and hook his leg at the same time. In a heap he landed on his back, sword no longer in his hands. Belrus breathed heavily as he felt the tip of his own blade rest against the centre of his throat.

The wanderer spoke calmly as he pinned the guard down. 'Collect your friend, get on your horses and leave here. I will not feel the need to report this to your superiors should you promise to never come here again.'

Belrus looked up at his enemy with burning contempt; he knew their bluff had been called. They had no real authority. The Duke was a dying man and the Grandcaptain of Dain had no care for what went on in the fringe villages. With blood trickling down his chin from a burst lip, he answered, 'We will go.'

Minutes later a groggy Belrus loaded his newly conscious comrade onto a horse. He then mounted his own steed and turned away from the others. Neither guard spoke nor looked back as they left via the west road.

The young stranger strode over to where his broken staff lay. He bent down and inspected the wood, cursing under his breath. He could feel the eyes of the woodsman behind him.

'Sir, I wish I had the means to repay what you have done for us. Will you have supper with me and the boy?' asked the large woodcutter. He was a little intimidated by this wandering do-gooder but felt it right to offer.

The lone fighter looked to the sky, through the trees, where he could see rain clouds approaching. He had only recently dried out from two hard days in storm and didn't fancy another drenching. 'Yes, that would be appreciated.'

'Do you have a name?' the woodsman asked, as they walked towards the door of his meagre cottage, trying their best to reach the entrance before the rain started.

As they walked, dried leaves crunching underfoot, the wanderer thought a moment and gave his answer. 'Leif... You can call me Leif.'

Chapter 5

I T HAD not been Sir Oakheart's intention to witness the execution. It just so happened that the hanging was taking place at the gallows in the square adjacent to the south gate. He rode at the head of the column, flanked by the other four departing Knightguards. Behind them marched an army of one hundred and fifty Meridian fighters, each carrying a spear in one hand and a shield in the other. During the last council meeting it was *agreed* that the number travelling to Inverwall would be cut by fifty men.

Sir Talon was first to break the silence amongst the knights. 'This has been some morning for the townsfolk; first the public execution of a traitor, and now a good portion of the city's defences riding out through the gate. What must they be thinking?'

Nodding with agreement, Sir Oakheart continued to ride towards the open gates. Out of his fourteen Knightguard companions, these were the best he could have picked. They were skilled in combat, schooled deeply in battle strategies and each he knew were willing to give their life for the Realms. If the choice had been his, he would have left Meridia with the knowledge Sir Nolan, Sir Talon or Sir Lenath would be in charge of her defences. Instead, Sir Blake was left with the command, much to Oakheart's annoyance. The Knightguard Commander quickly pushed these doubts from his mind and proceeded through the great iron framed gate.

Men, women and children threw flowers into the path of the

knights. Sir Oakheart was again lost in thoughts: *Are we really riding to our doom? Of course we are, and how do these people reward us for our sacrifice – by throwing flowers at the feet of our horses? They know nothing of what we ride against. They think we will return heroes, with word of victory and the decapitated head of Badrang the Dakha Butcher.* Oakheart jerked back from the dark reaches of his mind.

They had been marching for twenty minutes before they cleared the final building of Meridia's outer district. The sun blazed stronger than it had the day before or even the day before that. Oakheart thanked the gods they had decided to forego their plate armour for the march. Instead they each wore a white jerkin emblazoned with the Orellia family horse. Their capes draped down, shading the hind quarters of the beasts carrying them to their almost certain demise.

'What a heat, Oakheart!' claimed Sir Talon. Tradition dictated, the Knightguards were to call one another by name, no need for the "Sir" – as they were all equal within the company, even if Oakheart was leader. 'If I'd have known this would be the weather, I might not have been so quick to volunteer.' Talon had been the first to accept this suicide mission. Five years Oakheart's junior, he would be celebrating his thirtieth birthday on the road in two days' time. He was brave, strong and could only be matched by a few Knightguards in a duel.

'Are you saying you would have let a bit of sun put you off the idea of killing some Dakha?' laughed Sir Lenath. During the council meeting the previous evening, it had been *agreed* that Sir Lenath would take Sir Blake's place on this mission. Sir Lenath was a huge man, and the only Knightguard not to carry a sword. Instead he sported a double-edged battle-axe, which he slung across his back menacingly. Over the years he had gained a little weight to his midriff but that did not stop him from being one of the most dangerous fighters in the Realm.

'Hmm, well when you put it like that, I guess a little sun isn't so bad,' Sir Talon replied.

'You pups complaining about the sun, makes me laugh,' Sir Nolan interrupted. 'Would you rather rain? Or snow? Or thunder? We have a long journey ahead of us, so let's pray the sun is our biggest worry.' Sir Nolan was the oldest of the group, he was in his late fifties and did not let the younger members forget it. He had passed up the chance to be Knightguard Commander year after year until Oakheart finally took the position. Sir Nolan had always seemed to like respect without the added responsibility of being Commander. His laziness seemed to coincide naturally with his growing age.

'Easy, old boy, only a minute out of the city and you are calling us pups. Just remember, if you insult us, who is going to be rubbing mixture into your tired old joints at night!?' Sir Shale laughed. He was the smallest and lightest of the group. He was kinder than most, and on his day would give even Oakheart a hard fight with his tricky fighting style. He did not care greatly for the traditions of a knight and spent most of his time amongst the smallfolk of Meridia, conversing and laughing in *The Laughing Prince Inn* or fishing in *The Pond of Reflection*.

'Keep laughing, pup, and you will have the flat of my blade across your backside,' replied Sir Nolan with laughter in his voice.

'Quiet.' Oakheart turned his head to face the older Sir Nolan. 'Depending on their hearing, the soldiers behind you will start spreading word that the Knightguard are nothing but a bunch of mercenaries, who can't stand one another. We all like a laugh, but with these men marching to almost certain doom, I would rather them not see us make a joke of it.' He turned back in his saddle and pulled a few strides ahead. 'Talon, come with me.'

Sir Talon pulled ahead and caught up with the thought-riddled

Oakheart. 'So are we to discuss Inverwall? I thought we went over everything at the council already?' Of the Knightguards, only Oakheart and Blake were usually permitted attendance at the weekly council meetings. An exception was made for Sir Talon the evening prior.

'Talon, what I am going to say will not sound good but you must hear me out.'

Talon gave a thoughtful nod and Oakheart continued. 'Last night at the council, I finally made judgement on something I have feared for months. When I suggested that Blake would be coming with us, he immediately declined.'

Talon nodded again, signalling his full attention.

'When you and the three behind us were asked, they accepted with no hesitation.'

'Are you saying Blake is a coward?' asked Sir Talon.

'I'm saying he is a traitor!' replied Sir Oakheart.

Talon looked stunned but did not rush to the aid of Sir Blake. 'But why did you leave him with the Queen? If he is a traitor, surely he will seek to do her harm? You had the authority to *make* him come with us.'

'I thought the same thing, Talon, but would Blake make a move with Badrang still to the south of Inverwall? Would he risk capture and execution at the hands of our brothers? And at this moment, Blake could do a lot more damage in Inverwall than in Meridia.'

Sir Oakheart waited a moment for his companion to process this new information before asking anything else. He could see his comrade was pondering and wanted to give him enough time to think logically. 'What are your thoughts, Talon?'

It took Talon a few seconds before he replied. 'I agree with you. It all makes sense to me now. The man has always been an outsider. He has no friends within our order; I know for a fact Locke and Canmore can't stand him. Can't think of anyone within the city that likes the man. Unless you count some of those conceited nobles he likes to rub shoulders with. So, what are you wanting to do about him?'

'Nothing, it is not him I want to talk to you about. You were right the first time; we are still to discuss Inverwall. The plans I outlined at the council yesterday are not my true intentions,' admitted Oakheart.

.

Chapter 6

THE WOODSMAN'S name was Hilvard and he had lived alone with his son ever since his wife had died giving birth. Much like the exterior, the interior of his cottage was plain and measly. A warm stone fireplace crackled violently, breaking up the sound of the rain hammering against the thatched roof. Dotted around the cottage were small leaks where the water would drip through. The cottage was obviously built a long time ago and it looked like it needed some maintenance or would soon collapse.

'More stew, Leif?' asked Hilvard, while pushing a ladle into the thin soup-like mixture.

'I've had my fill, friend,' Leif replied. If he was being honest, he could have had another three bowls of the water that tasted like stew, but it had not taken him long to realise the extent of the woodsman's poverty. 'With this rain, I would prefer not to sleep in the wild if I can avoid it. Would I be able to trouble you for a space on your floor? I promise I will be gone as soon as the weather improves.'

Hilvard suddenly felt embarrassment and was ashamed he had not offered this earlier. 'Of course, of course! By all means, Leif. It's not very comfortable but I hand-carved that armchair over there by the fire. It might give you a better sleep than the hard floor.'

'Thank you, Hilvard, you are a very hospitable man,' replied Leif, grateful for the offer.

Although darkening, the small cottage was proving a nice warm refuge from the cold rain outside. Small, overused candles burned on the table and above the fireplace, giving little to no lighting. As Leif reached over for his cup of water, he heard the woodsman's son speak.

'What's that around your neck?' The boy pointed to a small rune necklace resting on Leif's partially exposed chest. 'What do the markings mean?'

'Idris, mind your manners! We do not ask questions like that!' Hilvard said assertively, his face showing a mixture of sternness and embarrassment.

'It's quite alright. I have no problem with questions. Although I was hoping one of you could tell me what it is. The necklace and sword belonged to my father, I never met him.' Leif smiled as he answered. He had never set foot in these lands and was hoping these Realms would give him the answers he sought.

'That's like me and my mum. She died giving birth to me,' Idris said emotionlessly; this was clearly something he had become desensitised to.

Hilvard coughed as he looked at the rune from a distance. 'Can't say I know anything about that, I'm afraid. Your best bet is in town.'

Leif did not linger on the subject any longer. 'Well I am on my way to Dain. How much further am I to travel? I seem to remember the guards mentioning it.' He tucked the rune necklace back into his jerkin, out of sight. 'It can't be far?'

'No, it's not far at all. It is just over a day's journey west of here. Would take you less if you don't stop for camp. If I could, I would take you there myself, but I have so much work to do. I can point you in the right direction; give you some supplies and a blanket or two?' said Hilvard before he was cut-off.

'Just the directions will be fine,' said Leif, smiling at the generosity of the man he barely knew. 'Hilvard, you are a good man.' Leif was beginning to tire, clearly feeling the lack of sleep the night before. 'Would you mind if I rested? It will be an early rise for me tomorrow.'

'Certainly,' said Hilvard, before standing from the table. 'Idris, say goodnight to Leif!'

'Goodnight Leif!' said Idris, rubbing sleep from his own eyes.

'Goodnight!' Leif replied kindly.

Leif slept a long five hours and woke before dawn could crack. He gathered his possessions and left the cottage well before the woodsman and his boy could wake. The air was cold and damp, and he could see his breath on the wind. He turned onto the western path and began the day's walk to Dain.

The young wanderer had been travelling for two hours before he could see the first beam of light peeking through the trees. Leif began to think to himself: *Will I find answers here in the Meridian Realms? He must have come from somewhere? I have three major cities to search in these lands – Dain, Meridia and Inverwall, not to mention all the smaller towns and villages.* He had also heard rumours of a monastery to the far north at the base of a snowy mountain. He looked down at his chest where the necklace was out again, almost mocking him. The carving illustrated three vertical lines with one diagonal through the middle, from bottom right to top left.

Leif felt it was time for breakfast when he stopped and dived into his leather duffle. Yesterday he had two half rotten apples, probably fully rotted by now, and a stale loaf. When he opened the bag and felt its contents, Leif could not contain his smile. He tipped the bag and out poured four new apples, one fresh loaf of bread and a tasty looking dried fish. With the food laid out in front of him, Leif spoke aloud to himself. 'Thank you again, Hilvard.'

Leif pulled apart the last of his stale loaf and began to eat. At the same time, he slipped his hip knife from its sheath and sliced one of the new apples into quarters. He ate for five minutes and listened to the birds sing their morning song.

It was now dawn back at the cottage and Hilvard woke. He stumbled through to the open kitchen where he could see the dying embers of the fire. Leif had left; he was sad but had expected as much. He made his way towards a pot he would use to boil some water. As he grasped the cast iron handle something glittered in his eye. The sun bounced off his kitchen table and blinded him for half a second. He rubbed his eyes and walked towards the light. He could not understand what he saw. He rubbed his eyes again, this time in disbelief, hoping it was not some cruel dream. Three gold coins, more money than he had ever made in his lifetime, lay stacked on the surface. A note adjacent read:

"Thanks for the directions".

Chapter 7

I T HAD taken the rest of the day for the survivors to reach the western shores of the Meridian Realms. The air was clean and warm, and the sound of sea birds echoed through their ears. The waves lapped back and forth from the sand as the group clawed themselves away from the perilous water.

Roar threw himself against the wet bank with exhaustion. He was conscious but could hardly move. 'We will rest here an hour.' He breathed heavily on his back, looking at the darkening sky. 'I want no fires. Huddle together to keep warm. If you're feeling up to it, you can get started on a camp. Again, no fires.'

Of the thirty men who were counted when they first regrouped at sea, only eighteen men had made it to shore. Those who were not taken by the creature from the deep had given up to exhaustion and drowned.

Torquil sat up, one short sword missing from the two sheaths on his back. Using all his remaining energy he withdrew his single sword and clutched the blade in his arms. He looked to his left and saw a sleeping Roar. He then looked to his right and saw the rest of the survivors. This was the heaviest loss The Wolves of Glory had ever suffered.

He glanced back out to sea, hoping to watch Rommel emerge. Exhaustion finally defeated him, and he collapsed back onto his sand mattress.

Roar was first to wake. He looked at the moon high in the sky and realised they had slept for too long. 'Everyone, on your feet,' he shouted.

Most of the men were quick to obey. Others decided to ignore the command. Two were dead.

'I want you all off the sand and up there. Strip off your wet clothes and start a fire,' Roar ordered.

'Thought you said no fires?' said one of the crew from The Old Maid.

Roar wheeled around with an angry scowl painted on his face. He would never have suffered such an insolent comment from one of his men; the crew member would be no different. He snarled with authority and pointed his finger. 'Is your Captain still alive?'

There was no answer from the crew member.

'Then you take orders from me, so get up that bank and gather some wood for the fire.'

There was a lot of dry dead wood just beyond the treeline, allowing them to build a large body-warming fire. Roar had made the conscious decision that a fire must be made. Better to be spotted by hostiles, than killed by the cold. As he watched the flames, he cast his mind to Rommel. Thinking of his old friend saddened him. They had argued a lot during the last few years together but in their prime they were a formidable partnership. Looking back, he understood he was getting grumpier with age and Rommel had only ever tried to help him with that. Rommel had been like a brother to him.

Roar had already decided this would be his last action as leader of The Wolves of Glory. He would get these men to civilisation and leave them from there. As the night thickened, he could feel his eyes beginning to drop and he blinked slowly. He blinked slower again, and again until he was fast asleep and *unaware*.

The first thing Roar did when he woke was spit on the grass to his side while rubbing his eyes open. It did not take him long to realise there was commotion in the air. Alerted, he lifted his head and could see the outline of Torquil standing and scratching his head with his sword drawn. Roar leapt to his feet and ran to his comrade. 'What's going on, lad?' he asked.

Torquil turned to Roar. 'Two men were taken in the night.'

Roar immediately bent a knee and scanned the ground. He could see the unmistakable tracks of two dragged bodies. 'I was afraid of this.' Roar turned to the west. 'Everyone to the beach! We are heading south along the coast.'

The group gathered what little equipment they had left and followed their leader. As they stepped down onto the sand, Torquil caught up with his commander. 'What is it?' he asked.

'Could be one of two things.' Roar paused and made sure only Torquil could hear before he continued. 'Could be the wild forest people. They come out at night and eat man-flesh. They are barbarians; you cannot reason with them and you cannot bargain with them.' Knowing their rough location while at sea, he knew these lands were far from any road or town and rarely travelled by Meridians. This was the least civilised part of the Realm and Roar knew not even the capital city's army would march through Tornwood Forest without expecting to lose men.

Torquil kept calm and studied the face of his leader. 'What else could it be?'

Before Roar could give an answer, he spotted something. There was some fresh wreckage in the water. A dirty white sail was pinned down by some broken wood. 'Come help me look,' Roar commanded.

The remaining survivors ran towards the water. They pulled the sail loose and began to stretch it across the bare sand. As they unravelled it and it was spread flat, they examined the pattern. Marked atop the white sails, printed in red and orange, was the unmistakable markings of The Flaming Sails.

Torquil turned to Roar. 'I think I can guess what the other possibility is.'

Roar nodded. 'I feared it as soon as the Sea Scale attacked. If it had attacked us, it surely attacked them as well.' He looked to the south, then the north, then the south again. 'Yes, we must go south. Too much forest covers the north. I will not be taking us inland until I find out what took our men.'

'Commander, we were lucky to escape The Old Maid alive. Surely the Flaming Sails were not as fortunate?' said Torquil. He was amazed to see Roar so shaken up. In truth, he did not know much about the corsairs they had been chasing. He only knew what anyone else knew, that they were evil killers. The young Wolf wondered if they were really as bad as man-eating forest-dwellers that slept through the day and hunted at night. 'It must have been the woodland tribes.'

Roar turned back and stared at Torquil with something close to fear in his eyes. 'I pray you are right.'

Chapter 8

IT WAS the end of daylight when Sir Oakheart halted the column to make camp. This was their fourth night on the road to Inverwall. Tents were beginning to pop up all across the meadow. Oakheart and the other Knightguards had their tent raised and ready for the evening's discussion. To attend this meeting, they had invited the three Captains in charge of the one hundred and fifty soldiers.

'Everyone inside, I want our discussion over within the hour, we have a big march tomorrow,' said Sir Oakheart as the group sat beside a roaring fire just outside the tent.

When all were inside and seated, Sir Oakheart took a headcount of the attendees – Sir Talon, Sir Shale, Sir Lenath, Sir Nolan and the three Captains of the Meridian army. 'Good, we are all here. Going forward this will be my war council. I need not remind you, anything said in these meetings does not leave our group. Tonight, we are finally going to discuss our intentions at Inverwall.' Oakheart paused to allow acknowledgement from the group. 'I received a falcon from the city yesterday. Scouts report that Badrang's forces have stopped and are camped close to the Marble Mountains. As we expected they are showing no signs of movement north. He will be waiting for the rainy season, the perfect time to strike us head on.'

'Was the falcon from Steward Rhaneth? Does he know we are going to replace his leadership?' asked Sir Talon.

'Yes and no.' Sir Oakheart took a small scroll and began to read. '*Sir Oakheart,*

I am writing to inform you that we have doubled our guards on the wall in preparation of your arrival. I have had my scouts reach Badrang's forces two weeks to the south, they report an army fifty thousand strong. They are currently camped and show no signs of further movement. Tomorrow I intend to send an ambassador for emergency treaties, something I feel the Queen should have done sooner. We appreciate your impending arrival and will make space in the south fields for you and your men.

Signed Rhaneth, Steward of Inverwall, Warden of the South.'

'The pompous oaf!' remarked the older Sir Nolan. 'We ride to his aid and he says we will be sleeping in tents on the outskirts of the city.' The old Knight's face was beginning to redden with anger.

'We will not be sleeping in tents. And I can promise you, no one will be sleeping on the south side of the fort wall,' Sir Oakheart replied. 'Our first action will be to send all civilians on a convoy north to Meridia. The Steward will also be among them.' The group murmured with agreement and Oakheart continued. 'Our main goal here, is to turn Inverwall into the impenetrable fortress it was two centuries ago.'

The group nodded with approval, already feeling brighter about their dark futures.

Sir Talon continued with the plans he and Sir Oakheart had discussed previously. 'Regarding the buildings south of the wall, we will have these ripped down and cleared. We need that area to be a killing-ground where our archers can hit their target easily. At the moment it would be too simple for an army to move through the buildings under cover, right up to the gate.'

Nodding, Sir Oakheart stepped forward and continued to explain the rest of the plan. 'We have a month before the rainy season is expected. This will give us enough time to raise two wooden walls to the south, stretching across the length of the main wall. We can have infantry between each of the wooden barricades. They will be shielded from the enemy archers at the bottom of the hill. With our archers on the high wall behind, they will have a perfect angle to hit the enemy as they move up the slope. When the first barrier is lost, we will have our men retreat to the fort. The second infantry will move forward and hold the enemy, giving the first platoon enough time to fall back.'

'Sounds like a good plan; might I make a suggestion?' Sir Shale asked.

'Certainly, Shale, this is why we are having this meeting,' Sir Oakheart replied.

'What if we were to coat the northern face of each wooden wall with fire-oil?'

The others listened with great intent.

'We have fire braziers stationed along the main wall for our archers. When a wooden barricade is lost and our men have fallen back, we have the walls set aflame,' Sir Shale explained.

Sir Oakheart had always thought the use of fire was unbecoming of a knight but in times of war you must be willing to go as far as your enemy. 'We would need to be sure our men had cleared the walls, but you are right. Badrang's forces will not find it easy crossing through the burning wood.'

Sir Talon paced back and forth, deep in thought. Turning to the three Captains stood together, he spoke. 'We will need two platoons of fifty down in the killing fields. They are the strongest soldiers in the Realm and will inspire greatness among the weaker Inverwallians. The third platoon will be on the main wall as insurance. If Badrang is victorious in the killing fields, we will need to prepare for ladders on the wall or a battering ram at the gate.'

Oakheart was happy with how the rest of the meeting went. They discussed the new training regimes the Inverwallians would be put through. Sir Shale and Sir Lenath had both volunteered to be the representatives of the Knightguards who would fight on the killing fields. Oakheart was pleased to have such fine companions on the road to his death.

Inverwall will still fall and when it does I must act. Sir Blake will grow closer to the Queen. He wished he had handled things differently in Meridia. *I should have had him arrested on the spot... But that would have led to a long trial which would have slowed my progress to Inverwall. No, it must be this way. Blake could not do any damage while Inverwall still stood.*

The evening was drawing to an end and the meeting had been finished. Sir Talon, Oakheart and Nolan sat out by the warmth of the dying fire. Sir Talon thought a moment then asked, 'What if Badrang proposes settling the fight with a *Battle of Champions*?'

'Then we will accept,' Sir Oakheart replied. A Battle of Champions was an age-old tradition used to settle wars without loss of armies. Each leader would select a fighter and these fighters would battle to the death. Thinking it is better one dies, than thousands. The losing army would then relinquish their lands to the victor.

'You know he will not honour it? If our champion kills General Malacath, he will still order the attack,' said Sir Talon.

'I know this, but at least Malacath will be dead.'

Malacath was Badrang's Chief General. Rumours had persisted the man was a monster, standing at over seven foot and sporting a two handed greatsword. His plate, midnight black, armour fringed with demon red skirtings. With supernatural strength and the speed of a man half his size he had never lost a fight, nor had he been knocked off his feet. From the Dakha Blacklands to Dain in the North, there was not a soldier who did not know the name of General Malacath and the fighting prowess he possessed.

'With Malacath dead, his men will have one less myth to believe in.' Oakheart paused a moment. 'We will also not honour the agreement if OUR champion is defeated.' He did not like it but it was for the good of the Meridian Realms. There was no way this war would be decided in a battle between two men.

'And who is OUR champion?' asked Sir Nolan.

'I am,' replied one of the knights.

Chapter 9

THEY HAD been walking for three days down the coast. Roar knew where the forests thinned they would be able to cut inland and either head north to Meridia or south to Inverwall. Either way, for the moment south meant salvation. On both nights travelling Roar had half the survivors sleep while the other half stood guard. They worked on a rotation, each managing three hours of rest per night. They had not been attacked since their first night on the beach but there was no doubt they were still being followed.

The night before, Roar had heard noises coming from the forest to the east, during which he had prepared himself for a fight and was ready to wake the men. Most of the survivors carried only daggers or makeshift clubs and spears by this point. However, some of the stronger swimmers had managed to carry their weapons to shore after *The Old Maid* had sunk and Roar was one of them.

The third day was coming to an end and they would need to stop and begin making camp. Better to stop sooner rather than later, giving them enough time to pick out as well a fortified area as possible. They had been fortunate with the previous night's positions. On one night, they slept with their backs to a sea cliff, giving them only one real direction to defend. The other, they were at the top of a large sand dune with the moonlight strong enough to pick out any intruders.

This was their third night and Roar doubted they would be

as lucky with the location. As they walked south the beach had narrowed. The forest to the East was as close as possible meaning the enemy could sneak right up close, before making their strike.

With an hour left of daylight Roar finally had the men stop and set up camp. They began the same process as before; the men paired off to collect firewood. It took half an hour before Roar was happy with their position. He had the men set up small fires along the treeline of the woodlands. These were used to highlight anyone or anything that would come from the cover of the trees.

Of the survivors left, only ten were Wolves of Glory, the others being crew from The Old Maid. The men would rotate the weapons among them depending on who was at watch. There were three longswords, two shields, two shortswords and two bows with a quiver of arrows between them. The guards would swap with the sleeping and the sleeping would guard when the moon was at its highest in the sky. The only two members of the group to keep their weapons at all times were Roar and Torquil. Both men preferred not to sleep for long, until tonight.

It was just past midnight and Roar could not fight his sleep any longer. He would be awake again in a couple of hours to take guard. *What would a little sleep hurt?* he thought and allowed his eyes to drop.

With most of the guards facing the direction of woodlands to the east and the others watching the sand trail to the north and south, it came to no-one's attention when *The Flaming Sails* emerged from the sea.

Each dripping wet and armed to the teeth, a group of twenty corsairs slipped amongst the sleeping survivors of The Old Maid. Each of the corsairs took up position, dangling a blade over the throats of the resting survivors, readying themselves for the attack.

Standing in the middle of the makeshift campsite, the Captain of the Flaming Sails raised his hand. Ready to signal the death of all the Wolves who lay sleeping, he called to Torquil who was standing guard with his back turned.

Panic ensued and all the defenders wheeled from their position to see the out-numbering enemy forces, each with a blade pinned against the throats of their once sleeping companions. No one dared make a move, as the Captain still had his hand raised. 'Good! So you have gathered this raised arm means your friends are still alive?!'

There was no answer from the armed survivors.

A wry smile appeared on the Captain's face. 'As soon as one of you moves, I drop my arm and every one of them dies.' He then took three steps to his left and lifted one of the survivors to his feet. 'Including this one, your pathetic leader!'

The tall Captain turned to the man he was clutching by the neck. 'Roar, isn't it?'

Roar looked at the Captain with a burning hatred and did not answer.

'Now Roar, how are we going to communicate when you won't speak to me?' The Captain spoke through yellow stained teeth, his pencil-thin moustache almost tickling each ear. 'I'm afraid if you don't start speaking, I will have to kill one of your men!'

There was still no response from Roar.

'Very well,' said Bruar, and rather than drop his arm he dropped one finger in his hand of five.

Just then a corsair at the back picked up one of the surviving members of The Old Maid. Using a rusty curved-dagger, the corsair opened a permanent smile across the crew member's throat. Blood tricked down his chest as the crew member gave his last gargling breath.

With the body thrown to the floor in front of Roar, the Captain spoke again. 'I steal, I kidnap and I kill, but one thing I don't do, Roar, is LIE.'

Roar remained silent still but fury burned deep within him.

'Now, let's start again. My name is Captain Bruar, leader of the Flaming Sails. Can you at least tell me your name?'

Roar stood in silence, his eyes fixed on the body of the man he scolded less than three days ago for not collecting firewood. He turned to face the taller man and spoke. 'Roar.'

With slanted eyes and a wicked smile, Captain Bruar replied, 'Hi Roar, it is a pleasure to meet you.' With his left hand and four fingers still in the air, he drew his right hand back and landed one heavy punch to Roar's abdomen. 'How long were you hunting us before the Sea Scale attacked you?'

Roar coughed as he tried to regain breath from the blow. 'A month.'

'It's funny how one month ago you would have never imagined it would be us hunting you.' The Captain looked around at the broken mercenaries. 'Might I suggest a little name change? Considering you have all followed this fool to your deaths, how does The *Sheep of Glory* sound?'

'Just kill us and be done with it,' Torquil called out from the back.

Captain Bruar turned to the young Wolf. 'Kill you? Why would we do that? Strong men like you are expensive!'

Chapter 10

L EIF HAD finally arrived in Dain. Progress was made slow by the rain and it had taken him just over the two days to reach the Northern Capital. The streets were alive with activity, as if making the most of the short dry period. Men and women rushed from stall to stall, making trades in preparation for the bad weather to continue. Some trading blankets for food, others were trading food for firewood.

Leif finally reached the door he was searching for, the Dain trade shop. He noted the carvings on the sign adjacent to the solid oak door – *The Finer Things*. He pushed down on the latch and entered.

The room was small, but amongst the tables was a treasure trove of items and trinkets. Swords, helmets, candlesticks, scrolls, anything you could imagine, *The Finer Things* had it.

Leif walked towards the keeper who had his back to him and was sorting a large tapestry that hanged down on the smallest part of the wall. Upon the tapestry was the family crest of Duke Delgath, Warden of the North. The silhouette of a large bear, rearing on its hind legs in front of a setting sun.

'It truly is beautiful,' Leif commented, trying his best not to give the owner a scare.

'Oh!' The shopkeeper turned with false surprise. Upon looking at the shabby garment Leif wore, he smiled. He then looked back to tapestry. 'Isn't it just, my boy?'

The keeper climbed down from his three-stepped ladder, dusted himself off and opened out a sweaty palm. 'Mr Potts, owner of The Finer Things.'

'It is a pleasure to meet you,' Leif replied and reached out his own hand for the customary shake. 'My name is Leif.'

'Leif?' asked Mr Potts. 'Do you have a family name?'

'No I do not,' answered Leif, instantly putting an end to that line of questioning.

'So what can I do for you, Mr Leif? I see you have a sword on your back, so no need for any weaponry. Let me have a good look at you.' Mr Potts took a step back and enjoyed his little game. Whenever he had a new customer, he loved to guess their requirements. 'You look like the kind of man that needs a little more comfort in his life. I have some new bedrolls over there in the corner, underneath the quill ink and beside the tapestries.'

'If only that was all I needed,' replied Leif with a smile. 'I have actually come to you for answers.' From his jerkin, Leif reached in and pulled out his rune-stone necklace and handed it to the short shop owner.

'Answers I can supply, my young man, but unfortunately they are often not cheap,' Mr Potts replied with the smile of a savvy merchant.

With his small stubby fingers, the shopkeeper studied the necklace, and then turned it over to see the markings. His smile vanished almost immediately. 'I'm afraid I must ask you to leave, Mr Leif,' he said, while thrusting the necklace back into the hands of his once would-be customer.

'Why? What is it? Do you know something about this necklace?'

'I'm afraid we are closed, Mr Leif, you must leave.'

'But what is it, Mr Potts? I have travelled hundreds of miles for answers. Please, you must tell me?' Leif pleaded.

'Please get out of here. I will have to call the guards if you do not leave!' replied a sweating Mr Potts.

'Very well, I will leave.' Before he took a step Leif looked at Mr

Potts and asked, 'Before I go, would you mind if I looked at those bedrolls you talked of?'

'No, you must leave and please don't ever return to The Finer Things.'

Leif left the establishment with no more words. This had been the first reaction of any kind his necklace had provoked. He was closer to an answer than he had ever been, and this frustrated Leif.

He decided to try his luck with some of the smaller stalls and independent traders in the market district of Dain. Many gave the same reaction as Mr Potts, while others pretended not to know and pleaded ignorance. *I am finally in a city that has answers, but no one will give them to me!*

For whatever reason, the people of Dain seemed to distance themselves from Leif, as if speaking to him would be their end. The firsts drop of rain could be felt when he decided to give up for the day.

Leif walked towards the steps leading to the Temple of Azmara, the goddess of compassion. He ran his scuffed fingers through the tall flowers on his right. He looked up at the small temple atop the small hill and sighed. He swept his shoulder length hair out of his face and tried to make himself look presentable. Before he could take a step, he felt a grip on his shoulder and then a sharp tug that made him change direction. Now face to face with an overweight guard with terrible breath and an extremely red complexion, Leif stood tall.

'Let me see your papers?' The guard reached out his hand. 'You're new round here, and I gotta make sure you are allowed to be here.'

'Unfortunately for both of us, I have no papers, my friend. I am a traveller, and do not plan on spending too long in Dain. I was hoping to have a drink and a night in the Inn, *The Barking Bear* I believe?'

'You don't drink or even sleep in Dain until I see papers!' said the guard, with more menace in his voice this time.

Leif could see movement out the corner of his eye. Other guards were making their way towards him. He did not plan on spending the night in the dungeons of Dain. He was ready to reach for the longsword strapped across his back when an elderly man approached them.

'It's quite alright, Sir, I can vouch for this one,' said the old man, with no further explanation.

The guard looked at the man and struggled to conceal he was clearly intimidated. 'Very well, but see he has his papers on him next time.'

After the rotund guard left and within seconds, Leif could hear him starting the same conversation again with another poor traveller visiting Dain.

Now alone with a man he had never met in his life, Leif was confused. He studied the face of his rescuer. The man was very old, but carried himself well. He looked healthy, with a well-kept white beard. 'Why did you?' asked the young wanderer.

'How would you like a drink?' interrupted the kind-faced old man.

Chapter 11

ROAR KEPT thinking back to the night previous. Why had he not thought about the sea? It was easy to see it now, but he had never been so angry with himself. *Would Rommel have thought of that? Would Torquil have, had Roar not been in command?* It was times like these that reminded Roar why he never wanted to be a leader in the first place. Now being taken south, the last of The Wolves of Glory were going to be sold into slavery. *No doubt some tribe chief or maybe even Badrang himself would have heard of the Wolves of Glory and fancied us fighting on his side,* thought Roar.

Roar took solace in his thoughts but knew there would be little chance of escape. *The Flaming Sails* outnumbered them. The corsairs also had all the weapons and all the food. It would be they who would be keeping themselves strong over the next few days. The Wolves of Glory were going to be half starved by the time they reached their destination.

He did not care; death waited for no man. Better to die a free man than live as a slave among the armies of the Dakha and Blackland hordes. The first chance he got, Roar would get hold of a blade and take as many of these corsairs with him. He was only hoping he would be near Captain Bruar when it happened.

Roar already hated the leader of The Sails. He had heard stories of his cruelty and knew there would be no mercy shown to those who caused him trouble during this march south. The stomach-churning crimes of The Flaming Sails had attracted a large bounty over the years. Many mercenaries had tried and failed to bring an end to these criminals.

Arms and legs bound by heavy rope, the Wolves marched through the wet sand. They had initially been asked to walk the dry sand further up the bank, but this proved too difficult as every few paces someone would fall, and progress would be temporarily halted.

In the morning, it had only been their hands that were tied together, but the last three crew members of *The Old Maid* had seen this as an opportunity to run for the forest. Their hunters had returned an hour later with their freshly decapitated heads. A lesson learned that even with free legs, they would not be escaping *The Flaming Sails*. The corsairs would not take the chance and added a shoulder length of rope to each of their ankles.

Captain Bruar marched at the head of the line, munching on the last of a roasted sea bird. He wiped his greasy fingers on his long leather jacket. 'Roar, join me up here a moment!'

With the bindings on his legs, Roar struggled to catch up to the leader of his kidnappers. He made it to the head of the column and was now matching the Captain stride for stride. He could see the dagger the Captain wore at the front of his unbuttoned shirt. Roar stealthily averted his gaze. 'Yes, what do you want?'

Tossing aside the last of the roast carcass, Captain Bruar spoke. 'Do you know where we are headed, Roar?'

Roar did not answer immediately but then with something close to a smile he spoke. 'South?'

The Captain ignored the wit. 'You are not wrong, but I will elaborate on your answer. Another four days south from here is a small bay. This bay caters to people like us, Roar. We will purchase a new ship and head further south to Blackland from there. Don't worry, these people like folk like you and me.'

'You and I are nothing alike,' spat Roar.

'Oh really, well tell me, how do we differ? You kill, I kill. You do it for the money, I do it for the money?'

'You kill innocents!' Roar said defiantly.

'Roar, in this world, no one is truly innocent. Are you that naïve? Over the years, how many of your own men have you had to kill, when the money just wasn't enough for them?'

'You know nothing of our past!' said Roar as anger flashed in his eyes.

'Well in the coming days, all nine of your men's faith will be tested. I will make them each an offer – swear fealty to me, joining The Flaming Sails, and you will be spared from the slave auction down in the Blacklands! I lost a lot of men when the Sea Scale attacked and I'm sure your men will make fine fighters.' Captain Bruar grinned at the solemn face of Roar. 'So who do you think will be first to give in, Roar? My coin is on your young comrade.' Captain Bruar paused and looked back. 'Torquil, isn't it?'

Roar remained silent a moment, then burst into hearty laughter. 'Ha-ha-ha-ha, you really think these men will fight for you?' Roar deliberately spoke so loud that all the men along the line heard.

The Captain was not happy; he had planned on making this proposal to each of the surviving Wolves one by one, and face to face. With one right punch he knocked Roar to the ground. 'You still need time to learn, Roar.'

He pinned the defenceless Wolf to the sand and began his strikes – right, left, right, left, his punches going into double figures. With each punch he could feel another bone in Roar's face crack. The Captain reached to his right and grabbed a heavy piece of driftwood off the bank. He lifted the club high above his head, ready to deal the killing blow before he stopped himself and regained his senses. He looked down at the broken face of the Wolf and smiled. 'By the Gods, you are lucky to be so damn valuable alive!'

A battered and bloodied Roar was left face up on the sand as the Captain stood and wiped his hands. Through the swellings already developed around his eyes Roar looked to the treeline of the forest. In a dazed state he tried to rise to his feet but fell back onto the cold wet sand. He could hear the outrage of the captured Wolves along the line, some fighting their captors to reach their battered leader.

With the last of his reserved strength, Roar managed to lift himself up onto one knee. He looked again to the forest. Although his vision was blurred, he was sure he recognised those eyes looking back at him from behind the trunk of a large tree.

Chapter 12

I NVERWALL WAS now in sight and Sir Oakheart could see the tall grey banners flying in the wind off the Northern Wall. It had taken fifteen days to reach the southern capital, which to all involved was a tremendous feat with an army this size.

Sir Talon rode next to his knight-brother. The journey had been easy with the weather favourable. Confidence was high with the troops and Talon could feel this when he spoke. 'It is truly a magnificent structure, the perfect position for a fortification.' He looked to both sides of the city where the mountains stretched as far as his eyes could see. No army was getting around Inverwall. 'It's a shame she became a city and weakened so much!'

'You are right, Talon,' replied Sir Oakheart. He also looked to the mountains and it reminded him how strong Inverwall could be. It has been three years since his last visit to the southern capital and times had changed. He did not think the city would be the site of a battle in his lifetime. Sure he had defended the Meridian Realms from eastern invaders, but the south had never posed any threat. Inverwall was always the perfect deterrent to the scattered Dakha tribes. He sat up in his saddle and cleared his throat. 'Two hundred years ago, Badrang would not have had a God's hope of breaching the fort.'

'I agree! Not only have they built out into the south fields, but the soldiers back then were of greater number, stronger, trained and disciplined.' Sir Talon continued, 'Will a month really be enough time to educate these men? Will we be able to train them to fight as selflessly as their ancestors did, to fight not only for themselves but the entire Meridian Realm?'

Sir Oakheart leaned back on his horse and began to think of the fifty thousand Dakha warriors. Since conquering the Southern Kingdoms and uniting all the Dakha tribes of Blackland, the Warlord now held the greatest army known to man. 'In one month, Badrang will charge the south wall with an army larger than ever before.'

Back in Meridia they had close to eight thousand defenders. Should Inverwall fall, the Queen would have to send word to Dain for more troops – perhaps all five thousand from the Northern Capital would be needed when the time came.

They were now passing through the gate and into the north courtyard of Inverwall. The fort was much smaller than Meridia or Dain. It had the basic foundations of an army camp, with the townsfolk living outside the walls to southern fields.

The grey stone Keep itself was double the height of the North and South Walls, with the mountains either side acting as defences of the east and west.

The knights were crossing the square towards the Keep and could see a group of Inverwallian defenders outside her great iron door. They were flying the grey and white colours of Steward Rhaneth. The only sounds to be heard in the courtyard were the squawking of crows in the high roofs of the main Keep and the distant rumblings from civilians past the South Wall.

As the Knightguards approached the Keep, one of the Inverwall Captains took a step towards them and spoke. 'Good day, Sirs, my name is Captain Thalue. We had expected more men to be with you.'

With one raise of his arm, Sir Oakheart halted the column and spoke. 'We had expected the Steward to be here to greet us; where is he?'

'He is eating, Sir and has only just risen from his chambers.'

'He has only just got up?' Old Sir Nolan commented. 'By the gods, it is past midday!' he added.

'Our lord was on a long and strenuous hunt the day before last. It tired him, but he returned with a great boar from the Balderstone Forest,' said Captain Thalue with suppressed shame in his voice.

Anger was painted on the faces of four out of the five knights. *How dare the leader of Inverwall enjoy such pleasures as a hunt when war was upon them?* Sir Oakheart thought to himself but he remained calm, as if he expected this. 'We will take one of the abandoned barracks on the south side of the square.' Oakheart raised his arm and made a gesture to the men behind him. Everyone, bar Sir Talon and Sir Nolan, moved towards their new accommodations.

Sir Talon then spoke to the Captain. 'We seek council with the Steward. Please inform him we will wait twenty minutes before we enter.'

Captain Thalue bowed his head and hammered a fist against his chest in the customary salute. He turned and entered the Keep with no words.

The three knights waited only ten minutes before entering the Keep. Through the corridors the decorations of banners, paintings and tapestries littered the walls; all were of Steward Rhaneth.

'This pup will not like the news we bring him,' Sir Nolan commented, as he looked at a particularly flattering painting of the Steward.

'I do not care if he likes it or not. We cannot have a man like this stay here!' Sir Oakheart replied.

At the end of the long corridor, they strode into a large dining hall. It was obvious this was no longer used to feed the defenders of Inverwall. Instead now, the personal relaxing place of the Steward and company.

At the far end of the hall, on the main stand, Steward Rhaneth sat. 'My Knights, welcome to Inverwall! I hear you have already acquired some new accommodation within my walls?' He smiled and added, 'Tired of roughing it out in the tents?'

'My Lord, thank you for the previous kind offer, but I feel it would be difficult for us to control the city garrison if we were camped on the outskirts of town,' Sir Oakheart replied, with a cool tone.

Rhaneth remained seated and continued to pick at what was left on his plate. 'So, Sir, you ride to our aid with a magnificent army of one hundred and fifty strong men!' The sarcasm was plain in his voice. 'I suppose you have guessed what happened to the ambassador I sent to Badrang?' He nodded towards a covered bucket on the other end of his table. 'Badrang sent me nothing back but his head.'

Sir Oakheart ignored the obvious distraction and continued with the point at hand. 'My Lord Steward, as you may know I have been granted complete control of Inverwall AND her defences.'

There was no reaction from Rhaneth.

'My first act will be to have all the women and children sent north to Meridia. During my travels the Queen has prepared some refugee areas within her walls. Your people will be safe.'

Rhaneth stood and poured himself a cup of red wine. 'And what of the men who can't fight, the farmers, the bakers and so on, what of them?'

'We have one month to train them,' replied Sir Oakheart.

'And what if they can't be trained?' said the Steward.

This was all Sir Nolan could take and he had lost all patience. 'Don't worry, lad, you will be sent north with the rest of the children!'

Rhaneth slammed his goblet hard against the table. 'How dare you talk to me like that, you forget your place, Knight?!' He picked up the jar of wine and smashed it against the wall behind him. 'I am the Warden of the South!'

Sir Talon interjected. 'No, my Lord, I'm afraid you WERE Warden of the South!' He held out a sealed scroll, stamped with Queen Orellia's family crest.

Chapter 13

S MOKE FILLED *The Barking Bear* as noise echoed through its tall ceilings. The Inn was large, its wooden interior warmed by the light of a roaring fire in the middle of the largest wall. It was becoming late, and the crowds were thinning. Most of its patrons were returning to their homes after a drink too many.

Sat at a table in the corner of the room, Leif cut into a meal of roast pheasant and fresh vegetables. The elderly man had introduced himself as Fathad, and was seated opposite and continued to sip at his third goblet of warm wine.

During the afternoon they had discussed the current state of Dain and its people. The Duke was ill and the city was falling into anarchy. Leif knew first hand of how the guards of Dain were treating the fringe villages. He had told Fathad the story of the woodsman and his son.

Fathad spoke of the struggles within Dain itself. The people were poor and getting even poorer now that the guards were doubling their taxes. Increase in duties had been introduced ever since Duke Delgath's illness. Fathad also explained how the Grandcaptain of Dain was paranoid at the thought of spies within the city. This was leading to the needless arrests of innocent traders and travellers. Anyone new in the city who did not have appropriate papers was called in for questioning and often not released.

The people within the city knew little of the war waging in the South. In truth, Dain had always considered themselves separate from the rest of the Meridian Realms. Instead of worrying about southern politics, they concerned themselves with the bad weather and the growing numbers of bandits operating in Moormire Forest to the North and West. As a matter of principle, Dain should serve the Queen in Meridia, but for as long as books were written and man spoke, it had been a Delgath that ruled Dain and its lands.

Leif was happy to converse freely, but he felt slightly unsure about this kind old man. He had not yet asked Fathad about his necklace. The thought of this nagged at the back of Leif's mind and he had his suspicions this elder knew of the runestone already.

Finally, after a long sip of wine Fathad spoke again. 'Now that we have got to know one another and the Inn is quieter, we can speak.'

Leif looked and nodded at him to continue.

Smiling, the old man returned the nod. 'I know you are not stupid and I'm sure you have gathered that I followed you for quite some time this morning. I heard your conversation with a number of shopkeepers in the market district. You say you have a necklace?'

There was a moment of hesitation from the young wanderer but it did not last long. Leif reached into his jerkin and leaned across the table for Fathad to study the rune. 'Yes, this belonged to my father.'

Upon hearing that comment, Fathad's eyes twitched. The elder studied the necklace thoroughly. 'Your father, you say?' He examined the rune for half a minute before he sat back in his seat and took another drink.

'You know what it is?' Leif asked.

'Not exactly, but I think I know who might. However, I must warn you, Leif, you must not show this to anyone else in Dain.'

Leif was as confused as ever. 'So, you must know at least something about it?'

Before Fathad could respond they were interrupted by a loud conversation taking place at the table next to them. 'Ugh! These bandits are at it again; the roads just aren't safe to travel anymore!'

The other at the table began to shout with agreement. 'Aye, where are the blasted bounty-hunters when you need them. Never thought I would say it, but I miss those mercenaries. I don't care who gets them, these outlaws need to be brought to justice.'

'The guards just don't care anymore!' said another voice.

'I agree, where are *The Gallow Ravens*, or *The Wolves of Glory*, or even *The Maidens of the Shield?*' added another member of the table.

'They are probably all off filling their pockets in the south,' said the first voice.

'Please, *The Maidens* wouldn't be seen dead in the Meridian Realms these days! They will be in the east,' interrupted another voice.

It was not long before the conversation began to quieten, but Leif could still hear the arguments continuing in quieter voices. He noted to himself just how bad the bandit problem must be in these lands if it dominates drinking time.

After the commotion had come to an end, Fathad continued. 'I only know that it is not something I would bring attention to. I have seen markings like these in the past.' He took yet another sip of his wine. 'And in the past, they have ALL caused problems. The people here are a superstitious bunch. The gods have done little for them in recent years and poverty is rife. The last thing they want is a mysterious wanderer coming to town bringing odd looking artefacts with him.'

'I understand,' Leif responded. He tucked the necklace away behind his undershirt. 'I am willing to do anything to get answers.'

'Good, then we leave tomorrow. We have just under a week's journey to the north west ahead of us.' He looked deep into Leif's eyes. 'That is, if you want to find out where that rune came from?'

Both men had adjourned for the evening and it was the morning before Leif knew it. The weather had not let up through the night, but he had been happy to spend the night in a warm bed within

The Barking Bear. It had cost him four bronze coins for the room and meal – three for the room and one for the full stomach. The Innkeeper was delighted to see the single silver coin Leif had produced from his duffle.

Leif was washing his face in the basin near the window when there was a knock on his door; he moved towards the latch and answered. 'Who is it?' he asked, as Fathad had instructed the previous night.

'It's Fathad, my dear boy, are you ready to travel?'

'I won't be long, just packing up the last of my things,' said Leif.

'Very well, I will be waiting downstairs enjoying one final goblet of wine.' Leif could hear the elderly man walking back down the wooden corridor outside.

He turned back to the bed and looked at his possessions. Firstly, he buttoned up the rest of his jerkin, next he donned his dark green cape and lastly he slung his father's longsword across his back. He looked at himself in the cracked mirror that hung above the wash basin. He was tidier than yesterday. With a night's sleep, a haircut and his beard trimmed, he felt less wild. He wondered if he looked anything like his father. He scooped up one more handful of water and splashed it about his face. Grabbing his duffle, he exited out the door and down the stairs to meet Fathad.

When they were ready, both men left the comfort of The Barking Bear and into the hammering rain outside. With their hoods up and arms folded they made their way towards the west gate, which would lead them out to the edge of Moormire Forest.

Chapter 14

THE WAVES crashed over Rommel's half-conscious body. During his struggles at sea, he had fought every inch for his life. Weighted down by his heavy boots and shortsword, he had managed to break the surface of the water for air. He had been fortunate enough to find the floating door that once led to the mess hall of *The Old Maid*.

On the beach, sea birds circled the old Wolf as he began to gather his consciousness. With seaweed draped around his neck and sand plastering his face, Rommel began to wake. Using his exhausted arms, he pushed down on the damp sand and lifted himself onto his knees.

Where am I, he thought to himself. Rommel knew he needed water. If he got to his feet and walked along the beach, he may find some small river that runs off into the sea. Rommel picked up a long piece of driftwood and used it to regain his feet; he then took a moment to catch his bearings. *Do I go north or south?* he wondered.

Rommel knew inland would not be an option with his current location. He turned south and began to walk. But by the third step he stumbled and fell; he needed to rest first before this journey. Raising his head he could see a group of large beach rocks to the south. It took him over a minute to regain his balance but he managed to stagger to the high stones sticking out of the sand. Through the rocks was a small stream running down into the salt water of the sea. He bent down and with cupped hands took four mouthfuls of cool fresh water.

With every bit of strength he could muster, he unclipped the brown belt around his waist. Next he removed all but his underclothes and stood with his back leaning against one of the high stones. After a couple of heavy breaths, he collapsed and slept.

It was the next morning before Rommel woke; he was fortunate the weather had been warm. He reached out and grasped his jerkin and was relieved to find his clothes were dry. With no other choice, he now felt he had the energy to start his journey south.

It was a struggle to begin with walking in the sand but eventually Rommel got into a good rhythm and progress was good for a man hungry and sore. He walked for an hour until he found it, a large burnt out fire bordering the woodlands to the east. Rommel bent a knee and studied each indent on the ground; he counted fourteen – the two nearest the forest had unmistakable dragging marks, and this worried him. As he struggled back to his feet he thought to himself, *If this was Roar and the rest of the group, they surely went south. North or south were the only option with the threat inland and I surely would have seen them if they walked north.*

It was another two hours before Rommel found a river of fresh water. A small stream leading out to the open water was all he needed to stay alive. He drank until he felt sick, then drank some more. Again, he could see the unmistakable signs of others passing through this way; *I must only be half a day behind them,* he thought.

In the days ahead he made good progress on his journey south but frustration was beginning to take over when he had to stop again for rest. He found shelter under a large tree bordering the beach and upon an open fire he cooked the crabs he had found during his journey. *These will at least give me a bit more energy to catch up with my companions to the south.* With each passing track it was becoming obvious he was following the survivors of *The Old Maid.*

It was Rommel's third day on the move when he realised he was not far behind *The Wolves of Glory*. As he looked at the sun beating in the sky above he reassured himself of his evening plans – *I must only be a couple of hours behind them so I will not stop for rest tonight.*

It was just past midnight when Rommel could see the glowing light of fires in the distance; he had finally made it. He quickened his pace and almost broke into a run. Just as he was about to call out, he spotted it. By the light of the moon he could make out the silhouettes of armed force crawling from the sea. He reached for the shortsword around his waist and was tempted to call out, but it was already too late – *The Flaming Sails* were in position. For the next two hours he watched as the corsairs bound and gagged the surviving Wolves. *Should I have made an earlier move,* he thought. *No, if I had I would have been joining my comrades in capture.*

He took upon the decision to try and sleep, tomorrow was another day and perhaps a chance would arise where he could untie a few of the Wolves and mount a comeback. He took off fifteen minutes north and slept in a secure hiding place away from any dangers of being spotted by *The Flaming Sails*.

The next day he followed the convoy heading south. He witnessed the three crew of The Old Maid make a run for it into the forest. 'Those poor lads, they are clearly going to be caught!' he whispered under his breath from the cover of some rocks. Sure enough less than an hour later a group of three corsairs returned, each carrying the head of a crew member.

It was midday when he witnessed Roar's beating. It was the most difficult thing he had ever had to watch in all his years. On numerous occasions he stopped himself from breaking his cover and trying to help his old friend. *I must wait for the right time; they clearly want to bring the Wolves to Brigands Bay alive! They would have killed him otherwise.*

Rommel knew the risk of transporting someone as skilled as his comrade alive. Roar would need only a small chance and at least three of these corsairs would be dead, one of them certainly being their leader Bruar.

'Hang in, Roar, it should only be two more days and you will have to head inland and cross Boundwater River,' Rommel said to himself.

Boundwater River was the largest river in the Realm and it spanned from the Western Sea, all the way through to the mountains at the edge of the Sand Kingdoms in the East. In a few days when the group would turn east to find the narrowest part of the river, Rommel intended to make his move. Hopefully Roar had seen him during the beat down from Captain Bruar. Rommel had tried to come out of cover as much as he dared in order to catch Roar's eyes. In the cover of the forest, it would be easier for Rommel to get close enough to the group while they slept and communicate a plan to his old friend. The river would be his last chance of freeing the survivors before they arrived at the Bay.

Chapter 15

I T WAS his second day in charge of Inverwall, and Sir Oakheart had gathered half the forces in the training yard. It was time to begin the conditioning of the city's defences. Flanked by the rest of his knight-brothers, Oakheart spoke to the twenty Inverwallian Captains who stood before him, awaiting their instructions.

'Thank you for your patience these last few days, but it is now time for action! In less than one month Badrang's forces will charge the South Wall, but we will have a few surprises waiting for him.' Oakheart studied the reaction of as many of the Captains as possible; most seemed to be listening intently. 'Firstly, all those in the fields to the south are to be pulled to this side of the wall. As of tomorrow, no one is permitted leave of the city unless we allow it.' He beckoned towards his Knightguard companions.

'We understand, Sir, and what of the refugees? When are they to be sent north?' asked Captain Thalue.

'The refugees have until this time tomorrow to gather their belongings, before the convoy north leaves,' Sir Oakheart replied.

Sir Nolan also spoke. 'And be sure Steward Rhaneth is with them! Along with anyone else who does not want to make a stand here!'

'It will be done, Sirs. What else will you have us do?' asked Thalue.

'The buildings to the south, they are to be brought down and cleared away from the wall. This can be done in two days' time, when the women and children have left,' Sir Talon responded.

Captain Thalue did not understand the logic behind such a request, but answered accordingly. 'I will have the men clear the fields to the south as requested. Does this mean the demolition of all the buildings?'

'Thank you, Captain and yes it does,' Sir Oakheart replied.

After the final plans were described to the rest of the attending Captains and they had all returned to their respective platoons, Oakheart gathered his knight-brothers within the council room in the Main Keep. 'We must be sure Steward Rhaneth and his family head north to Meridia. I have sent a falcon to the Queen requesting he be kept under watch.'

The Knights all nodded with agreement.

'To a man like that, the last few days have been a great defeat and his ego will have been badly damaged!' said Sir Oakheart.

'No more than the coward deserves! How many armed men are we sending north to guard the convoy?' asked Sir Lenath.

'Forty men should suffice; however, I want it all to be made up of the lesser local soldiers. They will not need to be skilled fighters if they stick to the main road to Meridia,' Sir Oakheart explained. 'We need all one hundred and fifty Meridian soldiers here; they will be vital in training the Inverwallians in the coming days.'

In the days previous, the knights had debated how to utilise the soldiers they had taken from the Northern Capital. It has been unclear whether they should split the troops up amongst the Inverwallian soldiers. It was eventually confirmed they would not dilute their strongest force amongst the masses. These three units from Meridia would stand strong in the killing fields and on the South Wall.

'These pups are weak, and a bunch of unfit layabouts! The Steward has let the defences grow fat and lazy!' said Sir Nolan.

'But this will all change when I get my hands on them!' He had never been one for tolerating laziness in military men. In his eyes, all men served a purpose and soldiers served the most important purpose of all.

Sir Talon was next to speak. 'Oakheart, we must discuss spies within the city. If Badrang has servants stationed anywhere in the Meridian Realms, it will be here in Inverwall.'

The other knights nodded in agreement.

Sir Shale spoke next. 'Spies amongst the soldiers will not be of importance as they cannot accomplish anything of greatness. We should turn our attention to those who work within the Keep. They will be closer to the five of us and either storing valuable information or edging a knife closer to our backs.' He continued with his soft-spoken accent, 'I propose we monitor all messages coming to and from the falconry. Also, we have visitors to the Keep sign in and out with their names at the main door.'

'Sounds like a good idea, lad – that way we will have a list of suspects if anything happens to one of us, gods forbid!' agreed Sir Nolan.

It was the next day and the refugees were gathered by the northern exit of Inverwall, ready to make the two-week trek to Meridia. They consisted mostly of women and children, with a small portion of men who were too old to carry a sword and shield. They all waited for Steward Rhaneth and his family guards. It had crossed the Knightguards' minds to use the family troops to defend the whole group, but that would have given the previous Warden of the South another reason to leave the civilians if he got the chance.

Sixty armed men and over a thousand civilians would be making the journey north, and still they waited for the Steward.

Eventually the Steward emerged with his entourage. He left the Greystone Keep, covered in his family jewellery and donning a long black gown. Over twenty servants followed him, each carrying what they could – paintings, tapestries, candle holders, chandeliers, goblets, jewellery. Rhaneth made his way towards his horse drawn carriage when he turned back to the Knightguard standing in salute. 'When it comes, I wish you all a quick and painless death. The Queen, Sir Blake and I, will ready Meridia's defences for when you all FAIL here!' Upon speaking these words, he knew immediately he had gone too far.

It was young Sir Shale who had heard enough of this so-called leader's venomous words. He strode towards the Steward and they stood face to face. 'Get in your box and get out of our city. You have already done enough damage here!' He turned and faced the servants carrying all the Steward's belongings. 'Each of you, drop those items and gather your own belongings for the journey ahead. You no longer serve Rhaneth and his family. We will send word to the Queen that you are all to be given accommodation and jobs in the Griffin Quarters with our Knightguard companions.'

'I will be sure to inform the Queen on how you speak to your superiors, Sir Shale!' Rhaneth barked as his servants dropped all the items.

Sir Nolan coughed loudly to clear his throat. 'Aye, well you can also give the Queen another two messages. The first is that the honourable Sir Nolan's final wish is to gaze upon her beauty one last time.' Sir Nolan turned to Sir Shale and winked. 'And you can also tell her, I suggest she give you regular naps and also have you burped regularly, to avoid any more vomit to emerge from your mouth. Now get out of here, you vain, pompous, pathetic excuse for a leader, before things turn REALLY nasty!'

The Steward stood open mouthed, dumbstruck by the words of the elderly knight. With an angry expression written on his face, Rhaneth, former Warden of the South, was loaded into his transport and sent to Meridia.

As the last of the refugees left through the Northern Gate an hour later, Sir Oakheart finally addressed Sir Shale and Nolan for their comments made to the Steward. 'You should not have angered him so. That's one less friend we have in Meridia.' He felt it was now time to tell Sirs Lenath, Shale and Nolan of his suspicions of Sir Blake. 'Come, I feel it is time we discuss the integrity of the Queen's current advisors.'

Chapter 16

THE RAIN continued to fall and the sound of heavy drops hitting the treetops above was somewhat relaxing, particularly when the forest floor was dry. The pine needles smothered the dirt below as Leif and Fathad made their journey towards Altnahara. Had it been up to Leif, they would have travelled to the North West Monastery by road. However, Fathad advised against it, explaining the risk of outlaws was too great to take the chance.

At night they would build up a large fire, making it unlikely wolves, bears or other predators would attack them. Through the day they made good progress, venturing even deeper into the forest. They had crossed two rivers and climbed many a hill in the last few days of their journey. The far north was filled with beautiful scenery and carried an abundance of wildlife. The area was largely untouched by man and Leif could understand why it had become such a haven for the fugitives of the Meridian Realms.

Fathad had spoken again of the growing outlaw population in the woodlands surrounding Dain. With the people growing tired of the corruption in the area, they would naturally turn to crime and flee to the wild. There were even rumours of a secret bandit village within Moormire Forest.

With Duke Delgath resigned to his bed chambers, Dain needed true leadership before the city was completely lost to disorder. The Queen in Meridia was too concerned with the Dakha uprising to the south to deal with the lack of rule in the north.

Fathad had also told the young wanderer of Badrang, Warlord of the Dakha. Leif wondered if the tyrant took Inverwall and Meridia, would Dain be safe. In any case, it did not matter for the moment, Badrang was too far away to worry about, and Leif still needed answers.

As they climbed through some particularly thick shrubbery, Fathad spoke. 'Tell me, Leif is not your real name?'

There was a small pause of silence.

'Come now, my boy, we have been travelling together for three days now.'

'No, it's not. I just adopted the name when I arrived in these lands at the woodsman's cottage I told you of.' There was another pause. 'Before that, I had no name. Thought it was best I kept the name for now. People look at you funny when you don't give them a name.'

'I understand, my boy. Who was your mother?' asked Fathad.

'I was an orphan. My mother did not have the money to look after a child,' Leif responded, showing no emotion as he brushed away a large branch.

'Did you ever meet her?' asked the elder.

'She is dead. The blue-tongue plague took her two years after I was born,' Leif replied, again showing no emotion.

'And why seek out your father?' asked Fathad.

Leif walked in silence for half a minute before he spoke again; he was hesitant to hand out true information with such free will, but he knew Fathad also had answers. 'My father was apparently a travelling soldier. He came through my home town and met my mother. It is likely he doesn't know I even exist. My mother stole the necklace and sword from him. If only she knew, no one in the village had the money to buy them from her. So she left them in the orphanage with me.' Leif continued after a brief pause. 'It is not his fault I spent my life without a mother or father; if he is alive I would like to find him.'

Fathad slowed the pace of their walk and stared at Leif. 'The life expectancy of a soldier is not great. However, if your father is alive I will help you find him.'

They were four and a half days into their journey when they found a stretch of water; it was too large to be a pond, yet too small to be a lake. The shadows of large pine trees loomed over the banks. The water was a bright silver and had a quiet atmosphere. Freckled trout were leaping for flies, disturbing its surface. The air was so peaceful and it made the two travellers want to sleep. Both Leif and Fathad scanned the treeline and to the east saw movement. Two young teenage boys were sat atop a large rock that protruded out into the water. Each boy cast a crude, make-shift fishing line into the glistening water.

Upon spotting the two travellers, the boys jumped upright and ran off into the woodlands behind them. Both Fathad and Leif looked at one another and nodded in agreement.

Fathad spoke first. 'We are too far from any village for these lads to have ventured this deep into the woods.'

'Do you think they are with the outlaws?' asked Leif.

'Nothing is certain but if I was a betting man I would have money on it. It's too late to catch them now and who knows how far their camp is. We should get moving in the opposite direction. Hopefully they will not see much point in pursuing us. Let's face it, neither of us looks like we are worth the trouble.'

Leif nodded and the two travellers headed west along the waterside in the other direction. 'How much further is Altnahara?'

'I am not sure, but considering we aren't going by road, I would say we still have the thick end of a week to go yet. If the weather is kind, we will be there quicker. We will start heading west now until we clear this forest. After which, it will take a couple of days to cross the marshlands.'

'It is a shame we did not make the full journey without being spotted.' Leif sighed.

'Leif, on this journey, it is not the bandits I am worried about,' Fathad admitted.

Chapter 17

ROAR HAD struggled to keep up the pace the last few days since the beating he had received at the hands of Captain Bruar. The swellings had reduced around his eyes but his broken jaw was proving to be the problem. He could not chew on the little food provided by their captors, but he was able to talk at a push. Roar was thankful that none of the Wolves had given in to the Captain's offer. Torquil was proving to be the strength the group needed, keeping morale high within the company.

It was night time and both Roar and Torquil whispered the plan they had come up with for when they were all going to enter the forest in a day or so.

'How can you be certain it was Rommel? You had just taken the beating of a lifetime,' asked Torquil.

'My eyes don't lie to me, Torquil, plus it's the only chance we have.' Roar paused to be sure a guard did not hear them. 'That's why, on our first night sleeping in the forest we need to sleep as far away from the group as possible. It will be cold as we will be far from the fire, but it will give Rommel a chance to sneak up to us in darkness. Hopefully we can talk to him then.'

Torquil nodded at his older companion and whispered. 'I'm glad you are still with us, Roar.'

After those words both men slept until the next morning.

It was the following day and they finally met at the neck of Boundwater River. So thick was the water that the travellers could not see the other bank. The noise of the flowing waves filled the air as it crashed into the sea. Jagged rocks and a small cliff separated the group from the water.

Captain Bruar was at the head of the line and stood next to Roar. He spat out into the great mass of water. He then turned and faced the old Wolf. 'Now, my friend, we head inland.'

Roar said nothing and only looked back at the Captain.

Bruar smirked at Roar's bruised face. 'How's the jaw? My men say you are struggling to chew your food. They say your friends have to soften it for you.' He could still see the fire burning in Roar's eyes. This was the first time they had talked since the beating. 'Granted it wasn't a fair fight, but you took a hell of a beating.' He smiled again. 'Took it like a real warrior.'

Roar stared at the Captain with burning hatred but before he could answer with what would likely get him another beating, Torquil spoke. 'How about putting a sword in his hands and see what the outcome would be in a REAL fight?' This time it was Torquil who was smiling. 'By the gods, I don't even think you would need to untie his hands. Just give him the sword and he would take you.'

The Captain continued to smile, ignoring the taunt from the young Wolf. 'Now, Torquil, be careful what you say to me. Next time, I will make you be the one to beat on Roar.' He laughed as the smile faded from Torquil's face. 'And you know how I could make you do it?'

Torquil said nothing.

'You don't know? I would give you a choice: beat up your commander, or I kill two of your men. Now don't ever speak to me like that again, Torquil,' said Captain Bruar, taking great delight in the expression on the faces of both men.

It was their first night sleeping in the forest. The survivors could hear the crashing of Boundwater River nearby, creating the perfect sound barrier for a conversation amongst them. Roar and Torquil slept on the outskirts of the group, far from the fire where it was darkest.

Torquil whispered to his commander Roar, who was lying on the ground beside him. 'Surely he will come tonight. If what you say is true, we will cross the river either tomorrow night or the next morning where it is narrowest.'

Two hours went by and it was just past midnight when Roar was woken by a small stone knocking his sore eye. Then another hit him in the chest, coming from a bush to his right. He slowly shuffled over to the bush, making it look like he was just adjusting his sleeping position. 'Is that you, Rommel?' he whispered.

'Yes it is. Don't wake Torquil. We do not want to bring attention to our conversation, old friend.'

Roar nodded and rubbed at his sore eye where the stone had hit.

'I am sorry I could not have helped you during the fight, if I had interrupted we would both be dead,' continued Rommel.

'Don't worry, you do not need to explain yourself. I understand why you did not interfere. You are lucky I spotted you on the beach,' replied Roar.

'I took the chance, and luckily the plan has worked so far. We must discuss the plan for when we reach the river ford. It is at its narrowest a day and a half from here.'

Roar did not reply this time, to avoid being heard.

'This Captain Bruar will no doubt go first with some of his men. You will be right after him I expect, with another load of corsairs behind you.'

'Aye, they will have us boxed in. What do you plan?' Roar whispered.

'When you are in the middle of the river, it will be neck high. I need you to all to drop under the water at my signal and let the flow take you down river.'

Conversation was paused as a guard patrolled round the perimeter of the camp.

When the guard had moved on Rommel continued. 'Bruar will not risk you drowning so will no doubt have rope between your legs cut. Unfortunately, I can imagine your hands will still be bound, however. You will flow downstream until you are well out of reach from *The Flaming Sails*.'

Roar thought a moment, and then replied. 'With our hands bound and a strong current, some of us may drown.'

'It's a chance we have to take, Roar; there will be no other chance until Brigands Bay,' Rommel whispered. 'A worse fate than drowning awaits you there.'

'You are right. Torquil and I will tell the men throughout the course of tomorrow,' said Roar quietly.

They then discussed the final plans before parting ways for the night.

The group had reached the river passing before nightfall the next day. They had made faster time than anticipated. This gave everyone one last sleep before they would cross. Rommel did not visit again, and Roar slept with more peace than he had since being on The Old Maid.

It was the next morning and the time to finally cross Boundwater River was with them. They all stood in a line near the bank of the flowing water when Captain Bruar ordered something no one had expected.

'I want these dogs to be bound together, in one long line. I want a length of rope to cross through each of their arms and legs. If one drowns, they all drown!' He turned and looked at Roar. 'This one knows the river is their only chance of escape!'

Roar and Torquil looked at one another – this had ruined their plans. As they were all bound together with the length of a man between them, Roar thought to himself. Racking his brain for answers he argued with his mind, *do we go with the plan? Has*

Rommel seen we are bound together? Will he still make the signal?
Just then, in a blur of unpredictability, a dagger emerged spinning through the air towards Captain Bruar. With sheer skill and balance, the Captain dodged by turning a full three sixty degrees and pivoting off his left leg. As he moved he allowed the blade to fly its deadly course into one of his men standing behind.

The sharp weapon buried deep into the corsair's throat. He clawed at the handle of the blade as blood poured down his chest. His red hands slipped over the blade as he tried to pull it out of his flesh. Gargling his last breath, he eventually fell to his knees and died.

As Captain Bruar barked orders to find the thrower, Roar studied the handle of the blade. He knew this steel hilted knife belonged to his friend Rommel.

Chapter 18

I
T HAD been a full day since Fathad and Leif spotted the two teenage boys. They continued to make their way west through the thick forest. The weather had again taken a turn for the worse and with the trees thinning it required the use of their capes. Climbing hills and pushing through bushes was not easy with a damp heavy cloak, but both men persevered. Fathad pondered if they should stop, make camp and allow the weather to pass. He hoped the weather was covering their tracks. He reassured himself and knew even the most coin-starved outlaw would not risk entering the Spectral Marsh.

'We are entering dangerous lands, my boy, the ground is damp. We can't be far from the marshes,' the old man said, as they stepped out into the start of the marshlands.

Ever since Fathad's comment the day before, Leif had been troubled by what Fathad was afraid of in these lands. 'By dangerous, you mean terrain or something else?'

'I mean a bit of both, my boy. We will soon be upon The Spectral Marsh. I think it is best if we rest here for a while and wait for this weather to pass. The cloaks are sheltering us from the rain, but with the damp ground we will get colder.'

Leif nodded in agreement and they set about making a modest camp site.

As the fire crackled under the cover of a large willow tree, the two men broke into a stale loaf of bread with some dried fish.

Leif was first to speak. 'What is the purpose of Altnahara?'

Fathad had been surprised it had taken Leif this long to ask some real questions about the Monastery. 'I cannot tell you much, Leif, other than it is like any other monastery. It is the place of worship, of discipline and art. As for its purpose, it is not my place to tell you.' He could see disappointment in the young man's eyes. 'But all will be revealed when we get there, my boy.'

'I understand, Fathad. Do you still think we are in danger of being attacked by outlaws this close to the marsh?' asked Leif.

'I would say the chance of an outlaw attack is small, but as I said yesterday it is not outlaws that worry me,' Fathad said, knowing what Leif's next question would be.

Sure enough the young wanderer spoke. 'What is it?'

'Again, my boy, it is not something I can tell you about. You must wait until we reach Altnahara.'

That was the last straw and Leif finally snapped. Usually a patient and calm man, he could not tolerate being kept in the dark any longer, especially considering the trust he had placed in the elder man. 'I am sick of waiting. You leave me in the dark as though I were some boy. I have spent twenty-five years on this earth, I have seen and done many things. Tell me what you know of this.' He took out his rune necklace and pointed it at the old man sitting next to him.

Fathad studied the face of the young wanderer and spoke. 'Leif, it was not a coincidence I happened to find you in Dain.' He paused, before taking a deep sigh and continuing. 'I am a Cleric from Altnahara. At our monastery we hold keys to knowledge and power. It was about a month ago when we felt your presence. I was entrusted to find you before *they* did.'

Shocked and more confused than ever, Leif was not sure which question he should ask next. 'Who are *they*?'

Fathad felt as though he had already said too much, but knew he needed to continue for the sake of his new companion. 'The Seekers,' he responded, solemnly.

Even stronger confusion painted itself across Leif's face.

'They are a group of supernatural beings who hunt those who carry hope for humanity.' Fathad's voice cracked as he spoke, he coughed and tried to continue with a calmer voice. 'That necklace around your neck, it belonged to a Dawnbringer, a worshipper of Amundsen and a keeper of knowledge. Dawnbringers are chosen by the gods to serve as protectors of our world.'

'The Seekers, The Dawnbringers, I have never heard of either of them?' said Leif.

'And nor should you have. The Seekers have not been seen by normal-folk for over forty years. With time, stories turn to myth and are soon forgotten,' Fathad explained.

'And are you saying I am a Dawnbringer?' asked Leif.

'Of that I cannot be certain. The bloodline has thinned so much, only a few can tell. Your father or anyone in your family could have acquired the rune by some other means,' replied Fathad, a thin expression of concern on his face.

Leif studied the rune around his neck and rubbed the markings with his thumb. 'Should we not keep moving? What if the Seekers find me here?'

'I cannot imagine them looking for you this deep into the wilderness,' explained Fathad. 'We shouldn't have to worry about anything tonight. I doubt even the spirits will bother us.'

Not able to get the Seekers from his mind, Leif continued. 'How many are there? Seekers, I mean.'

'I do not know how many ride in their hunt these days,' replied Fathad.

'You have seen them?' asked Leif.

'Yes, I have seen them twice, once as a child when they killed my father and uncle. The other time when I was about your age.' He took a mouthful of water from his pouch and continued. 'When I saw them last, they rode in a group of thirty. Before they appear, the air turns cold and thick; you struggle to breathe. A thin layer of red mist lingers on the ground and you can hear the faint screeching of tortured horses. There are few who can fight them, and fewer yet who even stand a chance of defeating them.'

Leif could see the distress on Fathad's face but asked in a respectful tone, 'Was your father a Dawnbringer?'

Fathad did his best to stay calm and remain emotionless. 'No, he wasn't, he served as a courier for Altnahara. But he was my father and meant more to me than anything. He was a great man.' As he spoke, he caught Leif's eyes. 'In the times to come remember these words. A man is not born, he is made.'

As they readied themselves to rest, Leif echoed those words in his head over and over again, until he finally slept in the darkness of the Spectral Marsh.

Chapter 19

THE DRILL squares were alive with activity as the soldiers of Inverwall trained under the new leadership of The Knightguard. It had only been a week since Sir Oakheart took charge of the southern capital, but the defences were already improving. The men worked in rotation – a quarter of the forces would be tearing down the buildings and structures south of the wall while the other three quarters practised combat and archery in the training yards.

None of the platoons particularly impressed the Knightguard at hand-to-hand combat, but there was one squad of fifty archers who seemed to know what they were doing with a bow. Their Captain, who went by the name of Guillow, had started a ranking system within the squad. Improve your rank and make the top ten, you would get a chance to drink ale at night, while the other forty would run laps of the courtyard. This ingenious leadership ploy did not go unnoticed by Sir Oakheart and the other knights.

It was midday and the Knightguard were patrolling through the training masses. They paid particular attention to one group of fifty men who were practising parrying and counter moves. They watched for half an hour as a tournament started with wooden swords.

One very large soldier with the nickname "Stonesword" had won eleven sparrings in a row and Sir Nolan could not resist.

The old knight took a step forward into the circle made by the surrounding soldiers. 'Right, lad, let me have a go at you.' He picked up a wooden sword and shield. 'And I don't want any of this "too old" nonsense. Give me your best or you will be doing laps all night!'

'Very well!' smirked Stonesword.

They began to circle round one another, each with their own fighting stance. Sir Nolan's sword was resting on the top edge of his shield, his eyes peering down the wooden blade. Stonesword had his shield close to his side with his sword-arm out on his right.

The larger man stood at six foot four inches, half a foot larger than the older Sir Nolan. As the fight commenced Stonesword lurched forward and made a downward swipe but the knight parried with his shield and took a nimble step back. The reach of the bigger man had prevented Sir Nolan from making a counter strike.

'If you didn't have your height, you would have been caught out,' said Sir Nolan.

The knight regathered his stance and awaited Stonesword's next move. It came, this time a little quicker. With a tight grip of his shield, the old knight wheeled around and caught the big man directly on the chin.

Stonesword staggered back and dropped his own shield. He could feel the heavy eyes of his comrades on him. He felt his face redden with embarrassment and annoyance.

'Pick it up, pup!' Sir Nolan said comically, nodding towards the wooden shield on the ground between them.

Stonesword gathered his shield along with his senses. He wasted no more time and rushed the knight again with a barrage of attacks, forgetting technique, coordination and poise. Three strikes landing hard on the knight's shield and the forth striking Sir Nolan's sword.

This was when the knight took his chance to counter. Sir Nolan moved to the left with the speed of a man half his age and struck the big man's sword-arm with the strength of a man double his size. The impact of the attack caused the big soldier to drop the wooden weapon.

Stonesword knew he was defeated. As he massaged his aching arm he bent down onto one knee and dropped his head.

Sir Nolan smiled. 'You're good, lad, don't get me wrong. You just need to remember to keep breathing during the fight. That will stop you from losing your head. If you lose that, it won't be long before everything else follows.' He tapped the larger man on the shoulder and marched back to his Knightguard companions. 'Size isn't everything,' he said as he winked at the large Sir Lenath.

'It would be a different story if you came up against me and Deathbringer here.' The big knight said as he tapped the leather-strapped handle of his two handed battle-axe.

'Whatever helps you sleep at night, pup,' laughed Sir Nolan.

They continued to monitor the progress of the training throughout the day until almost all of the platoons returned to their respective barracks. Again, forty of Captain Guillow's company were doing laps of the square well into the night. The Captain was among them this time. The Knightguard liked the way this man conducted himself. They all agreed they should speak to him the next day.

It was the next morning and Sir Lenath and Sir Shale were studying the sign-in sheet at the front door of the Keep. The larger of the two was first to speak. 'Perhaps we should have them write their purpose of visit, also?'

Sir Shale nodded in agreement. 'Wonder how many of them will actually visit the Keep then?'

'Something isn't right about this place, Shale. Last night when I was sleeping, I could hear muttering in the corridors outside my room. When I opened the door to see who it was no one was there.' He scrolled his fingers down the pages, counting the personnel who would have been in the Keep during that time. 'Granted it was probably just some guard patrolling the halls relighting the candles, but I don't mind saying this, Shale, I had Deathbringer by my side.'

'I agree with you. It worries me the damage it would do to morale within the city if one of us was killed during the night. The men need to believe we have sorted out the rat problem within these walls.' Sir Shale stared at Sir Lenath with a concerned look. 'It's only a matter of time before one of us falls.'

It was the afternoon council of the Knightguard and Sir Talon spoke about how the south killing-fields had been improving. 'We have cleared almost all the buildings and will soon be ready to construct the wooden barricades.'

'Good to hear it is all coming together. Shale, what news do you have from the scouts?' asked Sir Oakheart.

'I received a falcon this morning from the group we sent south. They report Badrang's horde is still unmoved. They will notify us if they start marching north,' Sir Shale replied.

'Good, so it still looks like we have a little longer before they arrive. Nolan and Lenath, how comes the training of the men?'

Before either of the knights could answer, the sounding of the southern alarm bell echoed through their ears. With no words, the five Knightguards charged out of the Keep and sprinted to the south wall. They felt the heat before they saw what it was. The great southern gate, the main defence against invaders, was engulfed in a deep red flame.

Chapter 20

I N T H E moments following the thrown knife, chaos had reigned. That was definitely not the signal Roar had been waiting for. He wondered what in the name of Sarpen Rommel was thinking to take on a group of twenty corsairs by himself.

Captain Bruar had sent out a search party while everyone else waited on the riverbank to the north, wondering who or what they would come back with.

The search party returned two hours later, with no head. 'Whoever that was, Cap'n, they know how to move about the forest without leaving tracks.'

The infuriated Captain paced back and forth, anger burning in his eyes. 'He must be one of the Wolves.' He turned to Roar and studied the face of the old Wolf. 'Why else would he be following us this far? The closest town to us is Brigands Bay, and I can't imagine anyone from there picking a fight with The Flaming Sails!'

'What you want us to do, Cap'n?'

'For now, Flint, we cross the river.' He turned again to Roar. 'And this one better pray his little friend doesn't appear again.'

It was a tough operation to cross the river, it had proved very difficult. The strong current tugged at the prisoners as they pulled each other through, kicking out their legs and arms as much as they could. Aside from a few coughs and wet lungs, they all made it across without drowning. As they climbed onto the mossy riverbank on the other-side they each thanked the gods. Wasting no time in moving out again, they marched south west in order to meet the beach again and follow the coast to Brigands Bay. The Captain had decided not to remove the length of rope binding the Wolves together, seeing it as another reason for them not to make a run for it.

Roar and Torquil walked together in the middle of the line whispering to one another.

'That was our last chance to escape. Tonight, when we are setting up camp, we are going to get close to the Captain. I'm going to go for the curved dagger he keeps in his belt. With any luck I will take him before his men get to me,' said Roar.

'You can't, Roar, there are too many of them,' replied Torquil, as quietly as he could.

Roar could see the fear in the young Wolf's eyes. 'Torquil, you must understand, if we make it to this Bay we will be as good as dead. Escaping from there will be impossible.'

It was close to nightfall when the line was halted. Captain Bruar was still in a foul mood and called for Roar to speak with him, while the rest gathered supplies for camp. The Captain stared at the treeline and smiled as his prisoner approached him. 'Do you think he is watching us now, Roar?'

'How would I know, you fool?' Roar replied. He knew his only hope of getting a hold of that dagger in the Captain's belt would be during a fight.

The Captain decided to ignore the fool comment and continued. 'I think he is watching us and I am going to prove it right now.'

As he spoke, Bruar drew back a powerful punch and knocked Roar to the ground, re-breaking his healing jaw. He turned back to the forest and called into the darkening wilderness. 'Do you like that!?' Looking back at his victim he continued to shout. 'This will make you come out!'

Torquil had the perfect view of the beating that was taking place. He watched in horror as Roar was struck again and again in the face, his head arching back with each blow. Blood splattered from Bruar's knuckles after each unblocked punch.

'You are killing him!' Torquil called out in anguish.

The Captain stopped and allowed a dazed Roar to spit out a mouthful of blood. 'Maybe I am beating on the wrong dog here? Flint, bring that young one.'

'Yes, Cap'n,' Flint replied as he grabbed the young Torquil by the back of the neck and dragged him over to the Captain.

The young Wolf was thrown at the feet of the brutal leader of The Flaming Sails. He spat sand out of his mouth and looked at his captor with courageous defiance. 'There are worse fates than death.'

It was the moment Roar had been waiting for. In a groggy state, he lunged at the Captain with his bound hands and grabbed the dagger from the belt.

Panic appeared in Bruar's eyes as Roar began pushing the blade towards his chest. With blood-soaked hands, the Captain pushed back at the dagger as it made its way closer and closer to his flesh.

'It's time for you to die, Bruar,' said Roar as he felt the power in his arms return to him with the adrenaline.

With all his strength Captain Bruar pushed against Roar's thick forearms, but even half-beaten the commander of the Wolves of Glory was too strong for him. Bruar knew he was going to die, and it was going to be one of his own prisoners that killed him. The Captain gasped a sigh of relief when Flint appeared with the butt of his cutlass and knocked Roar off him.

In the following moments Captain Bruar pulled himself back to his feet. He looked about the group and regained his composure. Running his fingers through his long greasy black hair, he looked down at the battered Roar. He let out a chuckle before drawing back and landing a heavy kick that caught the prisoner square on the nose, knocking him unconscious. Bruar turned to his saviour Flint and nodded with a smile. 'That Old Wolf almost had me there.'

The Captain had lost all patience and picked up the dagger from the sands. He strode across to Roar and grasped a clump of his hair and used it to lift his unconscious head. He looked back to the forest and raised the dagger to the throat of Roar. 'It's time for you to come out of your hiding place. If you don't, I'll kill him!' Before waiting for an answer, he added, 'Trust me, I don't lie and this one is proving more hassle than he is worth.'

Silence followed from the forest and the Captain smiled. 'Well, Roar, it looks like this is the end.' He pressed the blade against Roar's throat but before he broke the skin, he heard a call from the treeline.

Chapter 21

THE MARSHLANDS had proved difficult to travel through. With the rain as heavy as it had been, the water levels had risen in the lower parts, making some areas impassable. Leif and Fathad had stuck to the high grounds where they could, but with the water levels rising it made travelling at night impossible. Finding a dry site to make camp was proving as equally difficult.

'Should we not consider taking the roads the rest of the way?' asked Leif.

Fathad had not wanted to take the roads unless they had no other choice and this close to Altnahara the road was as dangerous as ever. 'What do you think we should do? I will leave the decision in your hands.'

Leif studied the expression on the old man's face. 'We should take the roads. If we continue through the marshes, we will surely drown or die from the cold.' He could see the worry on Fathad's face, but it did not alter his decision. 'What way to the road?'

'The road should be half a day north,' replied Fathad.

The two travellers had an uneventful half-day before reaching the road that would lead them directly to Altnahara. They decided they would not walk directly on the worn dirt road but would instead stay close by and follow it to the monastery.

The rain continued to hammer onto the two companions, but they made good progress. Arms folded with his hood up, Leif asked, 'Have the Seekers ever been inside Altnahara?'

'No, they cannot enter our monastery,' said Fathad.

'So, we will be safe there?' said Leif.

'Altnahara is the safest place in existence. That's why it was built, to protect the Dawnbringers and keep our knowledge safe,' explained Fathad.

'And what exactly makes Dawnbringers so special?'

'It is hard to explain, my boy. They are gifts from the gods. They hold the knowledge to bring darkness and evil to an end. Bringing Dawn to the Night as it were.' Fathad continued, 'That's why the Seekers hunt them, as there is nothing more evil than them.'

'And where did the Seekers come from?' asked Leif.

'They were put on this earth by Sarpen, in defiance of the other gods. It is Sarpen's wish to walk in our world and he uses the Seekers to help him with his quest,' said Fathad.

'I understand what you are saying but in my experience the gods haven't done much for anyone. In my hometown we had a shrine to Amundsen but like all such places it did little to help our poor people. The local priests would only use their words and actions to line their own purses.'

'Unfortunately it is like that almost everywhere these days, my boy. They are not true followers of the gods, only pretenders who do not remember that true values come from within,' explained Fathad.

Leif paused for a moment. He continued to think of the Seekers. He was growing fond of Fathad and he was sure he could trust him. 'I remember you saying their number changes – do people join them?'

'Yes, corrupted souls can join the Seekers' hunting party. They are the evilest of men, who have committed unspeakable acts. Sarpen rewards them by giving them unnatural long life, but they are bound to the hunt and his will for the rest of their days.'

'Can you kill one?' asked Leif.

'I believe it can be done, yes.' Fathad nodded, as rain water fell from the top of his hood. 'But that hasn't happened in my lifetime.'

The wind was picking up and Leif could feel the cold air slapping his wet face. He turned his head to take shelter and asked Fathad how much further they had to travel.

'We aren't far, should arrive tomorrow.' He stopped and looked towards a sheltered group of trees two minutes away from the road. 'We should stop and have some rest, it won't be long before nightfall is upon us.'

The two travellers again made camp, hoping it would be the last time before Altnahara. They created a makeshift barrier from the wind under the cover of the trees and removed their dripping wet cloaks. They were thankful their capes had kept their underclothes largely dry. Fathad had forbidden the use of a campfire this close to the road.

They had slept for a good five hours when it was time to make tracks again. The weather was mild, and the rain had stopped. The day passed quickly, and conversation had continued regarding the Dawnbringers and the Seekers. Fathad had also explained that the leader in Altnahara would be able to offer much greater details.

'We are close, it is just over this hill, on the other side of those trees. Only an hour to go,' said Fathad.

'Good to hear, but I must admit, for the first time in my life I am nervous,' said Leif.

'You shouldn't be nervous, my lad. Our leader is a great man, and he will sense that you are too,' Fathad replied.

There was a sudden mass of fluttering and Leif turned around and looked south where he could see a pack of crows take flight from the cover of a group of trees. He shivered and moved on while taking a small bite from the apple in his hands. 'It is a little colder than yesterday, but at least it's dry!' said Leif as another shudder shot up his back.

With the distant screeching of crows, Fathad stopped in the middle of the road. He seemed to be deep in thought when Leif asked him what was wrong. The young wanderer could see the old man's eyes scanning the dirt beneath their feet.

A light dusting of red mist littered the ground.

Chapter 22

I T HAD taken three hours to put the fire out and by then it was too late to save the gate. The timber was ruined and charcoal black. Thankfully no one had been hurt by the flames except for a few small burns. There had fortunately been no attempt at desertion, which surprised everyone considering the loss of the city's main defence. The Knightguards had expected that the soldiers would lose heart at this, but so far they remained loyal and strong.

Sir Oakheart paced back and forth in front of his knight companions and the twenty Captains he had summoned to the council room.

It was Sir Talon who spoke first and slammed his clenched fist on the table, startling some of the Captains. 'How did this happen?'

Sir Oakheart stopped and faced the group. 'We have a serious rat problem in this city and it's about time we do something about it.'

'What was the point in them burning the gate now? The army is nowhere near us. Surely they are worried,' said Sir Lenath.

Sir Nolan was next to step forward and speak. 'That gate will take half a week to repair. It is meant to slow down our preparations. However, you are right, brother, this was an act of panic. Badrang knows our plans are working and he needed to do something.'

'We need to find the culprit,' said Sir Talon.

'And how will we do that?' asked Sir Lenath.

'The guilty one will have burns on his hands. There is no way he would have been able to set something like that alight without the use of oil. He must have been close as someone would see him throwing a torch,' replied Sir Talon.

Captain Thalue of Inverwall was next to speak. 'Whatever is required of us we are willing. We are at your disposal as always. We will not stop until this traitor is brought to justice.'

'Thank you, Captain,' said Sir Talon.

Sir Oakheart had always known the city would be infested with spies, but this was proving worse than he had ever anticipated. They had recorded all messages sent to and from the falconry. They had guests sign in and out of the Keep, while also stating their business. He had even set up a pairing system among the soldiers, to limit the number of isolated individuals. Still, something like this had happened.

The rest of the meeting played out, and it was decided that all Captains were to inspect their men for burns. Unfortunately, it did not help that most of the men had assisted in putting out the fires and a lot had suffered from minor injuries. The barracks were also to be turned inside out in the hope of finding contraband items like oil or fire-starting items.

The Knights knew it was time to act against the spies within the city. If this was the damage the traitors were willing to do with Badrang weeks away, they knew they would be much more dangerous with the enemy forces just outside their door.

Scouts were still reporting an estimate of fifty thousand men in Badrang's forces. However, Sir Oakheart was still feeling positive and he knew that with the gate rebuilt, the killing fields to the south ready and the oil soaked wooden barriers they would have a great chance of holding Inverwall against any number. The men had been improving daily with the training regimes of Sir Nolan, and Sir Talon had almost cleared the fields to the south.

Sir Oakheart's mind began to wander back to Meridia. He wondered what was happening with the Queen. It was time he wrote to her instead of sitting procrastinating. He made his way up the winding stone steps to his bedchambers in the west tower. He entered the room and strode towards the desk near the window. After sitting, he picked up a quill and began to write on an empty piece of parchment.

My Lady Queen,

I hope this letter finds you well. I write to inform you of the progress made here at Inverwall.

Our plans are ahead of time and we have all but completed our operations in the south fields.

We had an incident today with the south gate that will postpone some of our other plans. It sometimes feels Badrang has as many men within these walls as we do.

We have decided that should Badrang offer us "A Battle of Champions" we will accept. With the force he possesses he will not honour the agreement should General Malacath fall, so we do not plan to either. It will give us a chance to take down this myth of a man and let his forces feel fear.

I wish I could be by your side in times such as these, but my true place is here with the men.

Sir Oakheart was coming towards the end of his letter and he could feel the overwhelming urge to tell his Queen his true feelings. He remembered their childhood together, their friendship. Every minute they had ever spent with one another filled his head like an overflowing stream. Fighting back tears, he resisted the urge and instead signed his letter.

With honour and loyalty.
Your Knightguard Commander,
Sir Oakheart

He rose from the table and heated the wax over the candle burning to his right. After he had left his print at the bottom of the page, he allowed it to cool and rolled the parchment up and sealed it shut.

Sir Oakheart then turned from the table and unfastened the white cloak from around his shoulders. After unbuckling his sword belt and dropping the sheathed blade onto his bed, he walked over to his wash basin and threw a handful of water over his face. He massaged his head and tried to get Queen Orellia from his mind.

As he rubbed the cool liquid into his tired eye, he was startled by a loud creak on the wooden floorboards behind him. The knight wheeled around quick enough to dodge the first swing of a sword. The blade crashed down onto the basin, spilling clear water everywhere. The knight then reached for his hip dagger and launched himself at the hooded assassin, whose face he could not see. With his right arm Oakheart tried to stab at the intruder and with his left he managed to grasp his enemy's sword-hand. The two were locked, hand in fist. They were each holding the opposite's weapon. Sir Oakheart could see the man wore coarse leather gloves.

The Knightguard Commander had already noticed that under his hood and cloak, the intruder wore an Inverwallian military uniform. He gave the assassin one large head-butt which sent them both crashing to the floor. He gathered his feet and reached for his bed. Grasping the hilt of his sword, he unsheathed the blade and spun round in time to ram the point straight through the traitor's stomach.

With warm red blood covering his hands and white tunic, he knelt down and lifted the hood of his enemy. He shook his head as he saw Captain Thalue's lifeless eyes staring back at him.

Chapter 23

C APTAIN BRUAR looked back at his line of prisoners as they approached Brigands Bay; he could not contain his smirk. With an already infamous reputation, this was his greatest achievement to date. Defeating and capturing one of the most recognisable mercenary groups in the land made his chest swell with pride.

The bay itself was a large cove that carved itself into the land. It held close to twenty corsair vessels, each docked on bustling wooden quaysides. The small village built on the bay was a refuge for all the scum of the Meridian Realms. Bandits and pirates alike would come from miles around to make their trade amongst the other outlaws. The market stalls were full of goods that criminals had stolen or killed for throughout the lands.

The Flaming Sails and their captives entered through the tall wooden palisade fence and into a lively street smothered with wet brown mud.

With a rag covering each of their mouths, Roar, Rommel and Torquil walked one after the other through the thick sloppy streets. The other eight Wolves of Glory, bound and gagged, stumbled behind them. They watched as fights broke out at each passing tavern. Grizzled old lawbreakers stared at the line of marching slaves as they guzzled down tankards of grog and mead. Other drunk inhabitants of Brigands Bay were dangling a few bronze coins at busty women sitting on a high balcony making crude gestures.

The stale smell of rotten food, sea water and excrement filled the air. The marching Wolves did their best to keep their vomit down.

The group passed a slaughter house that had a dozen dead pigs hung out to be gutted and skinned. Hundreds of flies swarmed the meat as a butcher within could be heard slamming his dull blade into flesh. The captives were so hungry that this didn't look unappetising.

In the days prior, Rommel had been beaten by the Flaming Sails. Bruar had to be certain Rommel was the last remaining free Wolf. It was only after The Captain had his men rip off two of Rommel's finger nails had he decided his new prisoner was telling the truth.

Rommel was thankful that none of his wounds were showing any sign of infection and they had scabbed over enough to allow him use of his right hand again. He hated Bruar, but he knew his hatred paled in comparison to what his friend Roar felt.

They marched through the town until they reached the docks. Sea birds sounded as they reached the wooden quayside of the harbour. A large-bellied, bald man came out from behind a darkened door on the main jetty. Roar and Rommel knew this man must be the leader of the port.

Captain Bruar bowed his head and walked towards the fat leader of Brigands Bay. 'Harbour Master, have you lost weight? It seems this last year has been kind to you.' He chuckled as he continued. 'You are a vision of health.'

'None of your fork-tongued comments, Bruar. What brings you here in such times?' As the Harbour Master smiled, the Wolves could see the few yellow teeth he had remaining.

'Unfortunately, we were attacked by a Sea Scale over a week ago. Just off the coast of Tornwood Forest.' The Captain turned and looked at the Wolves of Glory behind him. 'I lost my ship, but thankfully I managed to pick up this bit of coin along the way.'

'Hmmm, that's some walk for you. Going south to Blackland, are you? I take it you have come to me for a new ship?'

'My good Master Neg, you always were a clever one. You are indeed correct, we do plan on purchasing a ship and making our way south.'

The Harbour Master looked at the tall, thin Captain Bruar and smiled. 'I think I have a better plan for The Flaming Sails.' He could see that Bruar was intrigued and continued. 'On the day after tomorrow, we are having a large meeting with the other crews anchored here. I think it might be of interest to the great Captain Bruar and his band of fighters to also attend.'

'Neg, you always knew how to draw in my attention. We will make ourselves a cosy nest here in your beautiful town and wait for this meeting.'

The Harbour Master let out a large burp followed by a heavy cough. 'Tell your men I want no trouble here. They must respect the code; I want no murder here in Brigands Bay.'

That evening the Wolves slept, bound together in a small pig pen outside *The Rusty Dagger Inn*. The Flaming Sails had spent both nights drinking, sleeping and gambling in the tavern. From what the surviving Wolves could gather, Brigands Bay must hold thousands of outlaws and pirates.

It was late into their second day in the Bay and the group were huddled in the pig mud, eating some rotten vegetables. 'How could a place like this exist? Especially this far north of the Marble Mountains. It's a bounty-hunter's dream,' said Torquil.

'You are right, but there aren't enough bounty-hunters in the world to take this place,' said Rommel.

Roar was sitting quiet while the others conversed amongst themselves. Rommel and Torquil feared that the commander had given up all hope. 'Roar, do you not want some of these turnips? We need to keep our strength up.'

Roar didn't answer immediately but eventually responded with the use of his agonising jaw. 'What's the point? This place has finished us. Whatever it is these Captains will be discussing tomorrow will be unwelcome news for us.'

Downhearted after hearing his commander's words, Torquil grasped a particularly rotted turnip in his fingers. As he brought the foul-smelling vegetable up to his mouth he felt it break and some of the dirt and juices ran off his hands down onto his lap. The young Wolf wondered a moment and let his mind work. He began to rub the mushy turnips on the bindings around his wrists, squeezing the vegetable to get as much juice as possible. Quietly he then beckoned one of the pigs over to him. He coaxed the beast into smelling the soaked rope and sure enough it wasn't long before his plan worked. The pig began to gnaw through his binding until Torquil was able to break it in two.

Raising his two free hands up to his friends he chuckled. 'Well, Sirs, I think it's time we got out of here.'

In the next ten minutes they were all free from their bindings. They crouched deep in the mud amongst their grunting saviours, who were happily enjoying the rest of the turnips.

'Remind me to never eat pork again,' said Hunter, one of the Wolves, as he patted a pig on the back. 'Who'd have thought a pig would save a pack of wolves?'

'When do we make a move?' asked another voice, directing the question at Rommel.

In the time building up to this moment, Rommel had been giving their situation a lot of thought. He knew his friends would not like what they were about to hear, but he spoke anyway. 'Men, I know you have already been through much pain, but I must ask for one more day.'

There was immediate discontent within the ranks, some were even looking ready to get up and make a run for it.

Roar then interrupted the bickering with his gruff voice. 'Silence, all of you. This man risked everything to try and save us back in the forest. He could have turned the opposite direction and be living a quiet life the rest of his days. No one here moves until we hear what Rommel has to say.' He turned back to his old friend. 'Go on.'

Rommel nodded at his fellow commander and continued. 'We won't last long out in the wild without weapons, or supplies. The Flaming Sails will be straight after us, and we will not have time to hunt or fish for food.' He briefly scanned around at the group; most were now nodding in agreement. 'At this meeting tomorrow, no one will be permitted weapons inside. All the blades, bows, axes and clubs will be stored away from the gathering while the Captains talk.'

The old commander continued to outline his plan deep into the night until each of the Wolves of Glory were nodding with agreement. They slept peacefully, all ready for the next day.

Chapter 24

'**I** SAID, RUN, boy!'

Leif could hear Fathad shouting, but he could not move his feet. The echoing sound of tortured horses filled his ears as the heavy air filled his lungs. He snapped away from his fear and broke into a sprint. He was surprised how an elderly man such as Fathad could keep the pace, but they both ran alongside one another.

They could now hear the sound of hooves behind them as the horses screeched in agony. Leif dared not look back as the red mist about his feet broke with each stride. The sky had grown dark and grey in a matter of minutes and he could feel the freezing air penetrate his lungs.

'Cut through the trees, they won't be able to follow us on their horses,' Fathad shouted, as they ran off the road and into the forest. 'We aren't far from Altnahara. If we get there we will be safe.'

As they broke through some bushes and into shelter they slowed down to catch their breath. From the cover of the trees, they could hear the Seekers on the road screaming with annoyance. The two travellers slowed to a jog as they continued through the woodlands. 'Have we lost them?' asked Leif.

'No, we still have to go back on the road before we are at the Monastery,' said Fathad, with a calm panic in his eyes. 'They will be waiting for us to leave the cover of these trees. Look, you can still see the mist.'

For the next half hour, the two travellers worked their way

through the woodland, until they came to the final stretch of road between them and Altnahara.

'Look, there it is,' said Fathad as he pointed to the monastery atop a small hill, surrounded by wheat fields. 'I don't want to make a run for it, but we have no choice. When we are in the walls, it will protect us.'

'Let's go then,' said Leif, as he unclipped his heavy cape in preparation. He felt the cloak fall down the back of his legs and left the material lying on the cold ground. He unbuckled his duffle and tossed it aside, now ready for the sprint.

Rain began to fall, and a crackle of lightning could be heard in the near distance. The air was as cold as ever and Leif suppressed his fear. Both men nodded at one another, signalling the start of the run.

They were a dozen steps out into the road when the screeching started again, and the red mist engulfed their feet. They broke into a sprint as the horses appeared behind them.

While in full sprint, Leif turned his head slightly to look back. He saw a large group of spectral horsemen chasing them. They were approaching fast, and he could feel his heart pounding through his chest. He then heard a voice inside his head that spoke in a hoarse, ghostly whisper.

'We come for you,' spoke the voice.

Leif screamed in pain but pushed through and kept strides with the older Fathad.

The Seekers continued to scream as they chased their prey, getting closer and closer as they galloped down the road.

'We come for you both!' the voice spoke again.

Knowing there was no way they were going to make it to Altnahara, Fathad stopped in the road and in turn, so did Leif.

'What are we doing?' shouted Leif, as he took a few extra strides and stopped. He looked back at his old companion and their pursuers ahead of him.

'We are not going to make it. They are going to catch us. We must make a stand,' said Fathad as he unbuckled his sword belt and unsheathed his blade. The old man's gaze did not leave the Seekers as he threw his scabbard and belt aside to the wet ground. The sword's steel glistened as if it had the sun's reflection.

The Seekers stopped in the road in front of the two travellers. The largest of the group strode forward and dismounted his monstrous steed. He beckoned to Fathad and spoke. 'It is time for you both to die. By his word, we do not fail.'

The Seeker's voice was cold and relentless. It cut deep into the very soul of Leif. Obviously the leader, this Seeker headed the pack and stood tall, well over six foot. Clad in grey armour, the ghostly monster lifted the visor of his helmet to show a pale, rotted face. With jagged teeth that almost overlapped his lips, he spoke again. 'Sarpen calls for you.'

The young wanderer recoiled at the sound of the Seeker's voice but ignored yet another shiver up his spine. With young courage he stood forward and was now shoulder to shoulder with Fathad. With a firm right hand, he grasped the handle and drew the sword from over his shoulder. The blade whistled through the air as Leif took a fighting stance. The blade was ancient, and speckles of rust riddled the once immaculate steel. However, the hilt was spotless gold and the black velvet handgrip felt perfect in Leif's palms.

Before anyone could make a move, Fathad began to mutter under his breath in an ancient tongue. The mist around his legs began to whirl as Fathad clenched and opened his left hand repeatedly.

Leif tried to listen but could not understand the language.

The Seekers stared at Fathad with deep concentration as if anticipating an attack.

The leader then took a step forward and drew a serrated sword from his hip. He raised a hand, beckoning to its fellow Seekers to leave the fight to him. 'THEY ARE MINE,' it shouted with a hoarse voice.

Fathad continued to speak, only was now getting louder and louder until he was shouting in a language even the Seekers also did not recognise. The winds began to howl, and the earth trembled as each word cut through the air.

As the leader of the Seeker readied itself for its first attack there was a sudden burst of light from behind the two travellers. The light blinded Leif and sent the Seeker hurtling back towards the rest of its team.

The angry servant of Sarpen quickly rose to its feet and grasped its jagged blade. It roared at its enemy and launched forward.

Another beam of light shot from behind Leif and this time he covered his eyes to avoid the pain. The young wanderer felt the ground shake as Fathad's shouts echoed through his ears and the light burned his eyelids. The intensity in the air grew as he heard the Seekers wail in pain. The power grew and grew until just then, in a single moment, all was still.

Leif opened his eyes. His head was heavy, and it took a few seconds for his eyes to adjust back to the light. The air was calm and relaxed. No noise, no red mist, no Seekers. Leif turned to his left, and there was no Fathad. It was then, he collapsed.

Chapter 25

I T WAS the early part of the next evening and The Wolves of Glory sat in the wet mud alongside the pigs who had saved their lives. The group had loosely replaced their bindings and were eagerly awaiting the evening meeting of the Brigands Bay leaders. They noticed how busy the Bay had become as the streets and taverns were crammed with pirates. Another dozen ships had arrived in port, with each captain desperate to hear the harbour master's proposal.

It was not long before Captain Bruar appeared. He had donned his new clean clothes and looked at his most presentable. He walked past his prisoners with Flint by his side; he looked down at the pitiful bunch and laughed as Roar's bruised face caught his eye. 'Flint, I want you to stay out here and watch this lot until the meeting is over.'

After the Captain had left and entered The Rusty Dagger Inn to attend the meeting, Flint turned to the Wolves. 'What are you looking at?' He gathered as much fluid as he could and spat at Roar. He laughed as he watched the old Wolf wipe the saliva from his face. 'Correct me if I'm wrong, but the Captain has beaten you twice, right?'

Roar responded with a smile. 'Your time will come.'

'But not before yours.' Flint smirked as he took a seat near the fence.

Over the next fifteen minutes, the Wolves watched as the rest of the leaders in the Bay entered the Inn, each unbuckling their weapons before entering. 'They will be stored in a room close to the entrance of the building,' said Rommel referring to the weapons.

Another fifteen minutes had passed since the last of the guests seemed to have arrived. It was now time for Torquil to make his move. He made a faint whistle and called out to Flint.

'Me? What do you want?' replied Flint.

'Would you mind sitting somewhere else, your smell is rather unbearable,' said the young Wolf with a smile.

With a red face, Flint rolled up his sleeves, unlatched the gate to the pen and entered. 'Captain has given me permission to thrash you if you speak out of turn.'

As the pirate made his way towards the seemingly defenceless Torquil he was taken with sudden shock, when Roar appeared behind him, legs and arms no longer secured together. The old Wolf threw his hand over Flint's mouth to prevent him from screaming.

As the corsair struggled for breath, he bit down on Roar's hand as hard as he could. He could feel blood fill his mouth and run down his throat. The corsair needed air, but couldn't wrestle away from the Wolf's thick forearms.

Roar winced with pain as teeth sank deeper into his hand, but he refused to let go until his enemy was no longer moving. He dropped the lifeless body and looked down at the corpse. 'Seems your time was before mine after all.'

Removing his own loose bindings, Rommel climbed the pen fence and dropped down below the glowing light coming from a side window of The Rusty Dagger. He slowly lifted the latch, until there was enough space for him to hoist his body up and slip inside. He landed in a small room that held a large stove heater, most likely heating the whole building. Moving towards the door and slowly pressing down on the latch, Rommel didn't make a sound. He peered out and could see a large room to the right, another room across the corridor and to the left was the main door. From what he could hear, the conversation was coming from the main room. Patiently he waited for the opportune moment to slip across the corridor, the likely place where the weapons were stored. As clear as day, he could hear the meeting.

'So, now that introductions have been made, it is time we speak of this offer,' said Harbour Master Neg.

After the murmurs of agreement amongst the group died down, the unmistakable voice of Captain Bruar could be heard. 'Well you certainly have the attention of The Flaming Sails.'

Rommel could just imagine the smirk painted on the brutal Captain's face. The old Wolf commander, almost forgetting the weaponry, listened with deep concentration as Neg continued with his counsel.

The fat harbour master coughed and took a loud gulp of some mysterious liquid. 'We all know Badrang will take Inverwall and he has come to us with a proposal.'

There was a pause as the Captains talked amongst themselves, eventually allowing Neg to continue.

'He has offered us limitless gold if we all align ourselves with him and his southern horde,' said Neg.

'And what does this great warlord require of simple corsairs and outlaws?' asked one of the Captains.

The Harbour Master took another swig of liquid and burped. 'If we all combine our forces, we would amass a couple thousand soldiers. He is awaiting our answer before attacking Inverwall; he thinks his success will depend on our part in this.'

'Yes, but what does he actually need, Neg?' asked Captain Bruar, smugly.

As the harbour master explained, Rommel tried to keep his head at the shock of hearing the answer. The room was in uproar, some refusing and others calling in agreement. This was the chance Rommel needed. He used the distraction to slip across to the next room. Upon a long table, lay the outlaw guests' swords, daggers, and clubs. He bunched up a handful of sheathed blades, opened the window and handed them to the awaiting wolves in the darkness. 'Four more swords and that will be all eleven of us armed!' he said as he turned back to the table and buckled a cutlass around his waist. He was about to leave out of the window when curiosity took hold. He made his way back over to the door and listened to the conclusion of the meeting.

'Rommel, what are you doing?' Torquil whispered through the window as he watched his commander move back towards the door.

Ignoring his friend, Rommel peered through the gap in the door. He could see Neg standing from his seat, his fat belly bursting the buttons of his stained vest shirt. All the leaders of Brigand Bay, including Captain Bruar, raised their tankards of grog as the Harbour Master spoke. 'So, we are in agreement,' he snarled, looking around at the captains in attendance. 'We attack Inverwall from the north.'

Chapter 26

H E COULD hear songbirds chirping as he woke in a soft warm bed. Daylight peered through the blue-coloured glass of the window. As the birds continued to sound in Leif's ears, he lifted his head from the pillow and looked around for any sign of familiarity. He stared at the wooden door in the middle of the grey stone wall. Beautiful paintings hung on the wall either side, one of a peaceful apple orchard and the other an extravagant battle scene. Leif thought of the contrasts between both scenes and how the door was positioned neatly between them.

Before he could move, Leif heard footsteps from the corridor outside. The steps grew louder and louder until the door opened. As the entrance swung round it eclipsed and eventually covered the battle scene hung on the wall. Leif looked to the doorway and saw a hooded figure standing in the opening. The young wanderer made a quick move for the sword he usually kept at the foot of his bed, but it was not there. The figure made his way towards the bed and raised an old withered hand, beckoning for Leif to stop panicking. He lifted back his hood and a kindly old face smiled at the young wanderer.

'Who are you?' asked Leif. 'Where is Fathad?'

'Fathad is safe, dear boy!' answered the elder.

The combination of his smile and his voice seemed to calm Leif.

The aged man continued, 'My name is Master Rollow and this is our home.' He moved towards the window and gazed out to the square gardens. 'Welcome to Altnahara, Leif.'

Leif rose from the bed with his freshly rested arms and legs; he was in a white bed tunic and bottoms. His hair was shorter than before, and he was clean shaven. It was obvious they had washed him during his sleep.

'Will you walk with me? There is a waistcoat and gloves on the end of your bed there,' said Rollow and beckoned towards the white garments.

They both left the comfort of Leif's warm bedroom and headed out into a long stone corridor. Ancient tapestries littered the walls with a small burning torch every six paces. These torches were for keeping the interior well-lit at all times of the day. Both men made their way down the corridor in silence, the old master's white robes dragging along the wooden oak floor, giving the illusion he was gliding rather than walking.

After a few twists and turns in the long corridor, they came to a large double door, reinforced with iron latches. The old man unbolted the metal lock and opened the left door. 'After you, my boy.' He nodded towards the entrance and Leif advanced.

The young wanderer gazed in amazement at the large oval room. The high walls reached up to the dark rafters in the roof and the beams dangled beautifully-crafted chandeliers, each burning twenty white candles. On the left-hand side of the room, Leif saw a robed woman, similar age to himself, climb a ladder with a long stick in her hand. The stick was crooked at the end and burned a flame at the tip. The woman was lighting the candles on one of the hanging chandeliers.

Rollow saw the young wanderer stare at the woman. 'It is a full-time job. Keeping this place lit from darkness.'

Leif nodded with agreement and understanding that Rollow was not just talking about the candles. 'What happened to Fathad? Is he really ok?'

Rollow looked at Leif with sympathetic eyes and smiled. 'I know you worry for your companion, but I can assure you, Fathad is safe. You will see him soon, so please do not worry.'

'What was that light? Were the Seekers destroyed?'

'All will be revealed soon, my boy, but first you must eat,' said Rollow as they walked towards the centre stone table. As they approached the middle of the room, Leif was taken aback by the sheer temptation of the food in front of him. Freshly baked cinnamon bread, salted roast pheasant, garnishings of perfectly ripe vegetables. Honey-glazed carrots, lettuce, cabbage and roasted potatoes, all wafting their pleasant aroma towards the starving traveller.

'Please, help yourself. It is for you, after all,' said Rollow, with a little chuckle in his voice.

Leif was hesitant at first; he looked at the older man and remembered the words Fathad had said days ago. "Our leader is a great man, and he will sense that you are too." He nodded with thanks towards the kind man. 'Thank you, Sir.'

For the next fifteen minutes Leif sat near the end of the large table and feasted harder than he had for years. When he was full he washed his meal down with a goblet of mature red wine made with the grapes from the monastery's vineyard. He turned towards Master Rollow who was just returning to the room.

'I gather you enjoyed that,' said Rollow.

'I must apologise; my manners must have been forgotten back in the wilderness. Thank you again for all you have already given me,' replied Leif.

'Please, my boy, there is no need to apologise and you do not need to thank us. You are welcome to anything within our home.' He smiled at the young man and continued. 'I understand Cleric Fathad has given you some information on what we do, and the reason we sent him to collect you?'

'Yes, he has told me, but there is a lot I still need answers to,' Leif replied.

'We all have much to learn, Leif, and there is unfortunately no way of knowing everything. Here in Altnahara we are devoted to the gods Amundsen and Azmara.'

'Fathad told me. He said you are the enemies of Sarpen,' Leif interrupted.

'You are correct, my boy.' Master Rollow rubbed his old hands close to the warmth of a table candle before continuing. 'Some of us here are Dawnbringers, the lost bloodline of the gods. We are the keepers of knowledge and power. In the past, Dawnbringers were married into royalty, they served the Realms as leaders or advisors.'

'How many Dawnbringers are here?' asked Leif.

'Well there is me, and three other Dawnbringers here in the monastery. We lead our monks here in their studies and worship.' Rollow looked at the concentrated face of the young wanderer and continued. 'Our goal in recent years has been to increase our number and find Dawnbringers when we can. The necklace resting on your chest radiates power, my dear boy. It is an artefact of light and it led us right to you. When it got close to our monastery it sent out a signal of sorts. We are lucky Fathad found you before darkness did.'

Looking down at the rune, he spoke. 'Did it come from here?'

'Yes it did, but it left us over three hundred years ago. With what I can feel, that artefact has seen more of this world than any of us,' replied Rollow.

Trying to keep himself from becoming disappointed, Leif wondered how his father found it. He rubbed the markings with his thumb. 'How many Dawnbringers are there in the world?'

'By our estimations, there must be fewer than twenty Dawnbringers left in this world, almost all of them our age. It is objects of power that draw us to them. More often than not, however, the artefacts have changed owner over the years, and are no longer carried by their true keepers.'

Leif thought long and hard. He thought of all the lands he had travelled at such a youthful age. He thought of his upbringing in the poverty of the orphanage. He remembered teaching himself to read and fight. He thought of his mother and his father. After clearing his head and throat he spoke. 'Am I a Dawnbringer?' he asked, with bated breath.

The old man looked back at him with eyes full of emotion. 'I am afraid not, my boy.'

Chapter 27

SIR OAKHEART walked the battlements as the warm southern wind caressed his unshaven face. He felt taking charge of Inverwall had already aged him by five years. He was physically and mentally exhausted by the preparations and training. Every morning when he woke, he would review battle plans and training regimes before heading out to the practice yard himself. He would train alone in the abandoned gardens behind the main Keep. For hours he would hit the mannequin, practising his already perfect technique.

On the wall he looked to the killing fields and studied the three wooden barriers stretching the length of the passes. 'It must work. We must defend Inverwall,' he muttered under his breath.

The great southern wall itself was around thirty-foot-wide and stood uphill, towering above the killing fields. *We will fit almost a thousand archers and swordsmen on this wall,* he thought as he looked to the valley below. *And another two thousand infantry down there, divided up behind each barrier.*

He thought of the men inside the wall. W*e would have another thousand who can defend within the walls if the gate is breached.* Sir Oakheart had remained confident that the south gate would not be broken. Production of the new gate had made timely progress. If anything, the new gate was stronger than the last, and was reinforced with steel layers integrated between lengths of seasoned wood.

The middle-aged knight returned to the main Keep within the next hour. The rest of the guards had been waiting for their commander to enter the council room. Since Captain Thalue's death five days prior, there had been no other attempt at sabotaging defences. Although that did not mean the Knightguard believed all was well. In the dead Captain's quarters, they had found a list of targets. Sir Oakheart's name headed the list, with Sir Shale's also further down the page before being signed off personally by Badrang. It was a mystery as to how the letter had got past the inspection process.

In the meeting room, the Knightguards of Inverwall discussed their progress. They each sat around the table, reading their notes and detailing their progress.

Sir Lenath and Sir Talon were confident the gate would be fully reconstructed within two days' time.

Sir Nolan was extremely happy with the progress made by the men in the training yards. He sighted Captain Guillow as the man most competent to take Captain Thalue's place in being the high captain of the Inverwallians. Guillow had gratefully accepted; however, along with his new duties, he continued to run the courtyards with his platoon and was still willing to take his place on the battlements with the other archers.

'The lad is some shot. Best archer I have seen since Karius of Lyrenhall was in his prime,' Sir Nolan explained, clearly impressed. 'Hit a target hundred yards up wind. Right in the neck. Couldn't believe what I was seeing!'

The other knights nodded with approval and Sir Shale rose to speak. 'Before I speak of the scouts, I would like to further Nolan's point. This young archer Captain is wise beyond his years. I believe he would serve us well sitting amongst the council? His input could be priceless.'

'I would not be opposed to Captain Guillow sitting amongst us. Do you agree, Oakheart? It is your decision in the end?' asked Sir Talon.

Sir Oakheart nodded. 'He can only be better than the last Captain we trusted.'

The Knightguard Commander then remembered back to the night of his attempted assassination at the hands of Thalue. When they had removed the traitor's gloves, they had found severely burned hands that had been treated by an apothecary within the walls. The apothecary responsible for the treatment had been brought in for questions but had treated dozens of men with similar injuries. The healer was under the impression the injuries had come from trying to extinguish the fire, not starting it. However, there was not a doubt in Sir Oakheart's mind that Thalue was only one of the men to light the gate aflame.

Sir Shale continued to stand and deliver his update on the scouts he had sent south. 'Our men have yet to report any movement. However, something to note, two of the men managed to infiltrate the camp under guise.' Sir Shale could see concern on his commander's face but was quick to explain. 'I made the decision not to tell you, Commander. I didn't tell anyone. I thought the fewer people to know, the safer our men would be.'

After a few seconds, Sir Oakheart nodded with approval. 'Continue, Shale.'

'Well, they did not manage to get too close to Badrang, but had heard from some of his men that the warlord has been entertaining a group of shaman. They say these men come from the bowels of the Blacklands. Badrang, Malacath and the Shaman are said to spend all their time in tents.'

The rest of Knightguard listened with great intent as the young knight continued.

'It seems likely that the southern warlord is seeking the aid of sorcery to win the coming war,' added Sir Shale.

This did not surprise Sir Oakheart or the others. It had always been a suspicion of the Knightguard that Badrang entertained the dark arts. Sorcery was not uncommon in war, though rarely used to success in recent times. Most armies relied on tactics or sheer number and over the years the art of magical warfare had been lost.

'It will not help him here. Since when can sorcery break down walls?' scoffed Sir Nolan.

'It may not be his intentions to break down the wall, Nolan. Maybe his plans are more sinister than that,' said Sir Talon before turning back to Sir Shale. 'What news of Malacath?'

Sir Shale paused a moment before finally answering despondently. 'The man is a monster. The scouts have assured me all the stories and rumours we have heard of him are true.' He looked around at his companions and sighed before reading the scout report. 'Over seven-foot-tall and wears black plate armour with red trims. This "man" carries a two handed greatsword with one arm and wields it with the speed of a rapier. He kills for fun, even his own men at times. The only man who dares speak to him is Badrang. There is no hope of anyone killing this man in combat.'

'I doubt he even is a man,' said the large Sir Lenath worryingly, looking towards his Commander and Sir Talon.

'Well, if rumours are to be believed you might be right. He does not remove his helmet, and no one has seen him eat or sleep,' replied Sir Shale.

Sir Oakheart stood with an intense purpose and slammed his fist hard against the oak table. 'We are not to breathe a word of this to anyone. If our men find out the weapons Badrang possesses, it will be harder for them to stand against him.'

Sir Lenath stood. 'Do we still intend on going through with the battle of champions? Bearing in mind the absolute monster Shale's scouts have just described to us. The man has never lost a fight.'

The Knightguards looked about one another.

'But neither have I?!' said Inverwall's champion.

Chapter 28

ROMMEL HAD left the Inn before the first of the meeting's guests had finished their drink. The Wolves gathered in the darkness. Each of them was armed with a sheathed blade, either strapped to their hip or across their back.

'How do we get out of here?' asked Torquil.

'Straight out the main gate, as calm as you like,' said Rommel.

'But surely they will notice us immediately?' replied the young Wolf.

Roar interjected. 'And who is going to be looking for us? Our Captain is currently enjoying his flagon and the sound of his own voice. Will his men be on the lookout while they drink themselves into a coma?' The Old Wolf looked back to Rommel, rubbing his broken jaw with each hurtful word. 'Everyone will be as drunk as Dainman in spring. It will work.'

For the next few minutes The Wolves of Glory gathered themselves and cleared the muck from their faces. They washed their hands in a barrel filled with rainwater. They hushed deep in a dark alley adjacent to The Rusty Dagger Inn.

'Don't clean up too much, you want to fit in,' said Hunter, one of the Wolves.

They left the cover of the darkness and walked the road to the east gate. They passed inn after inn, each with their own unique name and noise. Arguments and fights were breaking out on the lower balconies. Crude comments were bellowed out by the patrons, aimed at the women wandering among them.

Still, the Wolves of Glory kept their composure and continued along the mud road, their worn leather boots squelching with each step. They were approaching the main gate, it was in sight and illuminated with the large burning braziers at either side of the open doors. 'Out that gate is our freedom,' said Roar as he winced with the pain in his jaw.

It was then, from the last Inn between the Wolves and the gate, staggered one of The Flaming Sails. He was wandering towards the group. The Wolves hesitated a moment but there was no other route – if they turned around it would look too obvious, so they continued to walk.

'Ho, lads, any of you got a couple bronze for me to keep this good night of mine going?' As he spoke he addressed Rommel. He swayed back and forth as he inadvertently barred the Wolf's path to the main gate. He looked about dazedly, drool and saliva running down his food stained chest and waistcoat. His greasy hair plastered to his head as he squinted and stared at each of the Wolves through blurry eyes. 'Have I see–' he burped and hiccupped loudly. 'Seen you fellas before? My name is Lacker. Lacker the Butcher of Banksfoot.'

'No, I don't think so, friend. We are new to the Bay and I'm afraid we are just leaving,' said Rommel.

'What about my coins?' said the drunken Lacker. 'You promised you would give me some. If you are leaving, you won't have any need for bronze.'

'We have no money, seadog. Now get out of our way!' said Roar, with anger in his voice. 'Or will I have to report you to your Captain? It would look mighty fine on the Captain of the Flaming Sails, his men wandering the streets begging.'

'I'm sorry lads, I meant no offence. I'll leave you to your night,' said Lacker, before staggering through the company. He was three steps away before he turned back. 'Before I go, what inn did you lot just come from? I need another place and by the smell of you, the place must be cheap.'

Unfortunately, one of the impatient and more panicked Wolves, named Jasper, answered with the only inn he knew. 'The Rusty Dagger, now be gone with you!' said the Wolf, before looking at Roar for approval.

Roar, Torquil and Rommel knew that it was a mistake.

'*The Rusty Dagger,* you say? Sounds like a good joint, but isn't that place closed tonight?' said Lacker as he felt himself sober up a little from his near drinking coma. He started to fumble and massage the cutlass around his waist. He looked around the group and caught eyes with Roar. 'I think I just remembered where I know you from.'

Before the Flaming Sail could speak another word, Torquil hurled a dagger through the air. The blade landed and thudded into the Butcher of Banksfoot's chest. The spinning blade had sent the corsair to the ground with one last outward breath in the form of a loud scream.

The patrons of the surrounding inns all heard the scream and came rushing out to see what the commotion was about. None of them wanting to miss out on a fight.

Upon witnessing the scene, and the dead body lying in the middle of the muddy road, a guest of *The Waveless Swell* asked, 'What happened out here? Is he not one of Bruar's men?'

Rommel looked back to the east gate. It was within running distance, and if they made it to the forest, no one would catch them in this darkness. He cleared his throat and spoke. 'This man gave us trouble, he tried to take our coin and went for his blade; we had no other choice.'

'That may be true, but Captain Bruar will like to speak to you, nonetheless. Although the old sea swine is never in town, he is a friend of the harbour master. We will have to bring you to him, tis only the rules.'

Rommel looked around at the buildings around him. He saw the crowd continued to grow. 'I'm afraid we won't be coming with you.' He turned and nodded to his friends, beckoning them to run.

With most of the pursuers drunk to the gills, the Wolves of Glory were making good progress and were unlikely to be caught by anyone behind them. However, they would have to cope with the two guards stationed in the centre of the open gate. Each outlaw carried a long spear and shield.

In unison, Roar and Rommel drew their longsword and cutlass respectively. They threw them through the air towards both guards. Rommel's cutlass buried itself deep into the skull of the first guard, killing him instantly. Roar's longsword crashed into the shield of the second. The guard wailed in pain as the blade penetrated through the wood and buried itself deep into his arm. Torquil rushed him and took his head off with a swipe of one of his shortswords.

Through the gate they ran, each of the Wolf Commanders gathering their swords as they passed. It wasn't long before arrows began to whiz past their heads from the outlaw town behind them.

'If we make it to the trees, we will lose them,' said Torquil. He took another four strides before calling out in pain as an arrow took him in the back of the knee. He slowed down to a limping jog and tried to push through the agony. Another arrow landed hard, this time deep into his back. He dropped to his knees and tried to reach round at the arrow in his leg.

'I got one of them!' shouted out a proud pirate in the distance.

Torquil then looked at his companions, who had stopped sprinting. He looked at them with tears in his eyes. 'Keep running, lads, you know I'm done for.'

Roar and Rommel could see the crowd of corsairs appearing behind the young Wolf and more arrows were flying through the air. Both commanders looked down at their young companion and nodded.

'You are a great man, Torquil,' said Rommel with an emotional break in his voice.

'Give them hell, Wolf!' added Roar with a respectful nod.

Both men turned away and, with the group, ran towards the cover of the forest.

After he watched the last of his companions disappear into the darkness of the treeline, Torquil pushed himself to his feet. He staggered a little as he felt his leg numb and his back throb with pain. He turned to face the onrushing horde of pirates and outlaws. Screaming the howling war-cry of The Wolves of Glory, Torquil charged his enemies with his two shortswords in-hand.

Chapter 29

THE OLD tower at the north end of the monastery gardens had been Leif's home for the last few days. He had spent hours upon hours in the ancient library of Altnahara, studying their traditions and history. Aside from a few small leaks, the tower acted as the perfect location to store the history of the Dawnbringers. A spiralling wooden staircase reached the very top of the interior, with countless bookshelves all around the inside of the tower.

Leif had studied the ancient history and rules passed down by the Dawnbringers. "The Battle of Kinship" was his current book of choice. He read at a solid-oak table on the second level of the tower. He could hear the nested birds in the high rafters above him as he turned page after page, carefully trying not to damage the old parchment with each turn.

During his time in the monastery, he had met all four of the Dawnbringers: Master Rollow, Quillion, Zander and Liliov, each of them over sixty and without children of their own. Of the four, he had liked Rollow the best. Quillion and Zander were the oldest two, both men the wisest of the monastery. Liliov was stern and strict but she clearly meant well. He was still not permitted to see the one man he worried about.

Fathad was somewhere in the monastery where Leif was not allowed. During his walks back to his room at night, he would take a different route each time in hopes of finding his old friend. Until they were reunited, he found it hard to fully trust the Dawnbringers with the same faith he had in Fathad. He had been grateful for the food and protection Altnahara had offered him. However, he had been disappointed with the lack of answers. Deep down he had known he would not have carried the Dawnbringer bloodline, but to hear it out loud from Master Rollow had nonetheless been disappointing.

Tonight, after his studying, Leif intended on searching the west grounds of Altnahara. Since learning he was not a Dawnbringer, he did not plan on sticking around the monastery too much longer. Out of respect, he decided he would also leave the necklace behind. It clearly did not belong to him or his family-line. Plus, the Seekers seemed to want it and he was sure it would be safe with the remaining Dawnbringers.

It was close to suppertime when Leif finished reading his last chapter. He closed the book, marking the page and made his way out the rickety old door of the library. It was a mild evening and the air was warm, the beautiful view of the gardens within Altnahara had still not become tiresome on his eyes. The hedges and flowers were trimmed to perfection, with a large lily pond in the centre. He could hear the night owls awakening from their day slumber as he walked the pebbled path to the mess hall. He passed other monks on his way to the main building, none offering a word of conversation as they bowed their heads with respect. Leif had learned that a lot of the monks had lived within the walls their whole lives, while most had been here from a young age. They all had an obvious respect for those who could live with the trials and misfortunes of the outside world, knowing their lives within the walls were simple and safe.

Leif entered the dining room, gathered a humble plate of stew and took a seat alone at the end of one of the three long tables in the centre of the room. He ate his meal in silence and watched the other diners talk amongst the tables in the hall. He envied their lack of corruption and the fact they had no first-hand knowledge of badness. He looked at the head table and could see the four Dawnbringers eating and conversing among themselves. Master Liliov delicately cut into some meat and slowly brought it up to her lips, only for the meat to fall from her fork and onto the floor below. The older woman scoffed with annoyance as she bent down from her seat to collect the fallen food.

Leif watched as one of the apprentice monks approached the table of four and spoke with a meal tray in his hands. Leif could not hear the conversation, but he could clearly see Master Rollow nod and give instructions. He watched as the monk turned and left the room, tray of food still in hand. Leif took this as his chance to find Fathad and rose from the table, leaving his half-eaten stew on the table behind him.

For close to ten minutes, he followed the hooded monk, staying a dozen or so paces behind to avoid being spotted. After a few stops along the way, the monk headed across the gardens to the west building, with Leif close behind. The monk entered with Leif following shortly after.

The young wanderer could hear the monk's footsteps turning left and he followed. He continued to trail the monk along corridors, downstairs, along more corridors until he saw the man enter a room.

Slowly and gently, Leif approached the door and pressed his ear against the wood. He was hoping to catch a word or two that would prove Fathad was there. He was surprised with what he did hear.

'I have some food for you, Grand Master.' There was no answer and the monk continued. 'Sir, you must keep your strength up.'

Hearing the monk walk around the room, Leif then noted the distinct sound of a tray being placed on a table. Still there was no answer from the other occupant within the room. Then the monk spoke again.

'Very well, Sir, I will leave this for you. Please try and eat something.'

Leif moved quickly before the monk exited and hid behind a corner down the corridor. He peered around the wall and watched as the monk closed the door behind and locked the latch. Leif could not help but wonder why they would lock their Grand Master behind a solid oak door. He contemplated trying the door but thought against it. He instead returned to his own quarters for the night, with his mind racing.

The following day during the lunch meal he saw the same monk leave the mess hall with another tray of food and return with the same tray as the night before, this time empty. This showed that whoever was on the other side of the door was at least eating something.

Later in the afternoon during his studies, Leif was invited to afternoon tea with the four Dawnbringers. He entered the room, small beams of light shining through the dense glass onto the dark wooden floors. The four leaders of Altnahara sat on one side of an eight-seated table.

'Please, sit down,' said Master Rollow, as he pointed to one of the middle seats opposite him.

'Thank you,' replied Leif as he sat on the chair.

'We have asked you here to thank you for your patience in these times,' said Master Rollow as he picked up the pot of honeyed tea and poured Leif a cup.

Leif took a sip and smiled as the warm tea hit his chest like a sweet hammer.

Master Liliov continued with a more serious tone and a firm expression. 'We have all agreed we would like to offer you a place within our walls.' Liliov studied the young wanderer's expression before continuing. 'We understand you have spent your life searching for answers. These answers we cannot provide, but you must know there are other questions in this world.'

Master Rollow cleared his throat and spoke next. 'You show great promise for someone so young, Leif. We would have you stay with us and achieve the potential we believe is within you. Altnahara can be your home and you will always have the freedom to leave whenever you desire.'

Master Liliov took a long drink of tea and placed the fine cup down on the table. 'What we are offering you is not something we offer everyone.'

Leif thought for a moment before responding. He had always desired to finish his quest to find his heritage but there was something about Altnahara that offered him stability. As the warm tea coursed through his chest, down his arms and legs, to the very tips of his fingers and toes, he smiled. He thought of all the travelling, of all the searching, and the trials of living in the outside world. He then thought of his father, of his legacy and where he came from. The young wanderer wondered if those were the answers he truly sought. Leif took another deep sip of his tea and gave the Dawnbringers his answer.

Chapter 30

T HEY KEPT moving the whole night since leaving Brigands Bay and the death of Torquil was weighing heavily on Rommel's mind and heart. He had not even discussed the meeting of the Captains with Roar yet and did not want any issues clouding their already tough bid for survival. He knew he was going to eventually bring up Badrang's offer with Roar, but he had to wait for the right time.

The group were camped in a small meadow, with a pleasant campfire warming their bodies. They had been lucky enough to reach some farmlands, where the owners would not miss a carrot or cabbage here or there. Roar had even taken a group of three Wolves ahead and had caught some rabbits. With the food and some good nights' sleep, they had regained much of their former strength and were beginning to believe the Flaming Sails had given up chase.

Upon dining that evening Roar finally asked what it was Rommel had overheard during his time in The Rusty Dagger. 'I think it is time we all know,' he said.

By the glow of the campfire Rommel explained Badrang's proposal and how the outlaws of Brigands Bay had accepted it. 'They will attack Inverwall from the north and the defenders will not know what hit them. Inverwall is a solid fortification and the defenders there will be well prepared for an invasion from the south. This surprise will cripple them, split their forces and cause panic.' He scanned the group as he added, 'Unless we warn them.'

There were murmurs of unhappiness in the group upon the proposition from Rommel. One of the Wolves named Jasper stood up from his seat, clearly irritated. 'Are you trying to get a laugh from us? This must be some kind of joke? Have you gone soft in the head? We should be heading north to Meridia, or better yet, Dain.'

Roar stood and faced the upstart eye to eye. 'If you want to stay a part of this company, you will watch your mouth. This is something that will require a lot of thought. Have a think a moment – if Inverwall falls there will be no Meridia or Dain.'

'Still better than moving towards the flames!' barked Jasper as his long blond hair glowed in the light of the campfire.

Rommel interjected before Roar exploded with anger. 'If we do nothing, our fellow countrymen will die at Inverwall. We are not military men, but we owe it to them to at the very least deliver this message.'

Jasper stared slant-eyed at the old commanders and smirked. 'I think my time in The Wolves of Glory has come to an end. Unless of course you have some bronze in those pockets of yours? You already got Torquil killed and I for one certainly won't be next.'

Roar was about to snarl back when Rommel again beat him to it. 'Are we in agreement then? You and anyone else who does not want to come to Inverwall will head north in the morning?'

Jasper nodded in agreement and walked over to a secluded spot away from the group, lay down and closed his eyes ready for sleep. Through the course of the next ten minutes, four of the others joined him, making their intentions to head north very clear.

The next morning the group split in two as expected. Not many words were spoken amongst the company. Rommel had a degree of sympathy and understanding for Jasper and the others. Roar, on the other hand, did not.

'Cowards. I find it hard to believe any of them fought next to us as Wolves.' He stared at the road ahead of them. 'There are now only five of us left, a broken pack.'

Rommel had tried not to think of Torquil's death but felt it right to discuss the young Wolf. 'We must not forget what happened back at the Bay. The boy showed magnificent courage, Roar. There is not a doubt in my mind he would have come with us to Inverwall.'

'How far away are we from there?' asked one of the Wolves.

'Three days, Hunter. Maybe a few more,' replied Rommel.

'Is it all farmland and forest until then?' asked Hunter.

'Yes, but we aren't far from Balderstone village, we will go there first on our way to Inverwall. As we all know, people do not always take kindly to mercenaries. We will need to keep a low profile. We can't afford any trouble,' said Rommel.

It was mid next day when they reached the outskirts of Balderstone. During the journey they had found enough time to clean themselves up. They did not look as menacing as they had done the day previous, but the bruising around Roar's face had turned an ugly yellow and purple colour. The cuts on his lip had scabbed over in hideous fashion.

'We will not stay long here. We have no money, and we do not want to draw attention to that fact,' said Rommel as the five companions approached the guard at the entrance to the village.

'Names and reason for visiting Balderstone?' asked the guard authoritatively. The man stood straight and was dressed in a rough leather cuirass. His round belly pushed over the side of his belt buckle which held up a sheathed longsword.

'My name is Rommel, and these are my four companions: Roar, Mallard, Hunter and Willem. We are just passing through on our way south.'

'And what is sending you south? Ain't nothing south but Inverwall and there is trouble brewing down there. Lot of refugees heading north to Meridia. It's going to be some fight against those Dakha barbarians,' said the guard.

The group did not answer.

Roar's battered face caught the guard's eye. He rubbed his hand against his stubbly chin and shook his head. 'You don't look like simple travellers to me.'

Rommel usually thought quickly in these situations, but was struggling to come up with a believable story. He thought deep and hard as the seconds ticked by and the group became more and more suspect.

Hunter quickly interjected. 'We are a travelling act; we preform stunts and re-enact famous battles and duels for coin.' He pointed to Roar's injured face and then back to his own cleaner appearance. 'As you can see, some of us are better than others.'

'Hmmm, never heard of this but it does sound entertaining,' said the guard and looked at the sword on the young Wolf's hip. 'And why do showmen need real weapons?'

Hunter looked at his companions and smiled. 'It makes the act more believable.'

Chapter 31

THE RAIN pounded hard onto the wet mud of the training yard as the men of Inverwall got in one of their last days of practice. Sir Shale's scouts had reported movement from the southern horde and it would only be a matter of days before Badrang and his army arrived.

'We will be ready to answer them,' muttered Sir Oakheart as he watched the defenders continue with their parrying and thrusting exercises.

The men had greatly improved under the training regime put into action by Sir Lenath and Sir Nolan. The Inverwallian soldiers were fitter, stronger and smarter than they had ever been. Each man showed sincere desire to defend the southern capital from the Dakha hordes.

Sir Oakheart walked through the water-filled yards as the rain continued. He eventually found Sir Talon at the foot of the high, newly built, main gate.

'She is quite a structure,' said the Knightguard commander.

'She is indeed, Oakheart; it will take something special to knock this one down,' replied Sir Talon with a smile. 'With Captain Guillow's archers directly above and to the right, it will be difficult for them to get anywhere near her.'

Captain Guillow had still been impressing with his leadership skills and had been granted attendance within the Knightguard meetings. He would lead the archers stationed on the wall. Behind every five bowmen would be a swordsman, ready for physical combat if ladders were to arrive. These swordsmen were also given basic healer training to treat any wounded archers on the wall.

'So let us summarise, Talon. We will have approximately one thousand men on the wall. We will have two thousand in the killing fields, and they will be led by Shale and Lenath,' said Sir Oakheart.

Sir Talon nodded with agreement. 'We will also have our last thousand men behind the gate, ready to help with the retreat from the killing fields.'

'Hopefully they will not be needed and the fire oil barricades will do their job,' interrupted Sir Oakheart, who had grown more and more optimistic about the south plains. 'The battle will last longer than a week and we still have to prepare for a battle of champions. Are you sure you will be able to kill him?' asked Sir Oakheart with concern in his eyes.

Sir Talon replied with only a confident smile, then lowered his eyes.

'You know I am happy to fight him,' added Sir Oakheart.

'I know you are and that is why you are commander.' Sir Talon paused a moment before continuing. 'You know it must be me. The men would lose heart if they saw you fall.'

This time Sir Oakheart did not respond.

'Not that I'm saying you couldn't beat Malacath, of course. It's just the men NEED you alive, they need your leadership. I'm not as important as you,' continued Sir Talon.

Although he did not like it, he knew the men would lose all hope if they saw their leader cut down in a duel before the battle even commenced. The chance to kill Malacath was too great to pass up and he had faith that Talon would be able to beat Badrang's general.

As night grew, the guards on the walls were doubled and the Keep was shut down to any new visitors. The chilly building wailed as the wind crept through the crevasses in each window. The noises caused by each gust made the ancient building seem more haunted than it actually was.

The Knightguards sat in the communal room together, each with a goblet of warm wine in their hands, talking of past and current members of their order. They remembered the old knights from long ago, like Sir Hugo of Dain and Sir Tilly the Unbreakable.

'Yes, but Nolan in his prime would have cut him down,' said Sir Shale.

'Against Sir Quinton the Righteous? You have to be joking!' scoffed Sir Lenath.

'That's a fight I would have paid to see,' added Sir Talon.

Sir Nolan chuckled with humility as the debate continued. He was secretly delighted to be respected the way he was. He never thought he was an amazing fighter, but in his younger years no man could match him.

'Did you ever have a spar with him, Nolan?' asked Sir Shale.

Nolan slapped his knee. 'No, it's a damn pity it never happened. The man was over seventy when I first joined the Knightguard. The old dog couldn't even lift a sword, let alone swing one. Least I'll be dead before that happens to me, pups.'

'Who says you'll be dead?' asked Sir Shale.

Chuckling as he spoke, Sir Nolan responded. 'I think we'll all be dead before too long, ha-ha.'

'Don't you think we should just go ahead and win this little war?' replied Sir Shale as seriously as he could.

The group burst into hearty laughter at the sarcasm in the young knight's simple statement.

'Oh, I hadn't thought of doing that,' said Sir Lenath. 'Suppose it would be simpler if we were to just beat Badrang. Then return back to Meridia and live the rest of our lives getting fat and lazy in the Griffin Quarters.'

'Looks like you've already had a head-start on that,' said Sir Nolan as he patted the giant knight on the belly, causing another eruption of laughter from the Knightguards.

Sir Lenath screwed up his face in friendly annoyance. 'I'm fat and you're old, so what? I can lose weight on my gut easier than you can lose years on your age.'

It was the first night they had all laughed since their days on the road and the laughter continued until Talon spoke. 'If you really think Blake is a traitor, how many more of us could be?'

Sir Oakheart swirled his goblet of wine around in both hands before taking a sip and answering. 'Well I can rule you lot out. You would make very bad traitors. Giving your lives for the people you were betraying.'

The group laughed again.

Sir Oakheart took a deep drink and continued. 'This brings me to a point I have been meaning to mention. When the time comes, and should Inverwall be lost, I am going to send whoever is left north to Meridia with this.' From his side pouch, Sir Oakheart retrieved a sealed roll of parchment. 'It is a letter, granting whoever I give it to the leadership of the Knightguard. It will also give him the right to arrest and bring Blake to trial for the traitor we are sure he is. This letter has to be given to Queen Orellia and no one else. As Talon says, we do not know if some of the others are with Blake.'

The knights looked about one another, each wondering what to say.

'Do you accept my decision?' asked Sir Oakheart.

Sir Nolan stood from his seat and drained the last of his wine. 'I'm with you, Oakheart.'

'As am I, Commander,' added Sir Shale.

Sir Talon stood sharply and drank the remnants of his wine. 'And me.'

There was a pause and the group looked to the tall Sir Lenath for his answer.

Sir Lenath looked about his friends and smiled. 'I am in complete agreement, brother. But I have one question: what if you are still one of the survivors? Should you not give it to her yourself?'

Sir Oakheart smiled but spoke in a serious tone. 'Lenath, my old friend. If Inverwall falls, so will I.'

Chapter 32

LEIF HAD continued his studies in the old dusty library within the north tower. For once in his life, he enjoyed the stability and security of a place to call home. Within the walls of Altnahara he felt safe and had no intention of returning to the outside world for the moment. For three hours a day the young wanderer would assist the monks of the monastery with their chores. This included cutting firewood, farming crops and lighting candles. Granted it was not an exciting life, but he felt relaxed and happy.

He had still not met the Grand Master, who they continued to keep under lock and key. The Dawnbringers continued to believe Leif was ignorant to the fact there even was a leader within these walls. The young wanderer continued to take orders from the four elders, even volunteering to go on the next supply run to Dain at the end of the week. They had gratefully accepted this, sighting his experiences would be useful to the clerics on their deliveries.

During his time at Altnahara, it had become clear that very few of its inhabitants knew how to fight. Leif was worried if the monks could even defend themselves during an attack. He knew something magical or mystical must protect the walls from the evil outside. It certainly wasn't the monastery's menacing reputation that scared away would-be attackers.

It was midday and he was out helping rebuild the stables on the east side of the gardens. The old wood had rotted over time and they were replacing the timber frame before the harsh weather really hit.

'We are four months away from winter, but it is good to get something like this done quickly,' said Master Zander as he kneeled on his walking staff. A keen builder in his day, he enjoyed watching as the young monks lifted one high timber beam up into position.

The construction made satisfactory progress and they would only need to finish off the back wall the next day. The frame was together and the roof completed. At the very least the horses had a place to stay for the night and would keep them dry should it rain.

Leif helped with taking the horses into their new home, counting twelve before locking each individual latch. As he reached the final stall, the occupying horse leaned over the barrier and knocked him on the arm.

The young wanderer looked into the eyes of the horse and smiled. The horse was a beautiful deep brown, apart from one speckle of white the size of a palm on its forehead. 'Hungry, fella?'

The horse moved its head and neighed, almost nodding.

Leif smiled again and reached into his pocket, producing a carrot he had taken from the vegetable gardens. 'You enjoy this,' he said and held out the carrot. He watched as the horse bit into the food gratefully and wrestled it from his grip.

Leif then turned and left the stables, but not before looking back at his new brown-haired friend. 'I'll visit again tomorrow.' He looked up at the name above the stall. 'Star, that's a good name,' he added, noting the mark on its forehead.

Over the next couple of days Leif continued to visit Star during his lunch hour. With the stables now finished, he was permitted to see the horse whenever he liked. Feeling an unexplained connection with the animal, he would always smuggle a carrot or an apple with each visit.

When the day came for the supply run to Dain, they were loading the cart with matured barrels of wine from the vineyard. Master Liliov was overseeing the operation and with her stern expression, explained the instructions. 'You are to supply two barrels to The Barking Bear, not a drop more. The rest is for the main Keep.' She watched as Leif and two other clerics loaded the container onto the back of the cart. 'With the money received, we need the items on this list.' She handed the scroll to Cleric Ulric and turned back towards the main building.

'All well understood,' replied Ulric.

Before the older Master entered the building, she looked back at Leif with something closely resembling a smile. 'Aren't you going to saddle-up Star?'

With his sword across his back, Leif readied his new friend Star and mounted the horse for the first time. He trotted out into the courtyard from the stables and drew his sword from his back. He whirled the sword about, loosening and stretching his arms. The other monks seemed intimidated but intrigued by the shining blade, glistening in the air. The young wanderer sheathed his blade and looked to the two clerics in the cart. 'Are you ready?'

With a nod Cleric Thomas gripped the reins and beckoned the horse to pull the cart forward. They exited the walls via the south gate with Leif riding by their side atop Star. He rubbed his chest where the rune stone usually stayed and was thankful he had left it back in his bedchambers.

'By road, it usually only takes us a couple of days to get to Dain,' said Cleric Ulric.

'And do we expect the journey to be eventful?' asked Leif.

The two clerics looked at one another then back to Leif before Thomas answered. 'What do you mean eventful? The bandits don't bother us, if that's what you mean.'

It was not bandits Leif was worried about, but he did not push any further. Although his two companions seemed to be the most experienced runners within the monastery, they did not fill him with confidence. Neither carried a weapon, save for a quarterstaff.

He was comfortable enough, but would have preferred a few more companions after his last ordeal on the road.

The first day of their journey did indeed prove to be eventless. They made timely progress, passing by a couple of farms on the outskirts of Moormire Forest. They spent the evening sleeping under the cover of the stars and exchanged stories amongst one another.

During their second day of travel something did happen. It was just after midday when, in the distance, Leif could see smoke rising from the air. He asked the two clerics to stay where they were, and he would go and investigate. He dismounted Star, gave the horse a pat and tied the reins to the cart.

'It will be nothing, Leif,' said Ulric.

'Probably some farmer burning overgrown roots,' added Thomas.

Leif did not agree. 'It will be safer if I check it out.' With no more words he made his way into the forest and followed the road by the cover of the treeline.

Less than a mile down the road, he reached an upturned cart with a stack of heather burning adjacent. The heather was creating the thick black smoke they had noticed. From the cover of a particularly large pine tree trunk, he watched for any movement coming from the cart. Leif thought to himself that the smoke was surely made for a trap.

For the next few minutes he remained motionless in the cover of a thick bush and waited for any signs of danger. Suddenly, he could hear noises coming from down the road south. A man sounded a full bellied laugh as another man came into view. Both were approaching the burning heather.

'Still nothing!?' called one of the men, sword in his hand.

Leif knew they must be bandits and he needed to get back to his cart. He did not want to take the chance on these outlaws letting them past. Even if Ulric said outlaws leave them be, it wasn't something Leif wanted to risk. He would go back and tell them to turn around.

As he took a quiet step backwards he was suddenly grabbed from behind. He felt the sharp point of a blade against his lower back which caused him to push his hips out and his shoulders back. Whoever it was they had the jump on him and he was at their mercy.

'Well look at what I've caught,' said a soft voice in his ear.

Chapter 33

THE FIVE remaining Wolves did not plan on staying long in Balderstone. They made their way through the small marketplace, looking for anyone who would trade some of their meagre possessions for something to eat. They had no such luck.

The town was small and surrounded by a wooden barricade. It must have contained close to a dozen buildings. Most of the inhabitants of Balderstone laboured in the mines a few miles east of the actual village. The others would work in the streets, also trying to sell what they could to the same customers day in day out. Since the south trade routes had been closed for the war, the town had suffered without passing traders. The town square was quiet as The Wolves of Glory made their way towards the main tavern within the town.

'Least it will be somewhere we can sit for a while,' said Rommel.

'I agree, and maybe if we give them Hunter, they will give us a couple drinks or a meal?' said Roar with a gruff smile.

'Your ego still hurting from Hunter's quick thinking back at the gate? Remember, in our little guise, you are the rookie,' said Rommel.

'I didn't mean anything by it, Commander, I just saw it as the only way we would get in,' said Hunter.

'I know you didn't, boy and if it wasn't for your quick thinking… I hate to think what we would have had do. I think it's time you all stop calling us "Commander". After all we have been through, we are equal in this,' said Roar. All the talking had hurt his jaw and he clamped his teeth hard together to take the pain.

They entered the tavern and immediately moved towards a table in the corner, away from the regular patrons of *The Flowing Goblet*. They each unbuckled their weapons before taking a seat at the table and began their discussion. The Inn was very busy and the crowds allowed each of them to talk freely.

'We are still two days from Inverwall,' said Rommel.

'When do we plan on leaving Balderstone?' asked Willem.

'In an hour, just sit back and relax, maybe try catch some sleep,' said Rommel.

Neither Roar or Rommel slept while the others rested their heads on the table or the back of their seats. This was the first time they had been able to relax their tired legs under some warm shelter. They had been sitting there for half an hour when a man approached the table.

'You lot going to buy anything?' said the Innkeeper. He was a small man, with a short frame. He looked like he was probably quite strong in his youth, but now he was older and weak. His arms were still thick but they had aged and the skin was loose. Walking with a slight limp, he stepped round the table.

Roar looked back at the owner, already trying to keep his cool. 'We are just resting; do we need to pay you for that?'

'I've got perfectly good beds. Why not buy a room, rather than use my tables?' said the Innkeeper.

'We aren't doing any harm. We are travellers and won't be staying long. We have no money to offer I'm afraid,' said Rommel.

'Hmmm, it's not usual for guests to come in here and not buy anything. If you are travellers, you must be hungry? When did you last eat?'

'This morning, on the road,' answered Roar.

'And what did you dine on?' asked the Innkeeper.

'Couple of vegetables. What business is it of yours anyway?'

snapped Roar.

'You are right, Sirs, it is no business of mine clearly,' said the Innkeeper as he turned and left the table. He returned less than ten minutes later carrying a tray with five hot bowls of soup and a crusty bread loaf in the middle.

'I'm sorry, Sir, but as we said, we have no money,' said Rommel.

'I know that, lads, but in these times it's good to help each other,' replied the Innkeeper with a smile. He placed the tray on the table which woke some of the sleeping Wolves. 'Help yourself, fellas. The name is Johnar; give me a shout if you need anything else.'

Each of the Wolves thanked the Innkeeper as he returned to behind his bar to serve a customer. They then turned their attention to the warm bowl of food in front of them. The Wolves did the best they could to live up to their name as they devoured the food.

'That's the first proper meal we have had since The Old Maid,' said Hunter, as he rubbed his warm ribs.

As he enjoyed the last of his soup, Roar looked towards the Innkeeper. Through the crowd he could see the owner was serving two new customers with their backs turned. Roar thought about the kindness shown by the stranger. He knew the Innkeeper would make little money each day, yet he still gave them the charity of food. Any doubt that they were doing the right thing by going to Inverwall was destroyed by this one single act of compassion.

The owner poured two tankards of mead and lay them on the bar top. 'Two bronze please,' he said, with an anxious voice. 'What brings you folk to town?'

Roar's heart stopped for a moment when he heard the customer speak. The unmistakable voice of Captain Bruar echoed in the Wolf's ears above the noise of the busy tavern. He turned to his side and nudged the other Wolves to take attention. They all shuffled and turned to shield their faces and listened intently.

In his usual smug voice Captain Bruar spoke. 'We are actually after some friends of ours, must be close to ten of them. One of them will have a badly battered face.' The Captain turned and looked around the busy Inn. 'Seen a group like that?'

With the reputation of The Flaming Sails, the Innkeeper knew immediately who this Captain was, and it did not take him much longer to realise who it was the Captain was after. He tried not to allow himself a natural glance over to the corner table. 'No, Sir, I can't say I have. Badly battered face you say, what happened to him?'

'That is of no business of yours, Innkeep,' snapped Bruar. With his slant eyes he took a quick scan of the room, but noticed nothing. 'It is a pity they aren't here, would be nice to see our old friends. My companion and I are just going to take a seat over in that corner; maybe we haven't missed them yet and they will be here soon,' said the Captain. Taking his flagon, he along with his comrade took a seat at the opposite corner of the Inn. A large drunk crowd separated them from the Wolves.

Roar turned to Rommel. 'Now we settle the score; the scumbag won't know we are here or that we are armed.'

'No, we can't, Roar!' replied Rommel as he tried to keep his voice down. 'Do you really think Bruar came alone? My bet is the rest of The Flaming Sails are outside, keeping watch. Do you not think he would have asked the guard at the gate the same questions? With your face, he will know we are in town.'

'There will be plenty time to settle the score; I am with Rommel. We should get out of here first.'

Roar replied through gritted teeth, 'You're both right.'

Half an hour went by, and still Captain Bruar waited at his table. The Wolves had not moved from their spot, afraid of being spotted. Thankfully the Inn stayed busy and the noise from the other patrons had only gotten louder. The Wolves knew they would not be able to hide in the corner forever before the Captain would grow tired of drinking and waiting.

After getting away from some arguing customers, the Innkeeper approached the group. 'I take it you lot want out of here?' He did not wait for a response. 'I think I can help you there. Not everyone knows this, but there are two entrances to my cellar.'

Chapter 34

'WELL LOOK at what I've caught,' said the soft voice from behind Leif. The point of the blade pierced Leif's leather waistcoat and tickled at his back.

'You have certainly got me at your mercy. So, am I a dead man?' asked Leif.

'That all depends on what you have for us. Is there any more of you?'

As he listened to the outlaw speak, Leif could tell it was a woman. 'Yes, two clerics from Altnahara. They are half a mile north, waiting for me to return. We are travelling to Dain for trading.'

He made the decision to come clean about his two traveling companions. He was positive the two clerics would be found regardless of his answers and would prefer not to antagonise these bandits with lies.

'Since when do monks carry weapons like this?' asked the woman. With her dagger still pressed against Leif's back, she unsheathed his blade and studied the weapon. 'It's a bit worn, but great to hold. Perfect balance on it. This would have been a fine weapon in its day.'

'You clearly know your blades,' said Leif, trying not to make any sudden movements as the cold iron of the bandit's dagger nipped at his skin. 'Considering I am unarmed, am I allowed to turn around?'

'Hahaha, you really think I'm that stupid? I didn't just arrive on the last caravan from East. Unsheathe the dagger above your boot and throw it over there.'

'It was worth a try,' said Leif with a chuckle, as he followed the instructions.

'I wouldn't be seeing the funny side of things if I were you,' said the mysterious woman. 'With my dagger pressed against your back and with all you own about to be taken from you, you must tell me what I've done to make you laugh.'

'Where do I begin?' said Leif with another chuckle. 'Even if you are bandits, I am convinced I am safe here. But if you were nothing but killers, you would have done me in and taken all my goods.'

No words came from the outlaw.

Leif continued with his usual calm voice. 'I have no doubt you will take all our valuables, but our lives? I think they are safe.'

The outlaw turned Leif around and at the same time sheathed her dagger. She was now pointing the young wanderer's longsword at his chest. The point of the weapon was only a few inches from where his heart was. Letting go of the sword with one hand, she brushed some of her hair out of her face.

'You are certainly an intelligent man. You are so clever you managed to get yourself captured by me, a common bandit. You are right, we aren't murderers but that isn't to say we have not spilled our share of blood. So do not test me.'

Leif tried not to stare at the natural beauty of the red-headed outlaw. Her face was muddy, her hair was unkempt and she wore a studded leather jerkin that concealed her womanly figure, but she was still attractive.

'What do you want me to do now?' asked Leif.

'You can take me to your companions, that's a good place to start,' said the outlaw. She then pursed her lips together and sounded a loud whistle. 'Warin, Emrest! I have someone here!' she shouted.

Moments later the two other bandits appeared through the bush. Neither looked to have much brains about them. Dressed in simple ragged tunics they looked at the young wanderer and laughed.

Emrest was tall and slim with dirty-blonde untidy hair. Warin was a short man, with a round barrelled belly and a bald head.

'He doesn't look like he has much on him, Fiora,' said Warin in a droll voice.

'No, but he has a couple of friends further up the road. They are priests from Altnahara,' she replied.

The two bandits looked at each other with slight worry in their eyes. They turned back to their leader.

'Altnahara? Are you sure we should be doing this, Fiora?' asked Emrest.

'Those folks aren't normal up there,' added Warin.

'Enough talking, now let's go!' replied Fiora with authority.

The three bandits, with Leif in front, marched the road north until they reached the halted cart. There was a picture of panic painted on the faces of the two clerics, as the four figures approached them.

During the walk, Fiora had taken Leif's scabbard from his back and was now wearing it over her own shoulder. She swaggered like a man as she approached the cart and spoke. 'The two of you, step down from there!' she demanded.

'But please, we are monks of Altnahara!? We know only peace!' said Ulric.

'Well I think it is time you were educated on other matters,' replied Fiora.

Both Ulric and Thomas stepped down from their seats on the cart. Each of the cleric's hands were shaking uncontrollably as they steadied the halted horses. Both men looked past Fiora and saw their comrade between the other two outlaws.

'Did they hurt you, Leif?' asked Thomas, with a quiver in his voice.

Leif shook his head and smiled. 'No, they haven't hurt me, but it is best we do as they say.'

Fiora turned back and walked behind her captive; with a heavy shove she pushed Leif over to his companions. She laughed as he stumbled but did not fall. Her laugh was quickly replaced with a frown when Leif turned back and looked at her with a smug smile.

'What all do you have then?' she asked.

'We only have the wine destined for Dain,' answered Leif.

Fiora smirked. 'I can see you also have a lovely cart and three fit horses?'

'Just take the wine, we all know you don't have any need for the horses. They are useless for travelling through the forests. You might be able to cover your own tracks when the guards are chasing you, but horse tracks? I think even the best outlaw in the known world would struggle to cover them.'

The young Fiora looked at Leif, with concealed admiration. 'Perhaps you are right. But how would we move the wine without the cart or the horses? We will leave that horse–' she pointed towards Star. 'But the cart and the other two are coming with us. We will be letting them go when we get back to our camp, so I'm sure they will turn up one day.'

In the moments to follow, the three bandits mounted the cart and Warin gripped the reins. He found a small duffle of gold coins used for buying supplies in Dain. 'They got some money here too, Fiora. Not a lot, mind you.'

Fiora looked at Leif and for a moment she hesitated. 'Put it in the back with the wine, I will have a look when we leave.'

'That money was meant for our people,' said Thomas.

'Well now it is for our people,' replied Fiora.

After the outlaws had inspected the cargo and they were satisfied, they had the three travellers from Altnahara empty their personal valuables into the back of the cart. The travellers weren't carrying anything of immense value, so it did not come as a problem to give anything up.

Leif continued to stare at Fiora. He hated how attractive she was.

Along with the softness of her voice, her ember-coloured hair did nothing to appease the uneasy feeling he had when he looked at her.

When it was time for the two parties to go their separate ways, not much was said. Leif's eyes had not left Fiora and he continued to stare with sheer annoyance. He hated the way she wore his sword around her shoulder, he could not forget the fact she had beaten him. He had had many dealings with outlaws and brigands in the past, but none had ever got the jump on him the way Fiora had.

Eventually, Fiora noticed him stare and in a parting barb from the back of the cart spoke. 'Hope you don't hold it against us. After all, in these lands, what choice did we have?'

The cart trundled down the road away from Leif and his companions. The outlaws had not long disappeared round the bend when Leif started walking south after them.

Keeping a firm grip on the reins of Star, Ulric called out to the young wanderer. 'Altnahara is this way – where are you going?'

Without turning, Leif answered, 'I'm going to get my sword back.'

Chapter 35

I T WAS midday when the sound of the south wall bell tower echoed in Sir Oakheart's ears. He was atop the battlements within five minutes along with the rest of the Knightguard. He gazed out to the south fields and noted the sheer size of the horde. Every inch of land in the distance was covered in the grey hazy colours of Badrang, Warlord of Blackland.

'Ready our horses, we will parlay within the hour,' barked Sir Talon.

The knights watched as tents and campfires began to appear within the hordes of the Dakha warriors. 'They are planning for an extended stay,' said Sir Lenath, also noting the sheer number of the southerners.

'It's amazing. It looks like a lot more than fifty thousand to me,' added Sir Shale.

'Ha! Could be one hundred thousand and they still wouldn't win,' laughed Sir Nolan as he patted Sir Shale on the shoulder. 'To think these fools want to pick a fight with us.'

The knights returned to each of their chambers after agreeing to meet in the courtyard in one hour's time.

Sir Oakheart paced back and forth within his humble room. He looked at the mirror on the wall and gazed into his own eyes. 'I must be strong,' he muttered, as he noted the bags appearing above his cheeks. He walked over to his bed and picked up his cuirass of chainmail. He raised it over his head and lowered it down until his torso was consumed. He then lifted his white waistcoat from the corner post of his bed and pushed his arm through the first slot and then the second. Oakheart then buttoned up the centre until Queen Orellia's family crest was clearly visible. He patted his chest before wrapping the thick belt around his waist. He looked down at the empty sword scabbard on his hip before picking the blade up from a table near the window. Sir Oakheart held the sword out in front of his chest; he could see himself in the reflection of the immaculate steel. The golden hilt glistened beautifully in the sun that cascaded through the open window. He took his griffin battle stance before swinging the blade about his person. He did not touch one piece of furniture as he moved the blade left and right, up and down. With a chuckle, Oakheart stopped and sheathed the blade before turning towards the door. He pressed down on the latch and exited, feeling as limber as he had for twenty years. The Knightguard commander was ready for a fight.

Within the hour, the five Knightguards along with Captain Guillow and two riders carrying banners, exited out the south gate on horseback. The flags of Queen Orellia and Inverwall flapping in the air as the group trotted out into the open south fields. They made their way past the wooden barricades and the men stationed behind them.

It wasn't long before they were clear and in the open, almost halfway between Inverwall and the Dakha army. They stopped and waited in formal silence until they could see a group of equal size ride towards them. The knights counted ten men, three flying flags; one flag for Badrang, one for Blacklands and the last flag, for General Malacath.

'I will do the talking, no one else is to speak,' ordered Sir Oakheart, as the rival group approached.

As the shape of the riders could be distinguished, they all noticed the unmistakable General Malacath. The monster of a man sat atop a giant steed, almost twice the thickness of the horse next to it. Sir Talon heard one of the Inverwallian flagbearers gulp loudly.

The Dakha stopped a stone's throw from the Meridians before three of them trotted forward. Sir Oakheart, Sir Nolan and Sir Talon did the same. They moved forward until all six men, three from each side, met in the middle. Badrang was not present.

Silence lingered in the air as the two groups faced opposite each other. Sir Oakheart finally spoke; he refused to look at Malacath and instead addressed all three of them. 'I see your leader is not here.' Even someone as stoic as Sir Oakheart could not control the surprise in his voice. 'We have a message for him and from your mouths he shall hear it. By order of Queen Orellia Kinlay and considering recent political events, please remove yourselves from the Meridian Realms. It is not our intention to continue with conflict, but we are ready should it be required.'

One of the Dakha raised out a hand, ignoring the Knightguard's message. He unravelled a scroll and began to read with his foreign southern accent. 'By order of Badrang, warlord of the Dakha, we demand the immediate surrender of Inverwall and all defenders.'

The three Dakha studied the reaction of each of the knights, who had all remained calm.

The reader continued, 'Failing to surrender, will result in the death of every man, woman and child within these walls.'

Again, the knights remained unfazed and Sir Oakheart answered. 'We respectfully decline surrender and would like to present an offer to your master. If he leaves now, and does not return until political negotiations are agreed, we will spare your lives.'

'I see negotiations will be going nowhere,' said the reader, almost laughing before continuing. 'My master had advised that should you not surrender, our next offer is a battle of champions. I am sure you would have anticipated such an offer?'

Sir Oakheart nodded. 'We had, yes.'

General Malacath finally broke his silence and bellowed with a deep tone from beneath his helmet. 'Well? What is your answer, puppet? Or do you need your woman here to answer for you?'

Sir Oakheart smiled at seeing the large general so worked up, but still did not like the disrespect shown to his queen. 'Of course, we have a champion ready.'

Sir Nolan scoffed. He did not like the disrespect shown by the General either, or the "puppet" remark. 'And who will be your champion – do you have a man worthy?'

The reader cleared his throat to answer quickly. He wanted to speak before the General discovered that this old knight had just insulted him. 'We also have a champion, I'm sure that question was not necessary,' he said with a smile as he turned and looked at Malacath.

After a moment of silence, Sir Oakheart spoke. 'So, we agree, a battle of champions will be conducted. The loser will surrender the battlefield.'

'We fight at dawn, puppet,' replied General Malacath.

Chapter 36

THE INN was crowded and as the afternoon grew late, its patrons became more and more active, brimming with sound. Songs broke out amongst the guests, men and women danced as the smoke-filled air obscured their vision. Miners returning from a day breaking stone entered the tavern and filled their mouths with liquid relaxation.

Still Captain Bruar sat at his table away from the busy centre of the Inn. He was still expecting a group of ten, not knowing The Wolves of Glory had split the day before. The remaining members of the Wolves had been fortunate enough to use this to their advantage. Sitting at the small table in the corner, they awaited the signal from the kindly Innkeeper.

Johnar moved about the guests. He took drink orders at the bar and conversed when he could with his regulars. He would collect empty tankards from tables and refill them for the next user. At one point he walked through the crowd with a handful of laundry. He then disappeared down into his cellar.

Rommel in a hushed tone said, 'They will be guarding the gates out of town, we will need to come up with something.'

They continued to wait and watch the surrounding crowd until finally the Innkeeper knocked on his bar bell for one of his staff to head to the cellar and collect more bottles of wine and rum. This was the moment the Wolves had been waiting for. They all rose from the table as the noise and commotion around them continued.

They made their way through the busy crowd, avoiding anything that would bring attention to them.

Rommel took a chance and had a look over at the Captain's table. He was still sat, smoking a large pipe and taking the occasional sip of mead.

The group had almost reached the corner end of the bar when they saw Johnar. The Innkeeper nodded, signalling for the five members of the Wolves to duck down and come around the back. He lifted the trapdoor and ushered them under the wooden floorboards and down a steep ladder to the basement.

As the last wolf entered the basement, the Innkeeper opened a palm and reached out his arm. 'May the gods protect you all.'

'Thank you again, Johnar,' replied Rommel, as he grasped the Innkeeper's hand and shook it before climbing down the remaining steps.

The Innkeeper did not close the cellar door immediately and waited for his own staff to return with the bottles of wine. 'Who were they?' asked the worker.

'They are friends of ours,' replied Johnar. He lowered the trapdoor and replaced the rug concealing it. He looked over to Captain Bruar and noticed there had been no movement; his plan had worked so far.

As the Wolves gathered in the dark dusty cellar, they could hear the noise continuing up above. Looking through the floorboards, they could see the Innkeeper still in his usual place and they realised all must be well. They made their way through the underground room until they saw a candle burning in the corner atop a table. Beside the solitary flame were five dark green hooded cloaks, a small bag and a scribbled letter that read:

Dear friends,
I knew you were running from something the minute I saw

you. If it had been the law that chased you, the guards at the gate would have arrested you there and then. When I saw Captain Bruar I realised everything. We have heard of The Flaming Sails and what this man has done. I refuse to let anyone else become a part of his horrible work. Please take these cloaks, they will help you outside in the town when darkness comes. The Captain is looking for a group of ten, so with these hoods you should hopefully slip past his men. The bag has a small supply of food, some bread, cheese and fruit. I wish I could have done more.

May the light of Amundsen and Azmara watch over you.

Johnar.

After they had all read the letter, they each threw a cape over their shoulders. Roar raised a hood over his head and at the same time ripped apart the note left by the Innkeeper. He knew there was a chance they would be caught, and he did not want Johnar to get into any kind of trouble. The Wolves made their way over to the cellar exit that would take them outside to an alley behind *The Flowing Goblet*. They crouched down and waited another half hour before they could see it was nightfall through the slats in the hatch door. This was the perfect time to make their escape from Balderstone.

Roar held up the latch and slid it along until it was no longer locking the double doors out into the alley. He slowly lifted the first door and popped his head up to check if the area was secure. He looked either side of the alley; all was clear.

One after the other, the Wolves climbed out of the cellar and into the back street behind the busy Inn. They slowly lowered the door behind them and regrouped before Rommel spoke. 'We need to stick together here. Hoods up and make a circle round Roar – he is the one who is recognisable.

The air was warm and damp as the group emerged from the shadows of the alley. They were thankful other travellers and occupants of Balderstone walked the dark streets of the southern town. It did not take them long before they saw the first outlaw from Brigands Bay. He wore the unmistakable colours and carried a broad cutlass around his waist as he spoke to a local woman in a provocative manner. The group ventured a little closer to the corsair before they altered their direction slightly and headed towards the southern gate.

'Always the same – we have to sneak out of some place without being seen. How many of them do you think will be there?' asked Willem.

What they saw at the exit made their hearts all sink simultaneously. A group of fifteen outlaws stood in the open, all shouting and laughing amongst themselves as the two town guards watched with overpowering cowardice in their eyes. These outlaws were clearly not members of The Flaming Sails but were certainly from Brigands Bay.

'The guards obviously know who they are, why let them in?' asked Hunter.

'The guards in this town are outnumbered. They wouldn't stand a chance if they said "no" to this lot. We are running out of choices here; what do you think we should do, Roar?' asked Rommel.

Roar rubbed his sore jaw. He looked about the group and gritted his teeth together. With his right palm he grasped the hilt of his longsword. 'I think it's time we fight.'

Chapter 37

EIF HAD been following the cart for hours when it finally left the main road and onto a smaller path. It was late afternoon and the sun was setting in the west and he could hear the day birds sing the last of their sun songs. The scenery and sounds were beautiful. *How could a land this beautiful, hold such conflict*, Leif thought to himself, as he watched the cart trundle its way through the trees. He kept a good distance from the outlaws. He was sure Fiora would have a keen enough eye to spot anyone following them.

Leif had spent years travelling through the wilderness and was an expert ranger. He could hunt, track and kill when necessary, but he had never felt the way he had when looking at the red headed bandit. He wondered if it was hatred? He wasn't sure, but he didn't like it anyway. Repeatedly he played the scene back in his mind. How could he have let someone creep up on him like that? With his years of experience in the wild, how did he not hear her coming?

Leif was accustomed to walking at night and had no problem with the lack of sleep. They continued to travel along the winding dirt path, deeper and deeper into the forest. The road thinned slightly with every turn of the cart's wheel. As Leif walked he heard strange noises coming from the darkness of the woods, noises he had never heard before. There were whispers in his ears like the distant cackles of an old woman. He put it down to the wind playing tricks and continued.

There was a piercing howl in the distance and Warin stood on the cart, before Fiora punched him in the ribs. 'Sit down, you fool, it's only a wolf.'

Warin sat back in his seat but continued to look anxious. 'I hate being out here at this time; should we not just make camp, Fiora?'

'We are only an hour away, what would be the point in camping now?' replied Fiora with a smirk.

'I just feel a bit safer with a fire beside me and my back to a tree,' said Warin.

'You don't really believe all the stories, do you? It was a wolf, and nothing more, now stop worrying,' barked Fiora.

Leif was beginning to struggle keeping up with the cart, his legs were tired, and he was hoping that wherever the bandits intended on stopping was close by. Eventually, in the distance, he saw a dim glowing light. As they approached closer he could make out humanly shapes. Each of these shapes carried a bow loaded with an arrow.

'It's Fiora!' shouted one of the bandit guards. 'Lower your weapons!'

As the cart trundled into the opening. Leif followed by the cover of the trees and bushes. He watched as more than a dozen outlaws came out of their makeshift shelters underneath the cover of the trees. They were all carrying lanterns, illuminating the area more than it should for this time of night.

'Where did you get this?' asked a broad handsome outlaw as he lifted the cloth covering the barrels of wine. 'How do you think we are going to sell this?'

'It's from a couple of Altnahara priests we met on the road,' replied Fiora. 'As for selling it, who said anything about that? I thought we could all use a drink.'

Laughter broke out amongst the other bandits, clearly impressed with the young female. The broad man, however, was not impressed. 'Altnahara is not an enemy, and there was no need for us to rob them. We can contend with the town guards, but the monks of the monastery?'

'You worry too much, Garrow, have a goblet of this stuff and tell me I was a fool. It's the best in the northern realms,' replied Fiora.

As the rest of the group cheered with glee, Garrow looked at the young woman with a grim expression painted on his face. 'You should not have done this. We do not know what powers they have. We need the small people of the realms to be on our side.'

Fiora looked at the large Garrow and smiled. 'Are we to talk about this somewhere else?'

Garrow nodded, and the two bandits walked shoulder to shoulder into one of the large tents under the cover of the trees, away from the crowd.

The outlaw camp set about unloading the cart and storing the barrels under a large shelter in the corner of the clearing. As it was late, most of the outlaws went back to their tents to rest. Leif counted half a dozen guards who were ready to spend the night awake. All six of them carried a bow, with a quiver on their back and a sword on their waist. Most of them looked either too young or too old to be carrying weapons. Leif thought back to his time in Dain, and how unhappy the people had been. Over-taxing and poverty could often lead to civil unrest, something he had read in one of the books at Altnahara. With the number of outlaws in this camp, it was a surprise to Leif that they had not been found by the guards. While Duke Delgath lay dying in his bed chambers, the local authorities had no intention of getting their hands dirty. The north would not get better while its leader was unable to settle its people.

Leif thought of all the times he had been in trouble with the law. In his younger days, his mouth would often land him in hot water with the authorities. He was in his early twenties now and had matured somewhat. He did not allow anger or annoyance to take control of him anymore and he knew when to keep quiet. However, in different circumstances, he could have ended up among these outlaws.

The outlaw guards patrolled the perimeter of their makeshift settlement as the rest slept and Leif watched. Fiora eventually exited the largest tent and strode across to her own, quite near the entrance. The young wanderer thought to himself for quite some time and waited until he was sure she would be asleep.

He moved through the trees until he was close enough to touch the tent. He was unarmed and outnumbered, but he wanted to get his sword back. He was sure it was his sword he wanted back and not his pride. It did not annoy him that it was a woman who had taken his weapon – he would have been equally annoyed if it had been a man. In the past he had given countless outlaws a lesson for trying to take what was his, but this was the first time someone had succeeded.

A guard on patrol stopped and spat beside the tent, before scratching his chin and moving on.

Leif waited for the outlaw to move out of earshot, before making his way around the tent and briefly into the light of the torches stationed around the border of the camp. He was not exposed for long, as he lifted the entrance to Fiora's tent and crossed the threshold.

Chapter 38

IT WAS still dark and an hour before the crack of dawn. Sir Oakheart dressed himself with a heavy heart. *Will this be the last day Talon draws breath?* He thought to himself. Sir Oakheart had been so confident of his Knightguard comrade winning until he had seen the monster that was General Malacath. He had hardly slept a wink through the night. He had been up and about his room for the past hour, pacing back and forth. *Talon is not fighting a man. He will not win, why have I let him do this?*

The Knightguard commander still had no intention of honouring the terms of a battle of champions. Should General Malacath fall to Sir Talon, he had no doubt in his mind that Badrang, Warlord of the South, would not honour the agreements. Oakheart had no problem with this. *Did Badrang think of agreements when he brutally murdered the Meridian herald we sent to Blackwood Keep?* he thought as he pulled his waistcoat over his shoulders.

When he eventually left the Keep, the courtyards were busy with activity. The troops were running to be ready for their position and the archers squeezing in an hour of training before ascending to the walls. Sir Oakheart was hoping to see Sir Talon before the battle, but he could not find his knight-brother. This did not worry him, however, as they had spoken heavily the night before. He would respect his Knightguard's wishes and only speak if he felt comfortable. He knew, like himself, that Sir Talon would prefer solitude in the build up to an important fight. It came to him that he had not seen any of the other Knightguards since the night before; he knew Lenath, Nolan and Shale would already be in position. As Nolan once said, 'Nothing instils confidence in a soldier as much as seeing his general ready to battle.'

Sir Oakheart thought again to himself as he walked toward the south battlements, *I hope at the end of today, I will be conversing with my old friends again.* He knew no matter what, the city would not fall today.

As he climbed the stone steps onto the wall, Sir Oakheart passed Captain Guillow. 'Where are you going, the battle is this way?' he said.

'Ha-ha, well I best go get the rest of my men then, they are still practising. Getting the bad shots out of the way before the real thing is upon us. Under pressure, the average archer always misses the first few shots,' replied the Captain with a smile.

'I guess I should be thankful you are far from average. I want you by my side before the fight; I will be close to the gate on this side,' said Sir Oakheart as he moved on. Before he reached the top of the stairs, he patted the Orellia family crest on his chest with an open palm. It was time for the war to truly begin.

Most of the men were in position; he looked down into the killing fields and saw the foot infantry behind each of the barricades. He could not see either of his knight companions, but that was not out of the ordinary in an army this size. He walked the length of the wall as the first glimmer of light shone from the sun rising in the east. The men looked in good spirits; he passed each solider and faced them eye to eye. He could see his presence was clearly boosting their morale. Within the next ten minutes, the rest of the archers arrived on the walls and took up position. Trays of arrows were placed along the battlements; they would not be running out any time soon.

Captain Guillow appeared beside the Knightguard commander

moments before the trumpets sounded. Sir Oakheart turned and saw a fully armoured Sir Talon emerge from the Keep.

Sir Talon's silver helmet sat atop his shoulders with his white cape cascaded down over his golden plated armour. His longsword rested by his side and his steel shield gripped his left arm. He marched through the courtyard towards the south gate. The knight looked up at his commander and raised a fist before pounding it against his chest in the Meridian salute.

'That is a man who knows how to walk with purpose,' said Captain Guillow, with complete admiration in his voice.

Sir Talon strode through the open gate as he breathed heavily through his helm. He wondered if there was ever a finer feeling than the moments before a battle. He looked at the men as he made his way through the killing fields. They all saluted him as he passed, one after the other, after the other. There was not an Inverwallian in the southern plains who did not admire the courage of the Knightguard.

'Give him hell, Sir Talon!' shouted one of the soldiers.

'Send him back to Sarpen!' called out another.

Sir Talon again raised his fist in the air and there was a mass cheer from the army of Inverwall. They beat their shields and sounded their horns in awe of this magnificently armoured champion.

'This is what I have lived for,' muttered the knight.

As he cleared the last of the foot infantry, he wandered out into the clearing away from the safety of help and cover. He could see General Malacath in the distance, marching towards him. His huge greatsword in the palm of his massive hand.

The General posed a menacing figure as he approached. He was more than a foot and a half taller than the knight and was dressed in his usual black armour with red trimmings. There was nothing behind his helmet, only a black abyss where his face hid.

'This is the end for you!' said the Champion of Blackland, as he slid his blade through the air. 'You will beg for mercy before I am done,' he bellowed.

The knight remained silent and unclipped his cape. The white cloak dropped to the dusty ground as the knight stepped forward and unsheathed his perfectly sharpened longsword. He swung the blade a few times, causing the sunlight to dance off the steel. When he was feeling limber, he rested the blade on his shield and took his battle stance. 'Let's go then.'

Chapter 39

THE NIGHT was quiet and damp. The last of the townsfolk had entered their homes for the evening but still the outlaws of Brigands Bay waited at the main gate.

Rommel studied the look on his old friend's face. 'Five of us, against fifteen of them?'

'It's time we make a stand, Rommel!' said Roar as he tried to keep his voice down. His hands gripped his longsword tighter with each word. 'I am tired of running.'

'We need to get this message to Inverwall – how would we do that dead?' asked Rommel.

Roar stared into the eyes of his comrade and loosened the grip on his sword. 'Then what do you propose, if not fighting our way through?'

'Maybe we should head back to the cellar and wait for all this to die down?' said Willem.

Roar let out a quiet laugh. 'Do you really think Captain Bruar will leave any stone unturned in this town when he doesn't find us? He is going to lose patience soon and I don't think we should be here when he does. Say he does find us in the cellar, what do you think he will do to the Innkeeper? I will not have any more innocent blood spilled.'

While the debate continued in the shadows of Balderstone, Hunter studied the group of corsairs at the gate. He thought of his companion Torquil and the demise he had met at Brigands Bay.

Hunter had joined the Wolves around the same time as Torquil and it upset him to think of his once strong friend. He thought long and hard before turning back to Roar and Rommel. 'I have an idea, but you are going to have to trust me.'

The Wolves looked at each other before eventually nodding at Hunter to continue. For the next five minutes Hunter explained his plan to remove the fifteen outlaws guarding the exit to Balderstone.

When all was agreed Rommel patted the young Wolf on the shoulder. 'Best of luck, my boy.'

Hunter nodded and walked out into the moonlight. He unclipped his cape and let it fall down his back. He took a deep breath and shouted. 'I am a Wolf of Glory and I will kill you all where you stand.' As he called out he drew the longsword from his waist and struck a battle stance.

The outlaws all turned to face this young fighter. They were shocked to see such bold arrogance from one man. Together they drew their weapons and took a step towards Hunter.

One particularly ugly corsair with a pointed goatee spoke first. 'By orders of Captain Bruar, we are to take you alive or dead.'

The corsairs started to slowly make their way towards Hunter. Each outlaw raised a blade, ready for battle.

Hunter smiled and returned his sword to the scabbard hanging on his hip. 'I'm afraid I won't be letting you do that.' He turned and ran into the darkness of a nearby alley. He disappeared into the night between two houses.

'Get him! Be careful, there will be more of them in there!' called out the ugly corsair, leading the outlaws after Hunter and into the darkness.

It was time for the rest of the Wolves of Glory to make a move. Led by Roar they charged at the gate, with weapons in hand. They made short work of the two remaining corsairs as Willem parried and crashed his shortsword through the chest of the first. The second was decapitated with one swipe of Roar's longsword. Not a sound was made as both corsairs fell to the ground.

The group waited a moment by the open double doored gate. They could hear shouting coming from the dark alley.

'Do you think they got him?' asked Rommel.

Roar's eyes did not leave the alley. 'I don't know.'

Each of the Wolves were relieved to see their comrade Hunter emerge from the dark alley and run towards them. With no words spoken and a nod exchanged, all five Wolves of Glory exited the south gate of Balderstone and onto the road to Inverwall.

With all the commotion now reaching out to *The Flowing Goblet*, Captain Bruar strode out into the open courtyard of the town.

'What is going on here?' Bruar asked the ugly corsair who had lost Hunter.

The corsair did not look at Captain Bruar and inspected his dead comrades. 'They managed to kill my men at the gate. These two didn't stand a chance.'

'And why were they left alone? Ten on two seems a tad unfavourable?' replied Captain Bruar, who remained calm. 'Where were the rest of you?'

'We were chasing one of them into that alley,' said the corsair as he pointed towards the darkness on his right. He turned around to stare face to face with the Captain.

'Ahhhhh I see,' said the Captain, with a calm tone on his tongue. 'My apologies, I didn't know you were chasing one of them at the time. Did you get him? I hope all thirteen of you gave him the hiding of a lifetime. Where is his body?'

'No, he got away. The coward hid in the shadows and must have sneaked off when we passed him. It wasn't our fault and anyway, Harbour Master Neg only sent us here to help you if we could. I don't take orders from you and neither do my men.'

'You are completely right, and I would never expect you to follow my orders. I must thank you for your assistance in these times. It has been a harsh few weeks for The Flaming Sails,' said Captain Bruar, with masked falseness painted on his face. 'But I must say, it is disappointing that we couldn't even get one of the Wolves before they left.'

'I agree; and did you enjoy your drink while we were out here doing your dirty work?' replied the corsair, causing the men behind him to snigger.

'Ha-ha! I did indeed. This is my kind of place.' The Captain turned and looked around the town buildings, exposing his back to his fellow corsair.

'Maybe you set up nest here, you seem about retirement age,' said the corsair.

With one swift flowing movement Bruar drew his cutlass and spun, taking the ugly head clean off the shoulders of the unfortunate pirate. A thick coat of blood hit the Captain heavily in the face as the head rolled to the ground near the other outlaws.

'I want those Wolves found!' he barked at the frightened corsairs. 'Now, how on earth did they make it through this town without being spotted?'

No one said a word as they stared at him with fear in their eyes.

Captain Bruar began to pace around the dirt square. 'Fools, the lot of you.' As he walked, he felt something move underfoot almost causing him to trip. He bent a knee and picked up the material with his blood-stained fingers. A cruel smile appeared on his face as he looked at the hooded cloak left by Hunter. He smiled because he had seen the dark green cloak before.

Chapter 40

I T WAS dark in the tent as Leif entered through the makeshift cloth door. There was a small candle burning in the far corner of the room where Fiora lay sleeping on a bed of sheepskins. He quietly wandered through the canvas, watching his footing to avoid making any unnecessary noises. He looked to the bottom of her bed and saw the studded leather cuirass she had worn earlier.

His eyes continued to scan the room for his sword, and eventually he found it. On the other side of her bed resting on a chest, sheathed in its scabbard, rested his blade. *Get the sword, then leave,* he thought to himself as he made his way quietly round the side of the sleeping bandit.

Again, he was drawn to the natural beauty of the red headed woman sleeping soundly on the pile of pelts. She wore a plain white shirt that was open at the top and her loose hair fell about her narrow shoulders. The chest was an arm's reach away from her head and he was going to need to get very close to her to retrieve his sword. As he moved forward he heard her turn onto her side and let out a small sigh; she was still asleep. He continued to move closer and eventually was able to reach out and grasp the hilt of his sword.

Just then, with a sudden flurry of movement, Fiora woke. At the same time, she drew a dagger from under her pillow and pinned it against the neck of the intruder. 'Big mistake coming here,' she growled.

He was not going to be outdone by her again. With his left hand, he swatted the blade away from the exposed skin around his neck. He dropped his sword onto the chest and with his other hand he covered her mouth to avoid the inevitable call for help.

Fiora bit deep into the side of his palm and punched out with her free fist. She bit down harder, but there was not even a flinch from Leif. She was beginning to fear for her life as his grip around her mouth tightened. Knowing that her life was now in his hands, she stopped biting and relaxed.

'I don't want to hurt you, I only want my sword,' whispered Leif, as he leaned in closer to her ear. 'I won't be taking any lives tonight, I only want the sword.'

She continued to remain calm as the hand around her mouth began to loosen. She stared into his eyes with burning hatred. Now she knew how Leif must have felt when she had caught him unaware. She had no doubt that if their roles were reversed, she would not be as gentle. She wanted to hit him again but decided against it.

'I promise you. If you scream, I will snap your neck and kill anyone who walks into this tent,' said Leif, as he looked into her hazel-coloured eyes. 'Please, don't make me do that. We do not need to shed blood over a simple sword.' He loosened his grip some more and allowed her to nod. 'I swear on the gods, I will kill them all,' he added with authority.

As he slowly removed his hand from around her mouth she took in a deep breath of relief. She believed him when he had said he would kill her and anyone who would threaten his life. She watched as he picked up his sword and threw the buckle over his shoulder; her brown eyes met his blue. She wondered if it was hatred she was feeling.

'Thank you for not shouting,' said Leif as they both looked at one another. 'Are you going to let me leave without problems?'

Fiora wiped away a small trace of his blood from her mouth and spoke in a soft voice. 'You got the best of me, I won't be stopping you.'

'Thank you,' he replied. With his sword now on his back, he turned from her bed and made his way towards the exit.

'Before you go, what is your name?' asked Fiora. She sat up on her bed with her messy hair cascading down over her shoulders.

'Ha-ha, I don't think that is something you need to know.'

'I think you owe me a name?' she asked again.

'Well, people have taken to calling me Leif.'

She moved to the end of her bed and looked the young wanderer up and down. Her lips pursed close together in something that resembled a smile. 'Well Leif, you enjoy that sword of yours. I will be taking it back before long.'

Leif smiled back and let out a small chuckle. 'I'll be waiting for you.'

He left the tent and into the dim light of the camp. He waited for a guard to pass before he made his way round the tent and into the forests behind.

Looking through the canopies of the treetops he spotted the stars and headed north through the thick bush of the woodlands. He had not been walking long before his mind wandered back to Fiora and her tent. He laughed out loud when he thought of her parting words. He wondered if it was definitely the sword she wanted back. Leif had never really felt attraction like this before. With her bad manners, and scruffy look, she had somehow found a way of interesting him. He pushed his mind from the scene inside the tent and kept moving. *It must be just after midnight,* he thought as he spotted the moon high in the sky. He planned on travelling for another few hours before he would stop for some rest. He knew at this time of night and with the cover of the trees it would be impossible to track him; he was safe.

Eventually he reached a small stream that ran across his path. He stepped down the shallow bank and bent a knee towards the water. He cupped a handful and brought it up to his dry lips. As he took a drink there was a sudden penetrating howl from behind him in the distance. With lightning speed, he reached for his sword and grasped the hilt tight. Wild animals had never bothered him in the past, but something about this howl sent a coarse shiver up his spine. He waited a minute, maybe longer, but nothing came. He released the grip on his weapon and turned. He stepped across the flowing stream and continued his journey north.

Without a horse, Leif had estimated it would take him over a day to reach Altnahara. There was something about being in these woodlands at night alone, that Leif did not like. He cast his mind back to his journey with Fathad and the trouble they faced with the Seekers. He rubbed at his chest where the necklace would usually rest.

Chapter 41

I T WAS General Malacath who attacked first; he strode forward with deceptive speed and made a downward chop with both hands, swiping maliciously towards the Knight of Meridia.

Sir Talon dodged the first slice of the two-handed blade and made a lunge with his shorter sword. The blade bounced off the heavy black armour, causing no damage to the flesh beneath. *That would have killed a man with lesser armour,* the Knightguard thought to himself as he dodged another large swing from the General.

As the two champions circled around each other, their footwork was immaculate. Sir Talon looked at the giant he was facing and noted for his size; General Malacath moved well. He scanned the black armour for any hint of an opening. At the hips and beneath the shoulder blades he spotted small gaps in the plate steel. The shoulder would be his next target. He waited for the giant to swing another attack. As the greatsword came crashing down, he lifted his shield and blocked the blow. Sparks flew into his helmet as he reached up and countered, he missed the opening and hit nothing but plate armour.

Back at the wall Sir Oakheart, with Captain Guillow by his side, watched as his companion and the monster from the south fought to the death. Without dropping his gaze from the battle, he spoke to the Captain on his right. 'Malacath knows Talon cannot hurt him.'

'But surely with all his attacks, he is going to get tired?' said Captain Guillow.

'Not this one, he seems to have an unnatural amount of strength,' replied Sir Oakheart. He watched Sir Talon stumble back dodging another downward slice. 'Come on, Talon, you should have made that counter,' he said under his breath. Sir Oakheart was surprised by the lack of speed shown by his comrade throughout the opening exchanges of the fight. Sir Talon was wearing less restrictive armour and the Commander of the Knightguard had expected him to move much faster.

Down in the battlefield, both fighters continued with their back and forth. The Knightguard was managing to move or block all the powerful attacks from the Champion of Blackland, while Malacath had only suffered a few scrapes to his black plate armour. The large General growled with every attack he hammered against the shield of Meridia. The knight would stumble back, before regaining balance and dodging the next blow.

The Knightguard was visibly tiring after the barrage of attacks and the chances to counter were becoming fewer and fewer. They circled round each other, and it was the knight who made the next move. He lunged forward and raised his shield up to his helmet, with his sword-arm he pushed out and caught the giant under the left armpit. Trickles of blood dropped to the dirt as the General took a step back and let out a grunt.

'Is that the sound of pain I hear coming from your helmet?' said the Knightguard as he readied himself for the physical retort of his adversary. He knew, one hit from his enemy and the fight would be over. The greatsword came, but it was slower than the previous attacks – he moved with relative ease and hit the General in the heavily armoured torso.

The fight continued for another five to ten minutes with both men exchanging attacks. Through the course of the fight, Sir Talon's shield had taken a battering from the opposite blade and it had begun to warp outwards at the edges. The knight noted this and tried to move rather than parry the giant's attacks when he could.

Back at the wall, Sir Oakheart continued to watch on with growing concern. He watched his friend swing and miss as Malacath dodged and parried his moves. Even with the injured shoulder, the General was still controlling the battle. He was not prepared for what was about to happen.

'What in the name of Sarpen is going on?' said a voice from behind the commander of the Knightguards.

Sir Oakheart turned his head from the fight for the first time and was now staring at a face he instantly recognised. Oakheart could not believe his own eyes: standing before him was a half-dressed, groggy looking, Sir Talon. He said nothing and took a quick glance back to the battle going on in the south plains. He briefly watched both fighters continue their exchange before turning back to Sir Talon.

'How?' he asked with a stutter.

'Good question, I was hoping you could tell me.' Sir Talon raised a goblet and around the rim of the metal was a light dusting of white. 'Someone must have drugged my wine last night.'

A thousand thoughts ran through Oakheart's head as he tried to process this new development. He looked back to the battle and watched as his champion, fully dressed in Sir Talon's armour, continue to fight the General of Badrang. He was next to speechless and he almost forgot the real Sir Talon was now standing next to him.

'Then who is that?' he asked.

'Your guess is as good as mine, Oakheart. Whoever he is, he is doing as good a job as I would be. He isn't dead yet,' replied Sir Talon.

On the field, both fighters were locked in combat and the momentum had swung back and forth. The mobility of the smaller man had been proving to hurt the large General Malacath. The knight had managed to strike the same area under his opponent's arm, and blood was now flowing freely onto the dirt below.

Malacath, however, continued with his assault and it would have only been a matter of time before the knight would make a mistake with his defence. Fortunately for the General that time was now.

The knight took a step to the left and crossed over his right leg. The General spotted this and rushed him, crashing heavily into the Meridian's shield. With his left hand, Malacath gripped the shield and wrestled it from the knight. Giving up ownership of the steel barrier, the Knightguard loosened his own grip and rolled out of the way. The monster from Blackland gave a hideous chuckle and threw the shield out of reach.

Sir Oakheart, Sir Talon and Captain Guillow all watched from the battlements, as their champion continued to move and parry with his longsword. The end was growing near, and all three men knew whoever this was, he stood no chance against the size of Malacath without a shield.

From their distant view, Sir Oakheart watched as the champion parried a blow with his longsword before taking a second strike across the thigh. Blood fell to the ground beneath the knight as he stumbled and dropped to his knees. The pain travelled up his leg, into his groin and eventually hit his chest. Malacath readied himself and drew back his blade for the killing blow.

Before the attack could land, with his last ounce of strength the Champion sprung to his feet and dodged the blow. Hammering a strike of his own into the midriff of the General, it did nothing.

The General returned the attack with a heavy punch from his armoured fist that caved in one side of the knight's helmet. Spurts of blood poured down the chest of the smaller champion followed by dying coughs.

Malacath let out a deep-bellied laugh as the Champion fell to his knees again. With blood covering the ground beneath them, Badrang's General removed the helmet of the defeated knight. 'Now you die.'

With thick blood running down his chin, a defiant face looked up at General Malacath through tired old eyes. 'All men die, and you will too, Pup.'

These were his last words before the final blow.

Chapter 42

LEIF HAD continued his journey north and was well on his way back to Altnahara. The two-day travel had proved uneventful. Leif had almost enjoyed revisiting his days as a wanderer. He could not help but reflect on how he had managed it year in, year out. Hunting in the deep forests of Helmdale, or fishing along the shores of Lake Redmure. However, his times in the east were not all happy memories. He would be harassed by local villagers and cast out of towns for the way he looked. For weeks he would go hungry, living on what he could find or sometimes steal from farmers. He was not proud of that part of his past, but knew he had little choice at the time. The last few years had been better. He had taught himself how to hunt and fish. He would pick up work here and there to make himself enough money to stay when and wherever he wanted. Since arriving in the Meridian Realms, things had gone from good to even better. He now had a place he could almost call home and was beginning to find answers to the many questions he had.

He was back in the sight of the Monastery and he felt a sense of happiness that did not come around too often in his lifetime. He felt he almost belonged at Altnahara and would do anything to preserve this ancient settlement. After more than three days away from his studying and chores, he was relishing the reunion with Star and his other friends.

As he strode through the long grass in the meadows adjacent to the outer walls, he could hear distant voices within. The longer he listened, the more the voices resembled shouting and arguments. He broke into a fast jog and reached the large double oak doors. He banged on the nearest, until a small slat in the wood opened at eye level. The two eyes looked back at Leif but did not speak; instead they unlatched the gate and allowed him to enter. He stepped through the doors and onto the pebbled courtyard.

In the centre of the gardened square, a large group stood in front of the four standing Dawnbringers. Some of the group were shouting, while others shook their heads. As Leif approached, the rabble began to quieten until eventually they were silent. Leif walked amongst them, towards the four elders atop the short podium.

The silence continued until Master Rollow raised a hand and spoke. 'It is good to see you alive, Leif. The rest of you, please return to your duties. There will be no further need for conversation.'

In the moments following, the crowd broke up and returned to whatever they were scheduled to be doing at this time of day. Some went to the gardens to continue harvesting the crops, while others tended to the animals in the paddocks. The winemakers returned to their workshops to continue the production.

Master Rollow pushed himself to his feet and spoke with quiet authority. 'Please come with us.'

Leif followed behind without saying a word; he did not understand any of what was happening, but thought silence would be better than conversation at this time. He followed the four masters into the building and along a winding corridor. As they made their way through the halls of Altnahara, other priests of the Northern Monastery would avoid eye contact with Leif. Each would bow their heads, pretending they were distracted by their task. It was obvious to Leif each of them knew what was happening.

The masters, along with Leif, continued to walk through stone corridors until eventually they came to a door, a door Leif was familiar with.

Master Liliov turned to the young wanderer before speaking. 'We have brought you to this room, as we feel it is time for you to know something we have kept from you.'

Master Rollow stepped forward and looked at Leif with apologetic eyes. He licked his elderly cracked lips before speaking. 'It was not our intention to keep this from you. You must understand we do not take outsiders into our home often and for this reason, we have been hesitant to tell you some things.'

Master Liliov looked almost annoyed at the way her fellow Dawnbringer had just spoken to Leif. 'We have nothing to apologise for, Rollow. As the elders of the Monastery, any decision we make should be respected by its inhabitants, whether they are permanent or only temporary.'

'I was merely telling the boy that it was not our intention to keep things from him. He has worked hard these last few weeks and had put his life in danger to help with the supply run,' replied Master Rollow.

'That may be the case, but as we have already discussed, he should not have left Clerics Ulric and Thomas. He went chasing the bandits for nothing more than a sword. What if he had got himself killed?' said Master Liliov, in a shrill voice.

The other two masters in the company did not answer and instead both men looked sympathetically towards Leif for an answer.

'Sirs, I meant no harm to you or anyone else within these walls. For the last ten years of my life I have had to fight for what I have. These bandits took something that belonged to me, and I saw this as my only chance of getting it back. I am not saying what I did was right, but I am saying it felt right at the time. I am not defending my actions, but surely you understand the sentimental meaning of this sword.' He paused a moment, unsure if he should continue but did anyway. 'It belonged to my father, and I was not willing to lose it.'

The Dawnbringers all stared at Leif with deep thought. Master Zander was about to speak when Rollow raised a hand. 'There will be no more talk of this. It is time you met someone, Leif.'

Leif nodded and caught eyes with Rollow, just before the elderly Dawnbringer produced a key from within the large pocket on the front of his robe and unlocked the ancient door. One by one, each of the masters raised a hood over their head and took a step back.

Master Liliov spoke from within the darkness of her cowl. 'You must enter the room alone and not leave until permitted.'

The young outsider stepped forward and pressed down on the latch. He heard the clang of metal as the door loosened and knew it could be pushed open. He pressed forward with his right arm and entered a poorly lit room. He closed the door behind him and turned to face a silhouette sitting in the far corner behind a table. The smell of pipe smoke filled the air. Almost afraid to speak, Leif moved towards the man and took a seat opposite him at the table.

'Hello Leif, it is good to see you,' said a familiar voice.

Chapter 43

IN THE afternoon following The Battle of Champions, Sir Oakheart had met with his remaining Knightguard companions and Captain Guillow. Watching a brother die had not been an uncommon sight during his time with the Knightguards, but this one had hurt more than all the others combined. Losing Sir Nolan could prove to be a heavy blow to the morale of the men within Inverwall. The elderly knight had commanded such a profound respect from all those around him, even his enemies.

During the meeting they had agreed a second parlay was to take place in the evening. They would ride out and speak again with the Generals of Badrang and ask for the body of their comrade and friend.

The four knights, along with Captain Guillow, mounted their horses in the moonlit training yard and made their way towards the south gate. As they approached the large double doors, a soldier of Inverwall approached.

Stonesword, a trainee of Sir Nolan's and one of his favourite defenders, reached forward and handed a sealed scroll to Sir Oakheart. 'Sirs, I have this for you. I was instructed by Sir Nolan to give this to you this evening. He had also instructed me not to open or read its contents.'

'Thank you, soldier; you have done him proud,' said Sir Oakheart.

'It is my duty, Sir. Sir Nolan was a great man,' replied the soldier.

'That he was, now you best get back to your platoon. There is plenty of fighting ahead of us.'

Stonesword did not waste any more time; he bowed his head and turned back to the barracks.

With the message firmly gripped in the palm of his hand, Sir Oakheart hesitated a moment. He wondered what he was about to read until assertiveness took over and he broke the seal and stretched out the scroll. He read in silence as the others awaited his verdict. His eyes moved down the paper as he pushed to hold back the tears that were forming. As he read, he thought of the knight who had welcomed to the Knightguard when he was no more than a boy. The knight who had backed him to be Commander. The man who gave everything for the realms he called home.

Brothers of the Knightguard,

You know I have never liked writing and to put this ink to paper has given me a heavy heart. I have done something that goes against our code and I must ask for your forgiveness...

Firstly, to Talon,

I must apologise to you the most for doing what I have done. You have your whole life ahead of you and our order needs you more than it needs me. I did not mean to cause offence to you and I hope the mixture has not given you a sore head.

To Sir Shale,

I wish I had your compassion and logic. You are a credit to us as Knightguards, and I am proud to have watched you grow into the knight you are today. If you ever doubt yourself or your ability, don't! Just laugh and call someone a pup – that's what I did.

To Sir Lenath,

You big brute! You are the strongest man I have ever met, and to have fought alongside you these last fifteen years has been a privilege. I will never forget our campaigns in the East and I take these memories with me to Amundsen and Azmara. Your wits will always be deadlier than your axe, no matter how much you sharpen her.

Lastly to Sir Oakheart, Commander of the Knightguards of Meridia,

You have always been the best knight in our history. I have lived through the reign of four commanders, and none have been as strong or as worthy as you. At times you will doubt yourself and your abilities, but remember I will always be with you. I have every bit of confidence that you will do what you can to save the Realms of Meridia. Please forgive me for my deceit. With seeing Malacath, I could not stand and watch another one of my brothers fall, when I could in their place. It was my time. Talon is more use to the order than I am.

Fight, fight for me, fight for Queen Orellia, fight for Meridia. Send these pups back to Sarpen!
Sir Nolan,
Former Knightguard of Meridia

As Oakheart finished reading the letter, he handed it to Sir Talon. He watched as the other Knightguards took their turn at studying the words of their brother. Sir Shale and Sir Lenath allowed their tears to flow freely with every word.

'He was a great old dog. Amundsen as my witness, I will take the head of Malacath before this war is over!' said Sir Lenath as he read the last of the note. He handed the letter back to Sir Shale. 'Here, lad, Nolan would have wanted you to keep it.'

'There is a special place on our wall in Meridia for this letter. It shows true courage and defiance in the face of tyranny,' said Shale, smiling as he thought of his old mentor. 'Surely now, Lenath, you agree that Nolan would have beaten Sir Quinton the Righteous?'

'I'm still saying nothing. Not going to give the old man the pleasure of me admitting I was wrong,' laughed the large knight.

Sir Oakheart allowed the men to remember Sir Nolan before he gave his instructions. 'It is time we ride out and face our foes again. I will take point, with Talon on my right and Guillow on my left. Shale, Lenath, I want you both to wipe your faces, I won't have the Dakha see any Meridian tears...'

As the Knightguards exited through the city gates they could see the archers on the wall watching their every movement. Sir Oakheart felt the men needed something to lift their spirits but knew nothing would come until the battle commenced.

As they reached the middle grounds between their city and the hordes of the south, Oakheart spotted two flags emerge from the masses. The silhouettes were illuminated by the light of the moon and as the riders approached, the Knightguard Commander noted that this time, General Malacath was not among them. He could see one of the riders carried a body on his horse, most likely the corpse of Sir Nolan. As one of the riders stopped and raised an arm of peace Sir Oakheart recognised him; it was indeed Badrang, Warlord of the South.

Chapter 44

'Fathad?' asked Leif, in disbelief of who he was looking at.

'Yes, it is me, although I may not look as well as I did before,' replied the old cleric as he sat across from his young friend.

Leif was confused and did not know which question to ask first. He thought for a moment, before he settled on his first question. 'What happened to you?'

'That is hard to answer, my boy. It is something I am not sure if I know the answer to myself,' said Fathad as he poured two cups of honey tea. The old man looked up at Leif before handing him one of the delicately crafted cups. 'I hear you have settled in nicely at Altnahara, Leif, I knew you would have.'

The young wanderer opened out a hand and accepted the tea gratefully. He took his first sip and remembered the sweet warm feeling coursing through his chest. As he took another sip, he looked about the dimly lit room. Three out of the four walls were stone with the wall leading out to the corridor built with solid oak. He looked back towards his friend and allowed himself a grin. 'Well I am glad you are safe anyway.'

'So am I, dear boy,' replied Fathad, as he also took a long deep sip of honey tea.

Leif continued to look about the room. He saw a desk smothered with parchments. A solitary quill and inkwell lay next to countless unsealed scrolls. His attention was drawn to the large fourposter bed parallel with the window, its immaculate linen sheets tucked neatly into the sides. Above the bed was a portrait of the man who sat across from the young wanderer. Fathad looked younger in the painting but through the brush strokes, Leif saw wisdom in the youthful eyes of his friend.

Leif turned back. 'I must ask you, you know I must... Are you the Grandmaster of Altnahara?'

Fathad let out a soft chuckle and sat back in his chair. 'I am indeed,' he said, before taking another long sip of tea. He coughed a little and cleared his throat. 'On the day I celebrated my sixtieth birthday, I was asked to lead these people. Amundsen saw it fit to put the fate of this place in my hands.'

Leif was silent. He did not feel betrayed. He somehow understood why everything had been kept from him. He nodded at his friend to continue.

'Indeed, it remains true, I am no Dawnbringer, Leif. I never have been, but there is something we must all come to learn. *A man is not born; he is made through the actions of a lifetime.* It matters not what family raised you nor the deeds, good or evil, committed by your bloodline. You remain the person you make yourself.'

Leif nodded with understanding admiration. 'So, you were a cleric, like all the others here?'

Fathad smiled again. 'Yes, I was a cleric. I kept my head down and worked hard. I would farm, and I would study. I did everything that was required of me. My work was noticed by my peers and with the blessing of Amundsen I was chosen to lead. Leif, for the last two decades I have led these people to the best of my ability. Yes, I have made decisions others did not approve of, but I have always done what I thought was right and followed my own conviction.'

'If what you say is true, and I have no doubt it is, this would make you eighty?' said Leif.

'Well, there is no flaw in your calculations. I have lived a good life here, we have lived on the good of the land and known no displeasure. Winter after winter we survive. We have never entered the conflicts of man and know nothing of war. Sarpen has no place within these walls and by the will of the gods it will remain that way. For twenty years we have been happy within our home.' Fathad coughed again as he topped up his cup with more honey tea. 'However, I am afraid my powers are failing, and time is finally closing in on me.'

'Was it the Seekers that weakened you?' asked Leif.

'Yes, my boy, but that was not your fault. So please feel no responsibility for this. When I felt the power of the stone that once resided around your neck, I was called to you. There is greatness within you, Leif. This is a greatness that has not yet ventured into the light and is waiting patiently for the right occasion.' Fathad coughed into a blood-stained kerchief. He leaned over off his seat and spat into the log fire burning to his right. There was a violent hiss as the moisture burned and dried in the flames. He sat back in his seat and gazed back at the young wanderer. 'I have taken it upon myself to coax this greatness out from the shadows. Will you allow me to train you in our ways? I have no intentions of training you to be a cleric and I do not mean for you to just read our history or water our tomatoes. You will be doing so much more than any of that.'

Leif studied the expression that painted itself across the face of the Grandmaster of Altnahara. He could not help but think his friend had doubled in age since they last spoke. He thought of all the running and searching he had done in his life. There was one thing stopping him from answering immediately and that was his father. He had travelled all his life looking for his father and was it truly time for a change in path? He finished the last of his tea and allowed the warm mixture to run down the inside of his chest and soothe the lower part of his belly.

'What is it to be, my boy?' asked Fathad, for a final time.

Without smiling and in a serious voice, Leif accepted. 'I want to know all you can teach me.'

Later in the afternoon, Leif set about putting his past life behind him. Taking an hour out, he bathed and dressed himself in fresh clothes. In his room he was given a large chest in which to keep the last of his belongings. They barely covered the bottom surface of the wooden container. He locked away his old life with a brass key which he tucked away into the front pocket of his jerkin. With a deep breath he left the comfort of his room, his father's sword strapped across his lean shoulders.

Before the day was out, Leif made a visit to the Altnahara forge at the far end of the large square near the main gate. He entered the dark dusky warmth of the blacksmith's office and approached a man sitting at a desk. The man's head was buried in some paper plans for what looked to Leif like some large steel structure.

'What is it you want then?' asked the blacksmith, without looking up from his plans.

'I was wondering if this was something you could repair?' asked Leif, as he unsheathed his sword and placed the bare blade on the desk.

The blacksmith, who went by the name of Bjorn, leaned back from his paperwork and allowed himself a good look. Moments later he stood from his table and gripped the sword by the handle. He ran his fingers up the worn steel and studied its imperfections.

'It seems like the steel is damaged beyond repair. I could re-forge her and put a new blade on the hilt? I have a busy schedule over the next few days, but I should be able to get this done within a week or so.'

'That would be greatly appreciated. How can I pay you for this service?' said Leif.

Bjorn let out a pleasant chuckle. 'That is not needed, laddie. We here at the monastery do not do things for each other only to gain something in return. We do it to help one another.'

Leif rubbed the coarse stubble on his chin and smiled. 'How about I help you out here for a couple of days? You said yourself, you have a busy schedule. I don't look like much, but you can get some work out of me.'

Bjorn laughed again, and his red cheeks swelled as the corner of his mouth extended up towards his eyes with a toothy grin. 'Well, laddie, that sounds like a great idea to me. When can you start?'

'I am free tomorrow morning. What are you needing done?' asked Leif.

'All in good time, my lad. We can talk tonight over a plate of something hot. I'll meet you in the mess hall at supper time,' replied Bjorn, with a friendly smile.

Chapter 45

ATOP THEIR horses, both leaders stared at one another. Neither Badrang nor Sir Oakheart was willing to break the silence first as a cold breeze swept in from the east. The clear plains were bone dry, and the wind swept dusty dirt up into the faces of all those in attendance. In the light of the moon, both groups faced each other, both ready for combat.

Badrang gazed into Sir Oakheart's eyes, trying to force the knight commander to back down. He was surprised by the strength this knight from the northern capital was showing. His gaze would normally break a lesser man. Badrang knew the aura he possessed and the charisma he carried with every word. Eventually the warlord raised an arm and the horseman carrying Sir Nolan's body dropped the corpse onto the dry ground below. With this sudden movement, Sir Lenath and Sir Shale's horses stirred and both knights regained the composure of their steeds. The warlord from the south looked to the Meridian group, he could feel the tension thicken and he loved every second of it. After running his fingers through his demonic black beard, he finally spoke. 'I can see by the archers you still have posted on the walls that you have no intention of surrendering tonight?'

'You are correct,' answered Sir Oakheart as he nodded and raised his own arm, signalling for Captain Guillow to collect Sir Nolan's body.

The Captain obliged; he dropped down from his horse and strode with officious purpose to the lifeless body. He showed no fear of the Dakha when he lifted Sir Nolan over his lean shoulder and turned back towards his horse.

Sir Oakheart looked back to Badrang. 'We thank you for returning his body.'

The warlord was expressionless as he gazed into the eyes of the large knight dressed in the white robes of Meridia. Still he did not seem to faze this defender from the north.

Tension continued to fill the area as Badrang spoke again. 'So, you truly do not intend on surrendering tonight? Imagine that, a Knightguard of Meridia not honouring the outcome of a battle of champions. What would your Queen think of your decision?' He waited a moment but did not let the defenders answer. 'We will give you the night to grieve your fallen comrade and come to your senses. When the first light of day touches your wall, we attack. The offer of surrender stands until then.'

Sir Oakheart looked about his company, puffed out his chest and spoke. 'We do not intend on surrendering to you, or any army you possess.'

The warlord removed the smile from his face in a frightening flash. Cool charisma was replaced with a terrifying expression. 'You know the number I carry with me. For every one of my attackers you kill, I have a dozen who will take his place. Do you really think you will win this war?'

It was now Sir Oakheart's turn to laugh; he watched Badrang grow in anger as he spoke. 'Tyrant, you know as well as I do... Inverwall was designed for times like this. Look at the width of our walls. Were they made for holding large armies? No, they were made for harbouring a small army of skilled fighters, who are trained to defend our Realm from southern invaders like you!' He could see the fury building behind the eyes of the warlord with every word. 'Now do not throw threats at me or my men. We know the numbers we have and we know the numbers you have. We will NOT surrender!'

Badrang contained his anger and breathed heavily through his wide nostrils until his head was clear. 'I have presented you with two choices and you have chosen the path of death. Your champion lost the battle, and by right you should hand over your weapons, surrendering Inverwall to me.'

'I must agree with you, Badrang, that in principle, we should honour the agreement. However, let me ask you something. Did you show honour when you murdered my Queen's herald in cold blood? The man you killed wore the colours of Meridia under a banner of peace. Do not question my chivalry when his blood stains your hands. We show respect to those who deserve it,' said Sir Oakheart with cool authority.

Again, anger flashed through Badrang's eyes. Not one part of him liked the way he had been spoken to. He questioned who this defiant knight was. 'It matters not. You will all drop before me in the end. Whether bending a knee or face down in the dirt, you will drop. Do you think you are the first to refuse me? The southern kingdoms invaded and pillaged my lands for centuries – I made them drop before me. The tribes of Blackland who would not join me, but they also dropped and swore fealty to me. Do you think you will be any different? I started this war to better my people, to give the Dakha what they deserved. I have created the largest army the world has ever known and you, Oakheart, you will be written into the history books as nothing more than a casualty of my greatness.'

'I will hear no more of this. My decision stands and we will await your attack tomorrow,' Sir Oakheart replied as he raised his arm again, signalling for the company to turn around and head back to Inverwall. As he turned, he did not drop his stare from Badrang. They were two enemies that would soon be locked in a battle of tactics, strategy and wit.

The group returned through the gates of Inverwall and Sir

Oakheart split from the rest of the company. He instructed a fire funeral to take place in the next hour for Sir Nolan and made his way towards the Keep; he needed to use the last of the night to think.

When he arrived back in his room, he moved towards the desk and began to write what could potentially be his final message to Meridia. He wrote of Sir Nolan's demise and the bravery the elderly knight had shown. He pondered if it was finally time to express his true feelings for the Queen. He allowed the quill to run over the parchment freely as his thoughts flooded down his arm and into his fingers. When he looked down at the parchment he supressed his sadness and decided against his heart's wishes. He now knew he would take his feelings for the Queen to the end. His love for her would die on the battlefield. When he was finished the letter, he sealed it into a scroll and got himself ready for a restless sleep.

It was before the crack of dawn and the south bell sounded through the city of Inverwall. The defenders collected themselves and got into position to make their stand.

Chapter 46

LEIF HAD been working with Bjorn for two days and was already developing a great friendship with the huge blacksmith. The young wanderer continued to learn the ways of the monastery, along with completing his daily chores within the hot clammy forge. He would help with the quenching of metal, holing structures in place, and had even been allowed to shape the odd horseshoe. In the evenings, he would dine with Fathad. During the teaching sessions he was taught some of the ancient words of the Dawnbringers. He tried hard to understand the enormous difference between his own language and the one used by Fathad against the Seekers a few weeks prior.

Leif learned of the power possessed within each word. Some even had the ability to manipulate light and air. Fathad had gone into extensive detail when describing the words. The old Grandmaster had stressed the control it would take to use such words. Like a spell, each word had an unearthly purpose, and could be used to contradict what others perceived as reality. With these words, Leif learned it was possible to defeat enemies of a supernatural existence.

It was nearly the end of the week, and Leif's sword was nearing completion. He watched as the blade was oiled for the first time and run over with a fine dry cloth. Bjorn turned to his young assistant and smiled. 'Looks good, doesn't it.'

'I am lost for words,' said Leif, as he gazed at the perfectly crafted steel. He could not wait to hold it in his hands. To feel his sword restored back to its former glory filled him with pride. He looked back at his friend with deep gratitude. 'Thank you, Bjorn.'

The blacksmith continued to smile as he put the last touch of polish on the hilt. 'Judging by the shape, this sword was definitely made in a nobleman's forge. The straight-cross hilt would suggest it once belonged to a lord or a knight. It probably spent the first part of its life in noble tournaments, or on some battlefield. May I ask how you acquired it?' asked Bjorn.

Leif paused a moment, unsure if he was going to be judged on his answer. 'It belonged to my father, he was a travelling soldier and my mother stole it from him before I was born.'

Bjorn said nothing, hinting for Leif to continue.

'I have had it since I was a boy. She was unable to pawn it in my hometown, so she left it with the orphanage.'

Again, Bjorn said nothing.

'I have never really seen a need to use the sword. It has more of a sentimental feel rather than a practical one,' continued Leif.

'So, you have never used it in combat?' asked Bjorn.

Leif looked at the older blacksmith and smiled. 'I wouldn't go that far.'

Bjorn frowned and stared into the young eyes of this one-time wanderer. 'How many people have you killed, Leif?'

'Why do you care?' replied Leif.

'Curiosity, and if I am completely honest, a little anxiety. I feel I should know more about the man I have done this for.' He pointed towards the newly crafted blade. 'What type of person would I be if I gave a weapon like this to someone who should not carry it?'

Leif studied the sword and caught his warped reflection in the blade, the double edge of the metal casting back a grotesque image of the young wanderer. He looked away from the weapon. 'Yes, it's true, I have killed men,' he admitted.

Bjorn did not react.

'But never without good reason,' he continued. 'At least, I always thought I had good reason.'

'You have regrets?' asked Bjorn.

Leif was growing annoyed with the questions coming from the usually jolly blacksmith. He tried his best to contain the anger building behind his eyes, but he could not. 'Only once did I regret killing. You must know I am extremely grateful for what you have done for me, Bjorn. You fixed this for me when you did not need to. I did not pay for this service and it was not your duty. You did it out of the goodness of your heart because I asked you to. But out of the goodness of your heart I ask you, please do not ask me any more of these questions. The world outside is not pretty, and it is not safe. There are people outside that would kill you and take all you have. This sword has protected me from these people all my life. I will not be judged. Not by you or anyone else. I have nothing but gratitude for the help, but you must not ask any more of these questions.'

It was clear to Bjorn he had triggered a nerve in his young friend. 'I meant no offence, lad. Honestly, I didn't. It's just not often I get to speak to someone who has experienced the trials of the outside world. My only knowledge of wars and conflict has come from the books in the library. The only fighting I know is when Cleric Thomas brings his horses over last minute for shoeing. You must have been through enough out there. You don't need some nosey blacksmith giving you a tough time.' He moved forward and patted Leif on the shoulder. 'I didn't mean to pry, laddie.'

'Thanks, Bjorn. I am glad you understand, and I am sorry for being so short tempered,' said Leif.

'Nothing to be sorry for,' replied Bjorn. 'You want to see temper, just you wait until tomorrow when Thomas needs that horse of his re-shoed.'

For the remaining part of the afternoon Leif worked under the light of the forge. He had learned a great deal while working for the blacksmith and enjoyed the entire process of steel craft. Bjorn had such a vast knowledge of metal considering he had never set foot outside the monastery. Although his body was hard, the blacksmith possessed a kind heart, and Leif did not hold any grudge against him at all. If anything, the young wanderer had grown to like him even more.

When Leif had finished his evening lessons with Fathad, he returned to his accommodation. His mind was alive as he undressed by the light of his wax candle. His studies, his duties in the forge, his new home, all these things dominated his thoughts. While rubbing handfuls of basin water into his tired muscles he practised speaking the ancient language of the Dawnbringers. 'Wjnald, forthrac, tormynd,' he muttered, as he massaged a particularly sore part of his arm.

With so many thoughts in his mind, he was surprised when he remembered Fiora. He wondered what she would be doing at this very moment. Would she be harassing some other innocent, running from the soldiers of Dain? Or would she be in her tent, getting ready for another night in the forest? Leif always tried to see the good in people and he was sure he had seen plenty in her.

Leif again thought of all the trouble brewing in the northlands. Without guards to keep the peace and without leadership for the guards, there would be no hope for improvement. With these thoughts in his mind, he knew what his next question for Fathad would be. He was going to ask why Altnahara has never helped with the Duke of Dain's health problems. With all the powers the Dawnbringers had, surely, they could do something.

The next day he was back in the forge and helping to shoe some of the horses. Thomas had been late again, and Bjorn had shown that temper of his.

'I knew you would be. I just knew it. I even said to Leif you would be late,' complained the blacksmith, as he grasped the foot of another horse. 'Okay, okay, just tie her up on that post. I'll see to her when I'm done with this one.'

Leif tried not to pay attention to the arguments as he finished fitting Star with a fresh set of footwear. It was not long before the two of them were alone again and Leif could speak more freely. It was not that he did not trust the clerics of the monastery. He just felt closer to Bjorn.

'How long have you been the blacksmith here?' he asked.

'Over twenty years. You think that's long – the blacksmith before me had been doing it for over fifty years before he died. He taught me everything I know. The different heats required for different metal. How to properly quench a metal to stop cracks from appearing. He was a clever man that one,' replied Bjorn.

'Must have been. This last week has given me a new-found respect for your line of work,' said Leif as he hammered in another nail.

'Glad to hear it. Hey, hey, hey! Hold still!' struggled Bjorn. Thomas's horse had begun to give out short kicks, making it very difficult to line up the shoe.

'So, in that twenty years, you've never been outside of Altnahara?' asked Leif.

'Not really. Sure, I've been out in the forests on occasion. To collect more wood or for a short walk. But never too far, no.'

'Well, that brings me to my next question. If I can get permission from the Grandmaster, how would you like to join me on an adventure?'

Chapter 47

THE SOUTH wall horn sounded hard in the ears of the Inverwallian defenders. The men had trained their whole lives for a moment like this, and not one man didn't know his place. They climbed the walls and got themselves into their positions. The killing fields below were alive with activity as platoon after platoon stepped into rigid formation. The archers strung their bows and notched the first arrow onto their strings. Each prepared for the orders of Captain Guillow.

Sir Oakheart was armoured in his plate cuirass. In the centre of his chest, Queen Orellia's family emblem shone immaculately on the perfectly kept steel. The morning breeze blew back his dark hair as he took his place next to Sir Talon.

'How do you feel, are you ready?' he asked.

'Today is the day we write our names into history. Today we meet these barbarians for the first time,' replied Sir Talon, who looked out to the invaders from the south. 'I have stood with you on countless campaigns, but this is the first time I have thought it could be our last.'

Sir Oakheart ignored the comment. 'Lenath and Shale are both in position. I could not have asked for a better group of brothers to fight with me in these times.' As he spoke, he too gazed southwards towards the advancing Dakha hordes. 'They will be within range of our archers soon. Guillow, remind your archers that no one is to fire until we give the command.'

'Well understood, Commander, I will have the word spread,' replied Captain Guillow, before taking off and moving through the archers stationed on the wall.

Just out of firing range, the Dakha halted their march. As expected, the southerners were not as armoured as the defenders, but they did not lack courage. They howled and screamed with passion as they smashed the rims of their shields with their weapons. The noise was deafening as they attempted to suck every inch of morale from their enemies. The coarse shouting grew louder and louder as each man roared like a wild animal.

With the narrow pass leading up to Inverwall, the Dakha stood in lines of a thousand and along every hundred men stood a General atop a horse. General Malacath took centre place, almost exactly in the middle of the ear-splitting southern army. The monster from the Blacklands stood up straight atop his own gigantic horse. With reins in one hand, and his greatsword in the other, the General bellowed out his own war-cry, drowning out some of those around him.

'His shoulder must be ok then,' said Sir Talon, as his eyes fixed themselves on Badrang's champion.

'It seems that way, but the man did lose a lot of blood against Nolan,' replied Sir Oakheart.

'How can he still lead the charge after those injuries? It must be dark magic, there is no other way of explaining it,' declared Sir Talon.

The Knightguard commander looked uneasily towards the massive General. He said nothing as he watched the monster swing his greatsword through the air with such ease, he may as well have been carrying a broomstick.

Sir Talon did not wait for a response from his friend. 'Shale's scouts had reported Badrang carried shaman from the Blacklands. I am sure healing someone like Malacath is well within their powers.'

'Their powers are nothing but myths, Talon!' snapped Sir Oakheart. 'There has never been any proof of dark magic, only stories from old women whose grandchildren will not behave. Malacath is a man, just like you or me, and I promise you, he will fall.'

The war-cries of the Dakha began to lessen until the battlefield was almost silent. Only the movement of weapons and armour or the light shuffling of feet made a sound. Not a word was spoken by the southern invaders as they waited for their fearless general.

Malacath rode out to the front of the masses. Without looking back at his army, he raised his sword high above his head and shouted, 'BRING THEM DOWN!'

This was what the Dakha had been waiting for and in unison, they took their first step forward. The drums began to boom, and the marching of feet could be heard, but still no one spoke. Methodically they marched towards the first of the wooden barricades where the infantry of Inverwall were stationed.

On the walls Captain Guillow stared down at the approaching hordes as they entered the range of his archers. He raised a hand without averting his gaze and held it in the air. The Captain looked to Sir Oakheart for the final instruction.

The Knightguard commander watched as the horde reached the marked distance from the wall. He turned to the Captain and gave a small nod.

The Captain dropped his arm and shouted at the top of his lungs: 'FIRE, MEN!'

The first wave of arrows was launched through the air. The accumulative sound of the five hundred whistling missiles virtually drowned out the noise of the Dakha drums. Just as the arrows hit their targets, Sir Oakheart watched Malacath. His eyes did not leave the general as two shafts hit the monster atop his jet-black steed. Both bounced off his impenetrable armour causing no damage to the flesh within. The knight watched as the general wheeled his oversized horse around and left the battlefield.

'He knows he is no longer needed. He cannot do anything while our arrows continue,' said Sir Talon while he watched the giant general disappear from view.

Throughout the advancing soldiers, men dropped like flies. If they did not die, they fell to a knee. Some would snap the shaft in two and continued through the pain, half of the arrow protruding from their flesh, while others cried out in anguish, pawing uncontrollably at the enemy projectile embedded deep within them.

The defenders on the wall wasted no time in loading another arrow to their bow. They launched a second wave into the air, then another, and another. Dakha dropped at will, as sharp pointed arrows punctured through their weak leather armour.

Spirited roars sounded from the defenders stationed behind the wooden barricades. They cheered on their flanking archers with every wave or arrow that passed overhead. Adrenaline coursed through their bodies as they eagerly awaited the wetting of their blades.

Sir Lenath watched as the first line of Dakha finally reached his troops behind the wooden barricades. The barbarians from the south made their way through the small openings in the wood and engaged in physical combat. Swords hit shields as both armies collided.

With only a few invaders able to make it through the gaps in the barricade at a time, they were quickly disposed of by the defenders within. That did not stop the Dakha forces from pushing in from behind. Still they marched, crushing their comrades between them and the brave defenders of Inverwall. Bodies mounted up at the entrances into the wooden palisades, but they were not all Dakha. Some Inverwallians had started to fall and their front line had begun to thin as more barbarians flooded into the opening.

Sir Lenath bellowed with valour. The time he had been eagerly anticipating had finally arrived. 'It is time for you to meet Deathbringer! Who's first!?'

He raised his double-bladed axe high above his head and brought it down hard onto a Dakha soldier who had been foolish enough to enter his range. The skull split down the middle like a chunk of meat under the slam of a butcher's cleaver. Blood exploded over the white armour of Sir Lenath, as he growled with glee. He drew back Deathbringer for a second swing, ready for the next attacker. 'You're next!' he shouted at another soldier. He stared into the panicked eyes of the Dakha, as he rotated his shoulders round, bringing the axe through the air with frightening speed. The blade sank deep into the flesh between his enemy's neck and arm. With little difficulty he jerked the axe loose of the dead man's flesh. He swiftly raised his shield high to block another invader's spear and countered with his third fatal swing of the day. He howled with unsettling delight, as his kill-count rose to three and blood coated his face.

The archers on the wall continued to notch an arrow and send it through the air towards the advancing swarm of southerners. They did not aim towards the barricade to avoid hitting their allies, but instead aimed out to the endless horde. Roars of cheer followed every shaft they sent. It was working, the invaders had not nearly begun to break the first platoon of defenders in the killing field.

'Is this all you can think of, Badrang, marching your men in a straight line towards us? Not very creative for someone with such a reputation. Don't think we have too much to worry about after all, Oakheart.' He patted his commander on the shoulder in an almost congratulatory celebration.

Sir Oakheart did not let himself smile; he knew Sir Talon was only trying to instil confidence in the defenders around them. He did not hear what else his companion had to say – he was too distracted by the sound of the north watchtower sounding its warning bell.

Chapter 48

THE GRANDMASTER had happily granted permission for their journey to Dain. Leif and Bjorn planned on travelling to the northern capital to replace the old hammer, tongs and quenching bucket that belonged to Bjorn's predecessor. They would also look to purchase a few other tools that would help the blacksmith with his daily chores.

Both men worked on assembling a two-horse cart; they rigged up the reins and began to load what provisions they would need for the journey. Leif rested his sheathed sword on the front seat and walked round to the back of the carriage, where Bjorn was loading four large sacks of apples.

'Master Liliov wants us to deliver these and those barrels of wine to the Barking Bear while we are in Dain. She has also given me this little shopping list,' said Bjorn. He pushed the bag of apples further into the cart and at the same time handed Leif a small crumpled scroll.

Leif took the paper and read it, before nodding and folding it away into his belt pouch. 'Suppose the people of Dain will be getting thirsty since they didn't get the last lot,' he said, as he helped the big blacksmith load one of the barrels into the cart.

When all was arranged, they headed out the south gate onto the road towards the northern capital. Leif was hopeful they would not run into trouble along the way. From what Fathad had said, it seemed the Seekers would not be reappearing anytime soon. He also knew the bandits were not entirely sure about robbing the monastery and doubted they would attempt it again. However, there was a small part of him that wanted to see Fiora.

Bjorn was excited to finally find out what life was like in a city. 'Will we stay for the night?' asked the blacksmith, as he smiled at the thought of the busy streets in Dain and all the different people he would meet.

'I don't see why not. The Barking Bear is a nice place, I stayed there the last time,' replied Leif.

'What about the people of Dain? Are the friendly? The way I hear it, most people don't like us monks. They worry in case we are going to curse them or bring them bad luck.'

Leif smiled at his friend. 'They are courteous, but I must admit, when they saw my rune necklace they were not so welcoming. Must have thought I was part of the monastery. So, I guess they do think we are going to bring them bad fortune. I think most of them are struggling without the Duke just now anyway.'

Bjorn turned and looked back at the concealed cargo within the cart. 'Maybe if you are bringing them all this, they will act a bit nicer?'

Leif again thought of his last journey along the road to Dain. He was still annoyed that he had lost the last shipment. He hated their kind, but he also pitied them. Throughout his life he had come across many bandits. Some were bad men who fled after committing an evil act. They would hide in the wildlands like animals, killing anyone they came across and taking everything. Others ran to the wilderness because they had no other choice. He was confident Fiora and her group were not bad people. After all, if they were, he wouldn't still be alive.

The two travellers from the monastery made good progress along the uneven dirt road. At night they camped by the light of the moon and slept under the shelter of the two-horse wagon. Leif did not sleep well throughout the night. He clearly still had doubts about their safety. Without truly falling asleep, he would keep an eye on the surrounding area and a firm hand on the hilt of his newly forged sword.

Two nights had passed since leaving the monastery, and they eventually reached the northern gate of Dain. As they approached, they could see two guards stationed outside.

'We come to deliver stores and buy goods,' declared Leif, as confidently as he could.

Both guards inspected the cart and sniggered between each other. 'So, you two have come from Altnahara? Do you know of the new trade tax?'

'Trade tax? Have you ever heard of this, Bjorn?' asked Leif, knowing full well that the blacksmith would not have a clue.

'Never heard of it' was the reply.

Leif turned back to the guards, who were now smirking with greed. 'Well there you have it; we haven't heard of it. But I'm afraid that means we aren't going to pay. Unless you two are going to try and make us?'

There was no immediate response from the Dain guards.

'What's it going to be then?' asked Leif, with smug confidence, trying his best to provoke an answer.

Both guards spotted the sword strapped across Leif's back. They found it intimidating the way the young wanderer spoke to them. Most travelling merchants would be too desperate and would not question made-up laws like trade taxes. Almost everyone they met was in such a hurry to do business they would pay any dues blindly.

After exchanging a glance with his comrade, one of the guards made an uneasy smile towards the two travellers and spoke as softly as he could. 'Apologies, we completely forgot, the trade tax does not apply to first timers in the city.'

Leif smiled and laughed lightly. 'I have been in this city before.

Surely, I am not exempt from such a rule?' He knew he had the two crooks worried.

The guards knew they had been found out and their bluff had been called. Although the soldiers of Dain could get away with most things, they did not want the hassle of an argument with this young stranger. 'We apologise, please enter.'

Leif was not satisfied. He wanted to teach them a lesson and was fighting the urge to give that lesson through the actions of violence. 'I must warn you both, I will not tolerate harassment. Whether it is directed at me or any other innocent man or woman who passes your way.'

Both guards looked afraid, and they still eyed the top of the sword that was strapped across Leif's back.

'I have a strong urge to beat you both. The only thing stopping me is the trouble it would cause me and my companion. Not that I would spend a minute in the cells after I tell your superior you were stealing money from the traders. It would just inconvenience me. I could always just report you anyway? I'm sure your boss wouldn't be pleased to hear you have been doing this, considering it is the traders that supply this city with food and drink. These lands need honest men to be in your position and it is time you both stepped up to the challenge. Or you could always step down from the position.'

Both guards remained silent and did not argue.

'Well, what's it going to be?' asked Leif.

They nodded in agreement and opened the gates. Both men dropped their heads and looked at the dirt around their feet. With nothing more than words, Leif had emasculated and embarrassed both men into feeling like naughty children.

'I have given you one chance, more than I have given people like you in the past. You will not get another, so don't waste it,' said Leif through gritted teeth.

Bjorn pulled the cart forward through the gates and they followed the main road deeper into the town. They eventually reached the large courtyard of Dain. The market district was not as busy as it had been during Leif's last visit, but that did not concern the young wanderer. He looked about the buildings as they continued to steer their cart in the direction of The Barking Bear. He continued to work from his memory of the northern capital, giving infrequent directions to Bjorn, who was sitting to his left. Eventually they could see the Inn; it was at the far end of the courtyard just past the townhall. Beside the townhall, however, both men saw a large gathering of people.

'What's happening over there?' asked Bjorn.

'Hmm, I'm not sure. Let's go and see what all the fuss is about anyway,' said Leif. He pointed over to a spot where they could drop their cart and tether the horses.

Both men began to make their way through the thick crowd of people.

'Must be something important,' said Bjorn while he squeezed past a couple of disgruntled townsfolk. 'Hope it's nothing bad,' added the Blacksmith.

For a moment, Leif's heart stopped when he looked up the stone steps.

Chapter 49

WITH THE battle continuing in the south plains and with the north watchtower's bell booming heavily in his ears, Sir Oakheart froze. He was trapped in a moment of indecision and tried to process what was now happening. After only a few seconds of hesitation he snapped into action. 'Continue without me, Talon, I will find out what it is.' The Knightguard commander turned to a group of soldiers on his right. 'You five, come with me.'

By the time Oakheart had descended the south wall, the watchtower was now beating its bell frantically. All six men quickened their pace to a run as they made their way across the courtyard to the foot of the northern battlements. With each stride up the grey stone steps a new thought crept into Oakheart's head. Had Queen Orellia sent reinforcements from Meridia? Had Duke Delgath sent men from Dain? One question dominated all other thoughts – would it be good news or bad news?

Upon reaching the top of the watchtower Sir Oakheart immediately scanned the meadows to the north. 'What is the meaning of this ringing?' he asked. It was then he spotted it. In the distance, just on the far edge of the fields, there was a small group of men approaching.

'I thought they might be spies,' said the bellringer. 'I am sorry for disturbing you, but I was instructed by Sir Shale not to take any chances.'

Sir Oakheart turned back to the watchman. 'You have done well. But if they ARE spies, they are poor ones to give away their position so easily. They look to be approaching us anyway. Allow them entry but they must give up their weaponry first.'

The watchman nodded. 'What are we to do with them – do you want us to lock them up?'

'Keep them under watch until this evening. I will speak to them then. For now, my place is on the south wall. These five soldiers here will help you with your watch. Stay vigilant, those men out there might not be alone.' He looked into the eyes of the watchman. 'If you see anything else suspicious, ring that bell again.'

With a nod the watchman saluted his commander. 'It will be done, Sir.'

Back in the killing fields Sir Lenath and Sir Shale continued to hold their line against the endless advancing horde. Both men were stained in a fresh coat of Dakha blood. Sir Lenath had killed a countless number of enemies, but for each one he would slay another two would appear into his view. Still the giant knight swung Deathbringer with deadly accuracy. He moved with the speed of a man who had just entered the battle and was showing no signs of tiring. He growled with every kill and the corpses piled up around him.

The Inverwallians surrounding Sir Shale and Sir Lenath were in sheer awe of the combat skills displayed by both knights. The defenders knew these men were trained to the highest standard in both mental and physical warfare, but not one man in attendance had expected such a showing. No other soldier came close to the potency of either man's skill. Not requiring the use of heavy armour, the knights would somehow dodge each attack. They would parry, thrust, move and counter, until the enemy that faced them lay lifeless on the ground.

Eventually numbers began to tell, and the first barricade was lost to the endless Dakha horde.

'Pull back!' shouted Sir Shale. He grasped a spearshaft heading towards his torso, pirouetted forward, and sliced the throat of the soldier who carried it. He felt the spear come loose and he jerked it away from the limp fingers of the dead warrior. With immense skill he twirled the spear around and rooted the point deep into another enemy who was attacking from the other direction.

Upon hearing the command to retreat, the Inverwallians backed away from the horde. Banner-bearers within each platoon waved their flags, signalling for the fire archers. Within minutes the first barricade was engulfed in high flames. Screams of death sounded from the invaders, as the men crossing through the gaps in palisades were burned alive. Their clothing catching fire like dry tinder. With the first wooden wall aflame, the Dakha were forced to fall back away from the heat and regroup to the south. This gave the Inverwallians enough time to retreat uphill behind the next barricade.

Sir Lenath ignored the call and continued to fight the Dakha caught between him and the flames behind them. He swatted away the thrust of one spear with his axe and returned by grabbing the man by the throat. He laughed as he squeezed, and ripped away a thick chunk of flesh, causing a burst of blood to spill over his arm. Next, he smashed Deathbringer down on an advancing southerner, carving halfway down the torso from the shoulder blade to bellybutton.

Sir Shale could see Sir Lenath fighting in the distance, as the rest of the defenders retreated. 'LENATH, GET OUT OF THERE!'

Sir Lenath continued to ignore the calls from his comrade and instead killed another two Dakha. Blood now covered his body, from head to toe, as he wielded his axe like a madman. He had long forgotten his shield and instead moved about his enemies, punching and breaking arms where he could. He growled at the next southerner who entered his view.

'I want you to give a message to your General. Sir Lenath is coming for him,' snarled the knight.

The Dakha warrior gritted his teeth and contemplated retreating. He felt the heat of the fire burning behind him. For a moment he thought jumping into the flames was more favourable than facing this knight who fought with the strength of ten men. He continued to hesitate until he made his ill-fated decision. He charged the large man, shield and curved sword in hand. He swung at Sir Lenath but missed.

'YOU FOOL,' roared Sir Lenath as he dodged the swipe with one easy step. He snarled as he brought Deathbringer through the air at a ninety-degree angle straight into the gut of the unfortunate soldier.

In a moment of surprise, he felt something behind him. For the first time that day, he had made a mistake and left a blind spot. His flank was not protected. He felt the grip of a hand on his shoulder. He wheeled about to attack but when turned he found he was staring face to face with Sir Shale. Through red, misty eyes he looked at his young companion.

'Did you not hear the retreat?' asked Sir Shale.

'Boy, I almost killed you!' barked Sir Lenath.

'We need you alive, Lenath!'

Sir Lenath snapped from his war-rage and gave a blood drenched nod. His head cleared long enough for him to come to his senses. 'Lead the way.'

They reached the second barricade and beckoned towards the men stationed there. The men they looked at could not hide the respect on their faces. Some even applauded as Sir Lenath turned back and faced the direction of the Dakha horde. He did not take a moment to rest. Instead, the big knight stretched his arms and moved Deathbringer through the air slowly, fighting off any small signs of fatigue.

Sir Shale called out to the soldiers around him. 'Be ready, men, that fire will not last forever. They will be able to pass through within the hour. I want the new men to move to the front. Those who are injured, head back towards Inverwall for treatment.'

The Inverwallians gazed with sheer admiration at the two heroes in front of them.

Chapter 50

Each of the remaining Wolves were permitted access to Inverwall through the northern gate. They were asked to hand over their weapons and allowed the guards to search them. They could hear the action of battle in the distance.

'We have missed the start then?' asked Rommel, as he unbuckled the shortsword around his waist and handed it to the Inverwallian guard.

'Yes, the barbarians attacked at dawn. Seems we have repelled their initial assault,' replied the guard. He was flanked by five armed soldiers of Inverwall, each with an uneasy look on their faces.

Roar was last to hand over his sword. He did not like the idea of being parted with it, but knew there was no chance he would be allowed to keep it. He remembered what it was like to be unarmed and at the hands of the tyrant Captain Bruar. Eventually he unsheathed the blade and handed it over to one of the waiting soldiers.

'I'll be taking this back soon,' he muttered through the pain in his healing jaw.

Rommel continued to try and be as friendly as possible. He smiled at the nearest soldier and spoke in his calm voice. 'We need to meet with the commander of this post. Can you please inform him that we bring him news regarding Badrang?'

Roar was the opposite and continued to stare at his weapon that was now in the hands of an Inverwallian soldier. 'It is information he will need!' he said, with obvious attitude.

'I am sure our commander, Sir Oakheart, will be interested to hear what information you possess but for the moment you must wait. He is currently on the south battlements; he will see you this evening,' said the guard before turning to the five soldiers behind. 'Please take these men to the barracks. Let them eat and wash up. Please stay with them at all times; they are not to go near weaponry.'

'This Sir Oakheart sounds like a trusting fellow. Are you sure you want to let men like us through your gates? Especially men that look like us?' asked Roar, with a smirk.

'Sir Oakheart is a great man and I trust his judgement. You won't be able to do anything with a watch on you. Now please follow these soldiers to the barracks.' replied the guard.

Roar scoffed and looked away.

'Thank you, Sir. You have my word, we will not cause any trouble. We are here to help,' said Rommel. He was first to follow the Inverwallian soldiers to the barracks opposite the main keep.

The mess hall within the garrison was empty, with all the soldiers manning a station to the south. All five of the Wolves grabbed an empty bowl and headed towards a large pot of stew simmering over a stone fireplace. They each filled their dish and tore off a piece of freshly baked bread. Under the watchful gaze of their five escorts, Roar and the rest of the group took a seat at one of the many empty wooden tables and devoured the food.

Rommel had warned the group not to tell anyone other than the commander why they were in Inverwall. Rommel was sure Badrang would have spies within the southern city and wanted to make sure their news reached the leader of the defenders. The one advantage the Wolves had in their favour was the southern warlord did not know of their existence or the knowledge they possessed.

Badrang would be counting on the element of surprise when his new army of outlaws and pirates attacked from the north. This was something the Wolves of Glory were desperate to take away from the warlord. None of them hated Badrang. He had never done anything to them, but they could not sit back and watch as their country fell to an invading army.

Roar's mind was still plagued by memories of Captain Bruar. During the journey south, he would have restless sleeps, dreaming of the chance at getting his hands on the tyrant who had beaten him nearly to death. He wanted nothing more to avenge his young companion Torquil. He wished things had happened differently back at Brigands Bay. He felt he would happily give up his own life if it meant extinguishing Bruar's. It had not taken the Captain long to become Roar's greatest enemy – it had all happened within the space of a few weeks. The corsair had gone from a quick bit of coin for a group of seasoned mercenaries to a nemesis Roar would do anything to get his hands on.

The five Inverwallian guards watched as the Wolves finished their meals in the quiet mess hall. Through the thin winds, they could hear their city brothers fight in the distance. Each soldier wondered how their allies were faring against the never-ending assault of the Dakha.

As the Wolves of Glory sat in silence, Rommel thought of how he would present the information to Sir Oakheart. He needed to make sure the commander of Inverwall believed what he said. The Knightguards of Meridia were known throughout the whole world and if this man was their leader, he must be a great warrior. Rommel knew the Knightguards were the best fighters and strategists in all the land, but he was sure Sir Oakheart would not have considered an attack from the north. As far as Oakheart was concerned, this new army did not even exist.

Before long, night had fallen over the city of Inverwall and the candles in the mess hall were lit by half a dozen soldiers. The Wolves had been well fed and had rested over the hours. They watched from a corner of the room, as tired and injured defenders would enter, grab a bowl of food, and collapse with exhaustion on their soft beds.

'It seems the battle is stopping for the night,' said Hunter.

'Yes, it appears so. Both armies know fighting at night is dangerous. Wars are even more unpredictable in the dark,' replied Rommel.

Roar rubbed at his bearded jaw. The joint was mending and wasn't as painful as before. He had managed the stew apart from the odd tough piece of meat. The cuts around his eyes were still scabbing over and he was beginning to resemble his former self. One thing that was not healing, however, was his voice. He had never been one for needless conversation, but these days he hardly spoke a word. When he did speak, it would usually be negative. Roar knew he wasn't the best travelling companion, but he had gone beyond the point of caring. All he wanted was to kill Bruar.

'You look like a man who has something to say,' commented Rommel. He passed his old friend a sheepskin pouch of water.

Roar returned his companion's look. He took a long drink and splashed a little of the cold water over his face. 'It is a warm night. Wonder how much longer this Oakheart will keep us waiting?'

Eventually a young man dressed in a captain's uniform entered the room. He looked exhausted and had clearly come from the south wall. He was of average height and carried a longbow in one hand.

Rommel turned towards the soldier and gave him a kind smile.

The Captain looked about the five Wolves and nodded. 'Our commander will see you now.'

Chapter 51

L EIF HAD the surging impulse to run up the stone steps and intervene, but for the moment he tried to remain calm.
Looking up towards the small square in front of the townhall both Leif and Bjorn could see the Grandcaptain of Dain. Slightly to the left, tied to a wooden post, and with his bare back exposed the lumberjack Hilvard stood.

'With the power granted me to by Duke Delgath of Dain, I sentence this man to ten lashings for the following crimes!' shouted the Grandcaptain.

Leif's heart began to race. This was a man who had offered him hospitality in a time of need.

'Bjorn, we need to stop this,' he whispered.

'Firstly, assaulting two soldiers of Dain!' began the Grandcaptain as the crowd continued to grow. 'Secondly, stealing money from the realm!'

Hilvard turned from the post and begged. 'Please, I've told you, the money was a gift from a friend. I didn't steal anything!'

With a stone expression, the Grandcaptain ignored the plea, smirked, and continued to address the gathering mass. 'And lastly, resisting arrest.'

Leif continued to listen as the crowd shouted with anger at the accused. Members of the enraged audience were throwing rotten vegetables at the innocent woodsman. Leif studied the expression on the lumberjack's face and could see the man was bracing himself for the pain to come.

'THIEF!' shouted someone from the crowd.

'CRIMINAL!' called out another.

Leif looked about and was incensed at how the people of Dain could turn on one of their own. Surely, they knew the state the city was in – they lived in it. He could not take any more, he nudged Bjorn in the ribs and took a step forward. They made their way to the front of the crowd.

'Bring out the Lasher!' called the Grandcaptain.

Moments later a large fat bellied man, wearing a black hood, emerged from the doorway of the town hall. It was unclear if the crowd cheered or jeered the punisher. The hooded man ignored the audience, and instead walked forward with confidence.

'Why does he wear a hood?' whispered Bjorn.

Leif looked at the Lasher, who was now testing his whip through the air. He did his best not to flinch at the loud crack. 'The hood is to prevent him being recognised in the streets. Do you think a man like that would live long in his line of work if he did not remain incognito?'

The Lasher tested the whip half a dozen times, deliberately teasing his victim. Leif could see Hilvard had kept his courage and had a stern expression on his face. It was the face of an innocent man. 'I cannot stand for this Bjorn.' whispered the young wanderer.

'What are you going to do?' asked the Blacksmith.

Leif scanned the crowd around him. They were still shouting in anger. He wondered if they were thirsty for justice, or were they thirsty for blood? He could not understand why men and women would be so quick to judge someone like Hilvard, someone who was similar to each and every one of them.

The Lasher took up his position, with his back now to the crowd. He threw the whip out in front, between himself and his bare backed victim. He gauged how far he was from the woodsman and took a small step back. He gave himself enough space to strike the target with optimum pain. The crowd had gone silent as they eagerly awaited the first lash.

With a deep breath, the hooded punisher drew back his whip. He exhaled and brought his hand forward with the same technique he had used every time in the past. However, this time, the whip did not follow and instead slid from his grasp.

The crowd erupted into laughter as the pot-bellied giant staggered forward and lost his balance, dropping to one knee. Enraged, the Lasher pushed himself to his feet and wheeled about to find a young stranger standing on the tail end of his whip.

Leif could see fury in the eyes beneath the hood. He smirked before bending down and picking up the weapon, coiling the length around in a circle.

'This must stop now. He did not steal that money either – it was a gift from me. And I was the one who beat those guards.'

The Lasher turned to face The Grandcaptain, awaiting instructions. He did not know how to react. There was clear confusion in his eyes, but the anger had not left him.

The Grandcaptain's expression was a clear painting of rage. 'How dare you!?' he shouted at Leif. 'You will be arrested and tried for this. Hand over the whip and unbuckle the sword around your shoulder. After we deal with this woodsman, your fate will be decided.'

The crowd remained silent, awaiting a response from this mysterious outsider.

After a few seconds, Leif eventually replied. 'No.'

'What are you doing, laddie?' whispered Bjorn on his left.

Leif ignored the Blacksmith and continued. 'I have not had to spend a great deal of time in these lands to discover the state the law is in. How long have you bled these people dry with overtaxing and charges? I will not let you punish another innocent man. I beat down two guards who were praying on the misfortune of a humble worker. These men were cowards, and cowards thrive under the guidance of someone like you.' As he spoke, he pointed towards the Grandcaptain in disgust.

The Grandcaptain was dumbstruck. He was ready to call for the city guards but remained calm. 'I see you wear the colours of Altnahara. Tell me why a monk would carry a weapon like the one you have on your shoulder?'

The crowd remained enthralled at what was taking place. This was more entertainment than any number of lashings could provide. They waited with bated breath for the young wanderer to respond.

Leif smiled again. 'I am no monk.'

The Grandmaster gave a twisted smile. He knew he had enough reason to arrest this newcomer but was happy to have so many witnesses. 'So, you stole the clothes? You are a criminal?'

Leif did not reply and instead he unsheathed his sword.

Chapter 52

SIR OAKHEART and Sir Talon were sat in the council chambers of Inverwall. They were dressed in evening wear as they discussed the day's activity. Sir Talon summed up the events of the first assault on the south wall.

'Shale and Lenath have reported the casualties in their foot soldiers were minimal for an initial conflict. Badrang has fallen back for the evening and will most likely not attack until the morrow. He understands, at night, his men would stand no chance against our arrows.'

'Good, it gives us the night to treat the wounded and regather our strength. Tomorrow I intend on joining our brothers in the killing fields. I need our men to see a leader who fights WITH them,' replied Sir Oakheart.

'Are you sure that is wise? We cannot risk losing you to a stray spear or axe,' said Sir Talon, with doubt in his voice.

'I will not stand by while our men die in the fields and I watch from the walls. The Knightguard Commander must make decisions and I have decided I will fight shoulder to shoulder with my soldiers. You will lead from the wall in my place. With Sir Nolan now dead, you are my number two.'

When they had finished summarising the day, Sir Oakheart instructed Captain Guillow to fetch the travellers from the north. He was intrigued as to what information these men held. Anyone coming in the direction of Inverwall, with all that was going on, deserved to be listened to.

Within half of an hour, the young Captain entered the council chamber, flanked by the five travellers.

Oakheart studied the men standing in front of him. Two were older than the others, but they looked like very capable fighters. One of the men carried a bruised face with healing cuts about his eyes. The man's jaw looked slightly offset and had obviously been broken recently. Sir Oakheart concluded that behind their weak exterior they looked like a tough bunch.

'Sirs, I bring you The Wolves of Glory,' said Captain Guillow.

Sir Oakheart beckoned towards the wooden seats across from the table where he and Sir Talon sat. 'Please have a seat.'

'Thank you, my lord. My name is Rommel.'

'So, Rommel, who are the Wolves of Glory?' asked Sir Talon.

Rommel let out a small cough before answering. 'It may not please you to hear this, but we are a group of bounty-hunters. We understand knights do not always approve of our methods.'

Sir Oakheart spoke quickly, to avoid any awkwardness. 'I have heard of The Wolves of Glory and know of what you do for the realm. Unlike our knight-brothers, we see the good you do for the people of our land. So please do not conceal any information from us. We need total honesty, now more than ever. Who else is amongst you?'

'Thank you for your understanding, Sirs. This is Roar, Willem, Mallard and Hunter.'

'I understood The Wolves of Glory was quite a big group? Where are the rest of you?' asked Sir Talon.

Roar snarled before his cooler comrade could answer. 'Mostly dead… The others just left. They didn't agree with coming here.'

Sir Oakheart looked at the healing bruises around the gruff Wolf's face. 'I see. Now please tell us why you have come here. You obviously have some information we need.'

Roar did his best to remain silent. He waited for his companion to relay the message to the knights. He did not like rubbing shoulders with the noble type and thought Rommel would be best at dealing with a situation like this.

Rommel cleared his throat and began. 'During our most recent contract, we took on Captain Bruar and The Flaming Sails. You may or may not have heard of them?'

'I know of The Flaming Sails,' replied Sir Oakheart before nodding.

'During our chase we encountered problems at sea and to cut a long story short, ended up as their captives. We were taken to Brigands Bay but managed to get away. However, before we escaped we were able to learn a valuable piece of information.'

Both Knightguards leaned forward.

'Please continue,' said Sir Talon with concern in his voice.

'The Harbour Master at Brigands Bay conducted a council. It was some kind of meeting between the leaders and captains. Anyway, they decided that with their combined forces they would attack Inverwall from the north. Under the coin and promises of Badrang, they will invade you from an angle you are not expecting.'

Both knights sat back in their chairs. Sir Oakheart's mind was racing, but he processed the new information quickly.

'Do you know the size of the force?' he asked.

'It must be close to two thousand. I know it's not enough to take the city, but it will surely be enough to distract your attention. He only wants to weaken your defences in the south.'

Sir Oakheart was not yet ready to give away any strategies to these five strangers, but he did nod with agreement. 'We cannot thank you enough for bringing this information to us. You have done us and our people a great service.'

'Thank you, but we were only doing our duty,' replied Rommel.

Sir Oakheart nodded again. 'Captain, please take these men to some unassigned quarters within the west barracks. They can rest there before they leave tomorrow.' Before he continued, he turned and stared at the damaged face of Roar. 'That is, unless they want to stay here and fight with us?'

Chapter 53

THE CROWD remained motionless as they awaited the next move from the Grandcaptain. They watched as this mysterious stranger stood defiantly before the gathering town guards. The crowd could see armed soldiers appearing from all angles, each of them ready for combat.

Leif continued to smile. With his drawn sword grasped in both hands, he moved slowly towards his woodsman friend. He shifted his gaze between the Grandcaptain, the Lasher and the guards of Dain.

The soldiers around him did not move quickly, in fear they would provoke an attack from the unknown warrior. They circled round the wanderer until all retreat routes were cut off and a tight perimeter was formed.

Still Leif moved, noting the position of each guard. He had only walked a few paces, but it had felt like an eternity. He counted the men around him. He had fought outnumbering enemies before, but never this many. Most of his combat experience had come against untrained bandits or reckless thugs. He had little experience dealing with fully trained, military men.

'No one needs to die here today,' said Leif, as he moved closer to the bound lumberjack.

Bjorn who had followed Leif slowly looked at the town guards who had formed a circle around them. The large blacksmith cleared his throat and spoke out. 'We come from Altnahara. We are peaceful and want no trouble here. This man is under the protection of our monastery, and by custom, you must grant us clear passage.'

'I'm afraid it is too late for that, Monk,' snarled the Grandcaptain. 'Your companion has gone too far. We respect the monastery and all they have done for our lands but as acting commander of Dain, I cannot tolerate such a flagrant disregard for our laws.'

Bjorn could see Leif reach the lumberjack and watched as his young comrade cut the ropes that bound Hilvard. The blacksmith turned back to the Grandcaptain and continued. 'Please, we will leave and no more will be said. No blood needs to be spilled for lessons to be learned.'

All three men were now standing in the centre of a closing circle of guards. Bjorn clenched his mallet-sized fists, while Hilvard rubbed at the chafings around his thick wrists, and Leif held his fighting stance. The Dain town guards were ready to attack at the order of their Commander. With their swords shinning in the light of the burning sun, they took another step towards the strangers.

Leif moved his sword through the air with lightning speed and cut at nothing but air; he shifted his feet and changed his stance. This startled the town guards. Leif was more than happy to prove to them he was skilled with a blade. If they attacked him, they would at their own peril. Leif smirked as two of the guards took a step back in fear.

'We are willing to leave without any further trouble,' stated Leif.

'You will not be leaving,' growled the Grandcaptain.

Leif looked about and counted more than a dozen guards. The crowd began to murmur with discontent, as if Leif's actions were beginning to win them over. He could hear some of the audience cursing the soldiers and he knew it would not be long before a riot would break out. Outnumbered and surrounded, he knew there was no hope of him beating all twelve of the soldiers by himself. Bjorn and Hilvard were both big men, but neither had any fighting experience, and Leif did not like the idea of them coming to harm. His mind began to race. If he was to surrender, it would mean his arrest. Also, Bjorn would be added to the list of innocent men in line for punishment. If he fought, however, he knew he would die, almost certainly with both his friends.

'What is it going to be then, rogue?' asked the Grandcaptain.

Leif turned to his companions and gave an appeasing smile. He turned back to the Captain of Dain and sighed. 'I will come with you, but only if these men are to be given safe passage to Altnahara.'

The Grandcaptain smirked. 'You are in no position to bargain. This goes beyond the lashings the woodsman was due. But if it avoids bloodshed, we will grant your friends the road.'

Leif turned to his companions and went to hand his sword to Bjorn. 'Please hold onto this for me. I am sorry for dragging you into this.'

The Grandcaptain quickly interjected and let out an obnoxious laugh. 'I'm afraid the sword will also be coming with us.'

Anger began to build-up inside Leif. He knew he had no right to push the issue, considering they were already willing to let his companions walk free. Including one who was yet to serve a punishment. He bit his lip and turned the point of the blade towards the stone ground. He pointed the sword down and allowed the guards to approach him. He was expecting to receive some rough treatment.

Three guards approached Leif. One grasped the hilt of the sword and brought it away from the traveller. The other two each grabbed an arm and began to lead Leif away.

The Grandcaptain smiled. 'You have made a wise decision, a decision that has spared the lives of your friends.' He raised an arm and another six soldiers moved in. In the moments to follow, both Bjorn and Hilvard were subdued and brought to their knees. 'I'm afraid they are also under arrest.'

'But you said they would be granted safe passage,' called Leif as he tried to struggle free of the tight grasps around both his arms. He felt the heavy blow of a fist land hard into his stomach. He let out a gasp of air before trying to re-catch his breath. The second punch was harder and put Leif on his knees. The guards lifted him almost immediately and hit him again in the stomach.

The Grandcaptain smiled smugly and spoke. 'We here in Dain do not make deals with thieves. Take these men to the dungeons; we will have them on trial tomorrow.'

It was then a voice called out from the crowd, then another and another. Leif could not make out what the new voices were saying, but he could see what they were carrying. Five archers emerged from the crowded audience, each wearing a hood. All five of the hooded figures had a strung arrow pointed at the Grandcaptain.

'Unhand these men! They are not going anywhere with you,' called a voice from behind the Bowmen.

The Grandcaptain sweated under the pressure of having five arrows pointed in his direction. 'And who commands this?' he stuttered, trying to sound as brave as he could.

'I do.'

One of the hooded saviours stepped forward.

'And who are you?' asked the Grandcaptain.

The figure took another step forward and lifted her hood, letting the material fall about her narrow shoulders while releasing her fiery red hair.

Chapter 54

I T WAS the second day in the assault of Inverwall and the defenders were as prepared as the first. It had not even reached the crack of dawn when the horde reappeared in the killing fields. The Dakha marched towards the upper wooden barricade as arrows fell from the sky like heavy rain. Hundreds had died during the first day but the morale amongst the attackers had not wavered. They had been told to expect casualties during battles, and like every other war in their past, this was no different. The Southern Kingdoms had resisted Badrang a year prior but had fallen to the might of the Warlord. There was not one Dakha who did not believe in their leader's cause – each one of them would die for the Badrang and his plans.

The archers on the battlements would continue to fire out into the endless hordes. As far as their eyes could see, the enemy's army covered the earth.

Captain Guillow had already killed a countless number of Dakha with his longbow. He would not follow the course of each arrow he fired; instead he would notch another quickly to his bow and fire at a new target. Between two arrows, he barked orders to the men around him. 'Aim for the head of the column.'

The horde eventually reached the wooden barricade and charged the defenders stationed behind. They growled their war cry as they met the shields and swords of Inverwall. Countless men died in the opening moments as both armies met for the second time in two days.

As per his intentions, Sir Oakheart had indeed joined his Knightguard companions in the field and was now leading the line against the charging invaders. Alongside Sir Shale and Sir Lenath, Sir Oakheart cut down his enemies with effortless ease. Not as big as Lenath, or as quick as Shale, Sir Oakheart was however the best of the Knightguards and one of the most all rounded fighters the Realms had seen in recent history. With his longsword in hand, he danced round attacks and countered with effortless ease. His footwork was remarkable as he dodged and parried the assault from onrushing Dakha.

As expected, the upper barricade was holding stronger than the first did. The steep slope below was proving difficult for the Dakha to climb and make any meaningful progress. The Inverwallian defenders at the top of the hill only added to the invader's problems, as they pushed back towards the Dakha, using the slope to their advantage. Numbers would eventually tell and before midday the invaders had reached past the wooden barricade and had spilled out amongst the Inverwallian defenders.

Sir Lenath was taken by his war rage again. He swatted away any enemy brave enough to go near him with frightening strength. His legend was growing with every kill as the soldiers around watched him with sheer astonishment. Still he called out for General Malacath as he cleaved enemies in two with Deathbringer. He wanted nothing more than to face the Monster of Blackland, for his axe to meet the giant's greatsword. Deathbringer was stained red with blood and interiors as it moved like lightning through the air. In his fury, Sir Lenath found himself separated from the rest of his men and he was now completely surrounded by enemy forces. He snapped necks, cleaved heads and opened guts as he fought like a madman. With the Dakha pushing on, and the large knight refusing to retreat back, Sir Lenath was now at least six enemy soldiers away from his

Inverwallian comrades.

'WHO'S NEXT?' he called, as he brought Deathbringer down through the helmet of a Dakha soldier. Just then, he felt the sharp pain of a serrated spear rip through his white leather armour and puncture the skin on his forearm. With the metal now embedded deep in his flesh, he reached out and grabbed the wooden shaft, yanking it out of his arm. With his free hand, he swung the axe through the air and decapitated the unlucky spearman. Again, blood covered his white armour, most of it his enemy's, but some of it his own.

'THIS IS FOR YOU, NOLAN!' he shouted as he swung Deathbringer in a circle, catching two more Dakha in the throat and chest. The impact sent the second solider cartwheeling back, knocking two others to the floor.

Through the melee, Sir Shale could see Sir Lenath surrounded by enemies. The young knight caught a glimpse of Deathbringer glistening in the sun before disappearing deep into Dakha flesh.

'OAKHEART, LENATH IS TRAPPED!' he called, as he sliced the neck of an attacking southerner. He dodged the next advancing enemy with a single step and stabbed with his longsword, deep into the abdomen of the Dakha warrior. With Sir Oakheart now by his side, the Knightguards began to carve a path through the attackers. Felling men left, right and centre, in an attempt to reach their comrade.

Sir Lenath continued fighting the southern invaders as they surrounded him from all angles. Each of the Dakha wanted to be the man to kill the Meridian giant, but so far all had failed. Attacking him with numbers had not yet worked, as he moved too quickly with his axe. Even with the open wound on his left arm, Sir Lenath moved like a man who had just entered the fray. His shoulders were broad, and he carried more weight around his midriff than years past, but no one yet could match his prowess in combat. He had taken his fighting to another level, a level neither Sir Oakheart nor Sir Shale had witnessed before. It was as though the death of Sir Nolan had granted him supernatural strength through the blinding mist of anger. He parried the sword of another attacker with the butt of his axe and brought the blade down through the invader's shoulder. Blood burst into his face as he growled into his enemy's dying expression.

As Sir Lenath was finishing off a particularly unfortunate Dakha soldier, he suddenly felt steel penetrate the chain armour protecting his upper back. He felt the sharp cold pain of broken skin, followed by the warming sensation of his own blood trickle down the inside of his clothes. In his fury, he pushed through the pain and turned, snapping the head of the spear from the wooden shaft. The pointed metal was still embedded in his upper back as he buried Deathbringer deep into the chest of the invader. He could feel warm blood running freely from his back and arm but still he fought with no fear or pain.

Sir Oakheart and Sir Shale continued to carve their route through the Dakha horde towards their comrade. As Sir Oakheart dodged and countered the blow from a southern sword he watched as the spear took Sir Lenath in the back. The sight of this sent the Knightguard Commander into frenzy and pushed him to quicken his pace. He swung his longsword perfectly through the air, killing multiple Dakha with each blow. It did not matter what foe he was fighting; his eyes did not leave his companion Sir Lenath. As he rammed the point of his sword through the belly of an enemy, his heart sank. It was then, he watched his brother fall to one knee.

Chapter 55

ROAR, ROMMEL and the rest of the Wolves of Glory had spent the night and morning in one of the abandoned barracks of Inverwall. They were each sharpening their new Inverwallian blades and donning themselves in war armour. Although not military men, each man was now willing to give their life for the Meridian Realms. Captain Bruar and The Flaming Sails had brought out the patriot within each of them. The barracks itself was dark and gloomy, with cobwebs and dust covering the weaponry and armour. The equipment had not been touched in decades, but that did not mean it was useless.

Roar grasped his new longsword, loving the power he held in his hands. He wondered if this was going to be the weapon he would use to kill Bruar. It was lighter than the last he'd carried, and perfectly balanced. The standard cross hilt made the blade narrower than what he was used to. He ran his fingers along the flat of the blade and looked at his reflection in the perfectly crafted steel.

Rommel was buckling his own sword around his waist when he noticed his comrade admiring the weapon. 'Lucky to have found something of such high standard in a barracks like this – surprised it wasn't snapped up already.'

The west barracks had proven to be a treasure trove of findings. With time, swords, shields, spears, and armour had all been lost in the halls of the abandoned armoury.

With the exception of Roar, each of the men now wore the colours of Inverwall and would fit right in amongst the masses sworn to protect the southern capital. Roar continued to wear his brown leather tunic over a layer of chainmail armour, with a fresh cream coloured shirt beneath. He had refused to wear the blue and grey of Inverwall.

Hunter had found a rounded shield with the Kinlay horse and crown painted on the front. He would carry this into battle and fight for the Queen he had never met. Now with having a few solid meals and a good night's sleep, the young Wolf was looking more like himself. It had always been Torquil who had shined in front of Roar and Rommel, but it was now time for Hunter to prove his worth. With a shortsword sheathed on his hip, he cut a menacing figure in the military armour of Inverwall.

'Are we all still in agreement, we are to fight with Sir Oakheart and his men?' asked Rommel.

'It is like you said, Rommel, there will be nowhere left to run if Badrang takes Inverwall. We must do everything we can to help these people,' replied Hunter.

'Aye, we have come too far together to split up now. I'm fighting with you,' added Mallard, who held two shortswords that would soon be strapped across his back.

Willem tested out his throwing arm, before picking up a javelin and launching it into a stuffed mannequin. He turned towards the others and let out a chuckle. 'Haven't done any fighting in a while. Will be good to kill for something other than coin.'

Roar could feel their eyes upon him to complete the agreement. He scoffed and sheathed his newly sharpened blade. 'I am not here to fight for a knight or a Queen. I don't even fight for you four. I fight for one reason: to finish what we started and kill Bruar.'

The other Wolves shuffled awkwardly.

With the conversation dead, Roar stormed out of the barracks and into the light of the sun. He heard the screams of war below the

South Wall. He turned and looked to the smaller North Wall. 'That's where I am going to kill you, Bruar,' he said out loud.

It was the afternoon, and Sir Talon granted the Wolves of Glory permission atop the Southern battlements. The sheer number of Dakha that stretched out to the distance surprised even Roar.

Rommel, who was well versed with tactical knowledge, noted the narrow valley and the slope leading up to the defenders. 'I see now why Inverwall has the reputation it has. I would say it is almost the perfect position for a fort.'

'I agree, but it has weakened over the centuries,' replied Sir Talon. 'The men here were weak before we arrived but look at them now,' he added as he pointed towards the soldiers fighting in the killing fields. 'They stand strong and brave against overwhelming odds.'

Rommel noted the tone in Knight's voice. 'Do you expect to win this war, Sir Talon?'

The Knightguard leaned on the battlements as arrows continued to fly along the length of the wall. 'Our custom dictates we fight for the throne and nothing else. Whether we believe victory is possible or not, does not alter the effort we give.'

'You expect to lose, don't you?' asked Roar.

Sir Talon turned to face the bruised complexion of the old Wolf. 'What do you know of war and honour, mercenary?'

Roar took offence at the words the Knightguard spoke. 'I know honour does not come from breeding, it comes from doing the right thing,' he replied, angrily.

'HA! All your life you have probably killed to line your own purse and now there comes a time you do the right thing.' He stared at the healed cuts and bruises and laughed again before adding, 'You are here to do the right thing, but for the wrong reasons.'

A flash of anger burst onto Roar's face. 'Do not push me, knight. The news we brought you saved your sorry skin. We could just have easily turned with our tails between our legs. We could have headed north when we learned of the assault coming, but we didn't.' Roar spat off the battlements. 'I am willing to fight with you, but not for you.'

Both men stared at one another as the war continued around them. Rommel was quick to step in and cool the situation and was quickly followed by Captain Guillow.

'Fighting amongst ourselves will accomplish nothing,' said Rommel and he pressed his hand against Roar's chest and greatened the distance between his friend and the Knightguard of Meridia.

Captain Guillow did the same with Sir Talon. 'I agree with him, Sir; we need to keep a level head. Sir Oakheart is down there fighting for us. What would he think if we were to start another fight atop the wall?'

'Mercenaries have no place in military uniform!' replied Sir Talon who had clenched his fist. 'I see you do not wear our colours? Your men should have done the same. You are not soldiers, just murderers fighting because you have no other choice.'

Rommel grabbed Roar by the shoulder and pulled him behind the Wolves. He also did not like the way Sir Talon was treating them. 'Sir, we came here to help. Last night you welcomed us to Inverwall and thanked us for the assistance. What have we done to offend you? We apologise if us questioning your faith in winning this war has upset you.'

Sir Talon breathed heavily and allowed himself to calm down. He brushed his blond hair back out of his face and forced a smile. 'I am sorry, please forgive my short temper.' He looked out to the killing fields. 'It may surprise you, but I wish I was down there with my brothers.'

Chapter 56

'FIORA!?' ASKED the Grandcaptain, who clearly knew the outlaw by name.

'I will not say it again. Unhand these men and allow them to walk towards us.' Fiora raised a hand and patted one of the archers on the shoulder and whispered something in his ear.

The archer released the string from his fingers and fired an arrow in the direction of the Grandcaptain. The missile sped past and buried itself deep into the door of the Town Hall. The archer laughed before restringing his bow and pointing another arrow at the sweating Grandcaptain.

Fiora smiled at the expression painted on the Commander's face. 'This one always did have a poor aim, but I promise the next one will hit its target.'

As she went to tap the archer on the shoulder again, the Grandcaptain wailed out in cowardice, 'Do as she said, release the prisoners!'

The soldiers scowled at the command, but they obeyed. They released their grips and watched as two of the three captives walked across the stone square towards the other outlaws.

Before Leif took a step, he turned and was now face to face with the guard who had punched him. He reached out and grasped the hilt of his sword and smirked. 'I'll be taking this back,' he said with his usual suave tone. He turned back to Fiora. 'That is, unless my lady wants it?'

Fiora did not return the smile and instead replied, 'Just get over here.'

Leif kept his smirk and strode across to the outlaws. He looked at the bruising around the eyes of Hilvard and felt a thought creep into his mind, a thought he almost didn't want the answer to. He wondered where his son Idris was. He knew, however, it was not the right time or place to ask such a question.

Fiora called out in her clean, commanding voice, 'So Grandcaptain Talowr, we will be taking our leave. I should warn you or your men not to follow us – you know as well as I do that you won't catch us.'

'You will hang for this, Fiora. I promise you, you will hang,' shouted the Grandcaptain.

'There are worse fates than that in these lands...' replied Fiora before disappearing into the crowd with her group.

As the last bowman disappeared from view, Talowr erupted into a vengeful tirade. 'I want those criminals found! Have every able soldier move quickly to each of the gates; they must not leave Dain!

'Yes, Sir,' replied a soldier on the Captain's left. 'Will that be all?'

'No. I want a platoon of thirty men assembled and sent to Altnahara. You lead them! I want you to find out who this stranger was.' A wry smile appeared on his spotted face. 'By any means necessary.'

Back with Fiora and the rest of the group, Leif spoke in private with the outlaw as they moved through the Northern Capital with quick pace. 'Surely he will have the guards at the gate stop us? There is no chance of us just walking out of here.'

Fiora was not interested in conversation and instead concentrated on the path ahead. She moved stealthily through the crowd. 'Less talking, we need to keep a low profile.'

'But we won't be going anywhere with the army of Dain after us,' said Leif.

Fiora ignored him and continued to lead the group towards the west side of Dain. They eventually reached an old abandoned mill in the far corner of the city. The two-storeyed foundations of the abandoned building lay ten paces from the wooden perimeter wall of Dain.

Leif turned to the she-bandit. 'Where to now? We don't have much time to make it to the gates before he will have soldiers there.'

'Do you always panic like this!?' replied Fiora, who was now smiling. She winked at one of her outlaw companions and turned towards the building. She led the group around the face of the mill to some overgrown trees and bushes behind. Lifting back one of the branches near the floor, she pointed out a stone, moss covered grate. 'This is how we get out. It is an old underground passage that leads out into the forest.'

Leif was hesitant at the idea of following the outlaws into an unknown dark hole in the ground, but neither he nor his companions had another choice. 'We are with you. But I warn you now, do not double cross me. If there is a trap waiting for us on the other side of this tunnel, I am killing you first.'

Fiora laughed before presenting a flirtatious smile. 'I would expect nothing more; I promise you there is no trap. You have a funny way of showing gratitude to someone who just saved your life.'

After climbing down the iron ladder into the watery depths of the old passage, the group lit three torches, two for the outlaws and the other was to be carried by Leif. Following the splashing of knee-high water, the sound of large rodents filled the dark air. Dozens of rats, panicked at the sight of the large fire-wielding intruders, leapt into the dirty water and swam amongst the outlaws.

Not worried about the rodents now swimming around his knees, Leif spoke with youthful confidence. 'So, you come and go from Dain through here? That would explain all the supplies you have at your camp.'

Fiora replied with a whisper, signalling for Leif to lower his voice.

'Yes, these old passages have not been used in centuries. A new drainage system for sewage and rainwater was built over a hundred years ago and this place has not been visited since. With time, the city forgot it even existed.'

'What brought you to Dain today? I doubt you came here with the sole intention of saving us from that Grandcaptain.'

Fiora looked back to the large woodsman. 'We were there to stop a grave injustice, but you beat us to it. Ended up saving more than just one innocent man today.'

'Well you have my gratitude. It looked a certainty we would be spending the night in Dain's dungeon before you intervened. I mean it, Fiora, I can't thank you enough.'

'Save your thanks, Leif. Like I said, we were there to save the woodsman; you just got in our way,' replied the outlaw, while swatting away a rat climbing up her hip.

Hilvard, who had not yet spoken, nursed a bruise under his left eye and shivered beneath his new cloak. 'My friends, I must thank you for helping me. Leif, I know you are troubled, but it was not your fault I was arrested. I have nothing but gratitude for you, and I hope you will allow me to follow in whatever journey you take. I have nothing left in this world.'

Leif's heart sank at the comment. He raised his torch up and watched as the flames danced in the tearful eyes of the giant Lumberjack. The young wanderer asked the question, even though he knew the answer already. 'He's dead, isn't he?'

Chapter 57

SIR OAKHEART would not allow himself to believe another Knightguard would die so soon. He screamed at the top of his lungs as red mist covered his vision. Longsword in hand, he carved a path of death. Dakha fell around him as the gold hilted weapon opened skin and severed bone. Blood covered the dirt around the Knightguard commander. With rage in his heart, he killed another four with complete ease, as Sir Shale fought by his side. Both men were given hope when they saw Sir Lenath rise again.

The giant knight snapped away from his approaching death and grabbed the neck of a smaller Dakha soldier who had been sent to finish the job. He squeezed with superhuman strength and felt the throat burst under the pressure. Blood exploded into his already stained face as he growled with defiance.

The Dakha were intimidated by the sight of this beast that would not die. The head of a spear was still buried deep into the back of the giant as they took a step back, creating space between Sir Lenath and themselves. Eventually a Blackland Captain arrived on the scene and looked at the giant knight who stood hunched over, covered in Dakha blood.

'Give me that spear. It is time to end the misery of this monster!' called out the Dakha Captain. He grasped the shaft of a javelin and was ready to launch it in the direction of Sir Lenath.

The Knight knew he was defeated and could feel the energy leave him. 'I am with you, Nolan, thank you for waiting,' he muttered.

The Dakha Captain grimaced as he brought his arm back, but before he could throw, a perfectly sharpened sword burst from his abdomen. He gurgled blood as he looked down at the steel protruding out of his belly. His eyes rolled back into his head as Sir Oakheart appeared over his shoulder.

The Knightguard commander pulled his sword back, as blood poured from the gut of the dead Captain. He looked to his fallen brother and shouted, 'You are not dead yet, Lenath, not without me.'

Sir Lenath gave as hearty a laugh as he could muster and watched as Sir Oakheart and Sir Shale went about killing the surrounding Dakha. Surrounded by the dozens and dozens of southern invaders he had slain, the giant collapsed onto the hard ground. As he rested his left cheek on the blood-soaked earth his eyes began to drop. Before his vision went dark, he watched the defenders of Inverwall appear, pushing out into the hordes, forcing the enemy to retreat.

Night had fallen and both armies had pulled back from the battlefield, both nursing deeper wounds than the previous night. The casualties had been greater for the Inverwallians, but all were thankful Sir Lenath was not amongst the dead bodies. The giant knight had been taken to the infirmary within the Keep and was being tended to by the best physicians Inverwall had to offer. The wounds he had sustained on the battlefield would have killed a lesser man and it had amazed all who had witnessed the man breathe after such injuries.

By candlelight the brave Sir Lenath lay in bed unconscious and still. By the side of the bed stood a freshly clothed Sir Oakheart, Sir Talon and Sir Shale. All three of the Knightguards had vowed to stay within the room for the night and would not allow their giant companion from their sights. It had taken the strength of both Sir Oakheart and Sir Shale to carry the injured knight from the war and both men were exhausted.

'He fought like a mad man amongst the enemy,' commented Sir

Shale as he wiped his own head with a damp cloth.

'I have never seen such fearlessness,' added Sir Oakheart.

'It seems our companion has defied the odds yet again. I have heard reports his kills were close to thirty. The man was possessed,' said Sir Talon, who had spent the evening taking reports from those stationed in the fields. 'Oakheart, I must tell you, our archers are losing hope. You know what it is like on the wall. With the number Badrang possesses, it seems an arrow is a drop in the ocean. I fear we will only last a week of this, and if what these mercenaries say is true, we will have to deal with a force from the north within a few days.'

There was no response from the Knightguard Commander.

'What are we to do?' asked Sir Talon.

Sir Oakheart's eyes had not left the unconscious Lenath until now. He turned back to Sir Talon and began outlining his plan. 'Tomorrow, we are to have a group of scouts head north and find out how long we have before the assault. We will use the infantry we have stationed behind the south wall and have them man the defences to the north.'

Sir Talon hesitated before asking, 'But what good are swordsmen on the wall when the enemy comes knocking at the gate beneath them?'

'They will be given bows and a large supply of arrows.'

Sir Talon was not convinced and did not hide the fact. 'But these men are not archers; I doubt most of them would hit the target one in three arrows. I feel victory in this war is almost outwith our reach.'

Sir Oakheart replied with confidence, 'Talon, I trust you, Lenath and Shale more than anyone in this known world. If we do not expect these soldiers to hit the target, one in three, we give them three times as many arrows.' As he spoke, he felt exhausted both physically and mentally. 'This brings me to my next point – we need to discuss this.' He reached into the leather pouch on his right hip and took out his scroll to Queen Orellia.

Sir Talon and Sir Shale looked at one another, both with heavy eyes.

Sir Shale was first to speak. 'What do you need of us, Sir? We are with you, no matter what your decision is.'

Sir Oakheart coughed and wiped back his dark hair. 'Sirs, I have already asked so much of you this last month, but now comes the hardest decision I have to face. I must send one of you north to take over at Meridia in my place. Talon is correct – with the attack from the north coming and our casualties to the south, Inverwall is already lost. It is now up to us to hold Badrang here as long as possible to allow Meridia time to strengthen its defences.'

Both knights found it difficult to hear but agreed with a simple nod.

'We are ready to die for you, Oakheart,' said Sir Talon.

'I have no doubt of that, Talon, but it is you who must go north. You are my equal in every way and will make a fine commander of the Knightguard. I am relinquishing this title to you.' He reached out his arm and handed the scroll to his knight-brother. 'You are to place Sir Blake under arrest and take control of the defences. Our fellow Knightguards will accept you as their leader; you are the best among us.'

Before Sir Talon could answer there was a knock on the heavy door behind them. Moments later the latch was pressed down and the two bounty-hunter commanders entered.

'We have come to pay our respects,' said Rommel, with his soft accent.

'Anyone who can stand face to face with death and spit in its eye, has my respect,' added Roar.

Chapter 58

I T WAS the next morning at Inverwall and the rain drizzled over the wet mud in the courtyards of the southern capital. An hour prior, the battle had again commenced in the killing fields. Sir Shale had returned to action and was as ready as ever to face the Dakha hordes. Knowing this was the day Sir Talon would leave for Meridia and become the new Commander of the Knightguards, Sir Shale had said his goodbyes and was now focused on the task at hand.

The giant knight Sir Lenath still lay unconscious in the tower of the Main Keep. He was under the watchful protection of the best healer of Inverwall. No one had expected him to survive the evening, but the knight was still full of surprises, and continued to draw breath.

Sir Talon had recruited a platoon of twenty soldiers. Each soldier was assigned a horse from the stables to ensure a quick ride back to the capital city. It had not been difficult to find volunteers to make the journey. Most of the soldiers had already seen combat in the south fields, and some even carried wounds. Sir Talon thought it would be good for these men to return home and bring their experience of fighting the Dakha with them. They could regale their comrades with stories and with first-hand knowledge of the southern invaders. It would help to educate the defenders in Meridia.

Within a small group on the edge of Inverwall, Sir Oakheart, Sir Talon and the Wolves of Glory conversed about their plans. The two Knightguards talked of the coming future and the finer details of what Sir Talon would do upon reaching Meridia. Sir Blake was to be arrested immediately.

The Wolves of Glory had also made some important decisions. This was the first day they would enter the fray and fight the invaders from the Blacklands. It had been decided by Roar and Rommel that they would honour the life of young Torquil; news must be brought of his death to his family back in Meridia. Roar, adamant he would not be leaving Inverwall until Captain Bruar was dead, had refused such a task. He, along with Mallard and Willem, would stay in the city and fight until the end. Rommel and Hunter were to go north with the new Knightguard Commander and the other soldiers. They were to be rewarded for informing the defenders of the impending attack from the north.

Roar and Rommel stood almost alone to discuss what the future held for each of them. Neither really knew what to say because they knew they would not be able to persuade the other.

'Well, my friend, are you sure you would not like to come? We can have that retirement we always talked of. The two of us, like the old days?' Rommel asked in vain.

'You know I cannot change my mind now...' replied Roar, warmer than he had been in the recent weeks.

Rommel faked a laugh to hide his pain. 'Ha-ha, I know. It was worth me asking though. It is better to ask the question and hear the answer, than to not ask at all. You will take care of yourself and the others, won't you?'

Roar did not answer.

Rommel reached out his hand. 'Do not let hatred push you to your death, Roar.'

Roar forced a smile and grasped his friend's hand and shook it. 'When did you know anything to push me anywhere?'

'I am serious, Roar. If all you want is Bruar's head, you will have lost before you even reach the battlefield. What is it we always told our recruits? Do not let the job become personal. We knew the type of men The Flaming Sails were before we took the job. We always knew there was a risk of capture. We made mistakes and cannot blame anyone but ourselves. We took to the sea and risked it all. We lost Torquil, we lost our whole group.'

Roar suppressed the urge to snap at his old friend, but knew he was right and instead just smiled. 'You know I want to settle the score and kill Bruar, but that is not my only reason. What the knight said to me yesterday hit a nerve. I feel it is time I did the right thing. Time for me to put the skills I have to good use.'

'I am one man you were never able to fool. And for the first time in my life, I am unsure if what you say is the truth. I have never seen anyone better with a sword than you, but you need to make sure your head is clear for this fight.'

'I can assure you: my head will be clear,' replied Roar before unsheathing his longsword and raising it in the sky. 'It has been the greatest pleasure of my life to fight alongside you. It is my only regret we will not die as we lived, by each other's side.'

Rommel smiled and unsheathed his shortsword from around his hip. He brought the steel into contact with Roar's longsword. They howled the war-cry of the Wolves of Glory, sheathed their weapons and put a hand on one another's shoulders.

'Go with grace, friend,' said Rommel.

Both men turned back and returned to the rest of the group, with no more words spoken to each other.

The remaining Wolves said their goodbyes. Rommel and Hunter mounted a horse each and gave their comrades a final shake of the hand. 'We will be sure ballads are written to honour what you are doing, brothers,' said Hunter.

'You do that, boy, and I will be haunting you from the grave. I couldn't think of anything worse than some good for nothing bard singing about me trying to woo some ugly wench.' Roar scowled, with a stern expression.

The group laughed and shared a smile for the last time.

The troops pulled their horses north and trotted towards the gate of Inverwall. As the last soldier exited, Sir Oakheart appeared at the side of the remaining three Wolves within the city. 'Men, it is time we write our names into the history books. We are going to die for something greater. You are all welcome additions to our defences.'

Although Roar did not like knights, he had a great deal of respect for this Knightguard. He seemed different to any nobleman he had ever met. 'Well, Oakheart, we are prepared to die. We are staying to fight. But on one final condition. When the forces of Brigands Bay arrive from the north, we are to be stationed that side. I have some unfinished business with them.'

Sir Oakheart smiled and reached out his hand. 'I understand, Roar. We all have our own General Malacath to kill.'

Chapter 59

L EIF AND Fiora were the first to emerge from the final stretch of sewer. The tunnel was again concealed by overgrown greenery and both led the way through the thick bushes. As Leif pushed back branches, he made sure to hold them to avoid it pinging back into someone's face behind him. He would pass the duty on to the next person and shuffle another couple of metres forward to the next thorny bush.

The rest of the group did the best they could to follow behind the two leaders. Hilvard and Bjorn conversed about their different lives. Hilvard spoke about his life as a woodsman and the back-breaking work he would do, for measly pay.

'How can someone who is so important to the community be paid so little? Firewood, timber and even parchment... All of it comes from you. At Altnahara, we are taught that trees are a gift from the gods and only the best among us are sent to collect wood from the forests. I am sure there will be a place for you back at our Monastery.'

Hilvard allowed himself a smile. 'I hope so, Bjorn. The city guards have taken everything from me.'

'Don't worry, we can use a strong worker like you,' said Bjorn with a soft northern voice.

As they left the cover of the thick bush, they stepped out into the open space beneath the canopy of the trees. Each of the group checked the area for any guards.

It took a few minutes before Fiora was satisfied and they could move on. She looked to the sky, and through the gaps in the trees she could see rain clouds approaching. She turned to Leif who was facing the other direction. She looked at his lean shoulders and shoulder length brown hair. She did her best to supress a flirtatious smile and instead spoke. 'This is where a decision must be made. On any other day I would have taken your valuables and the sword around your back. However, for what you have done for this man–' she pointed to Hilvard– 'you will not be harassed by us any further.' She hesitated a moment before continuing. 'Grandcaptain Talowr will have sent men to Altnahara. I doubt he will harm anyone, BUT in the meantime, it would be too dangerous for you to return to them. You would be putting your lives at risk, and the lives of your friends there.'

'I had gathered as much if I am honest,' replied Leif, who was now thinking of where he and his two companions could hide. 'Where do you suggest we should go?'

'I have a proposition for you, Leif,' said Fiora.

Leif said nothing, and only looked at the outlaw to continue.

'It is no secret that I do not like you, but again, I must commend what you have done for the people of these lands in the short time you have been here.'

Leif remained unfazed by either of the comments. 'What do you need of us?' he asked.

'Well, you have seen our camp and you know the number of us that live with us.' Fiora waited for Leif to nod before continuing. 'I propose you come and stay within our camp until the soldiers leave Altnahara and you are free to return. You can go back and convince the monastery to make a deal with us. We are to be supplied with goods. I am not talking expensive wines, or equipment. I am talking food. Believe it or not, the forest is not the rich bountiful place you would think it is. Without the ability to grow crops, it will not be long before our camp begins to struggle. Our numbers are increasing, and starvation can lead to disease. We would only ask for food and medical treatment.'

Leif turned and looked at Bjorn, the other member of Altnahara. 'We can always speak to our leader and try convince him. I know our Grandmaster is not happy with ongoing troubles of Dain. However, I have another part of this deal I would like to offer.'

'Go on,' replied Fiora.

'If all parties agree, our goal should be to fix the root problems with these lands. That means instead of robbing innocent traders and travellers, you harass town guards and stand up for the local villages.'

Fiora's face reddened but she controlled her anger and spoke softly. 'It has never been about robbing or theft. We have taken all that we need to survive. The wine we took from you was to numb the pain our men have experienced since fleeing from their homes. It was to make them feel better of the world that has taken everything from them.'

'Fiora, I do not aim to cause offence, but you need organisation. If we are to strike up a deal between your outlaws and our monks, there must be common ground. I know you are helping us in a time of need, but our Grandmaster will not stand for theft amongst the common folk. You need to lead these people, rise up and take back the homes of your people. You are correct, these lands have fallen into corruption. I spotted it the day I arrived, but what is taking from traders going to do?'

'It is not about taking from traders...' Fiora shouted, her anger erupting to the surface.

Bjorn stepped in to split them both. 'We will get nowhere arguing this. We do not know what our Grandmaster will say to your proposal.' He looked at the outlaw. 'In the meantime, Fiora, we are happy to accept your hospitality within the forest.'

Hilvard was next to step forward. 'I agree with him. We need help and Fiora is offering us safety. Will you have us? That is, if the offer still stands?'

Fiora calmed down after being addressed by the Woodsman and the Blacksmith. She did not look at them, and instead scowled at Leif. 'Yes, the offer still stands. Are you coming with us?'

Leif breathed heavily and felt the first trickle of rain fall and run down his nose. He looked to the she-bandit and tried not to find her attractive. 'Very well, we will come with you and we are grateful for the offer.'

Fiora burst into a sarcastic laugh. 'A wise decision, for someone who had only one option. Took you long enough.'

Leif slanted his eyes, clenched his fists and took a serious stance. 'But Fiora, if anything happens to one of my friends, I will kill you.'

'I wouldn't expect you to do anything else,' replied the red-haired outlaw.

Chapter 60

I**T WAS** now day four of the assault at Inverwall. The day prior had proven to be the same as the first two days, with casualties on both sides. Badrang's forces had still not reached the main gate to the south.

Sir Oakheart and Captain Guillow stood atop the battlements as the sound of war filled their ears. The air was thick with the smell of death as the clashing of swords and spears could be heard from miles around. Looking down into the fray, both men could see the Dakha pushing into both sides of the defenders in the narrow pass, but the Inverwallians stood firm.

'Badrang will grow impatient if he does not push us back through the gates this evening. If we have less than a thousand men by the end of today, I plan on pulling them back to behind the wall. It will be in the courtyards where we will make our final stand,' said Oakheart.

'And what of the northern assault, Sir?' asked Guillow.

'Scouts report the outlaw army should arrive tomorrow morning. I cannot see them wasting any time in attacking the smaller northern wall. They are not attacking us to win, they are attacking us purely to distract our attention away from Badrang in the south,' replied Sir Oakheart.

Captain Guillow nodded in agreement and strung another arrow to his longbow. He pulled back the string and let loose into the great mass to the south. The arrow buried deep into the skull of a Dakha soldier and the Captain frowned. 'Still after all my years in the army, it has never given me pleasure in extinguishing another man's light.'

Sir Oakheart ran his fingers through his hair as he gazed out into the southern horde. It looked as though there was even more than when they first arrived. Sir Oakheart had always known his mission south would have been his last, but he was always willing to die for his lady and queen. He spat off the battlements and gave a sigh. He thought of his brother Sir Talon heading north to Queen Orellia. He was ashamed for a small moment when he wished he could take his brother's place. He snapped from his selfish thoughts before grinding his teeth together.

'Captain, we will give these Dakha invaders the fight of their lives. You will lead the line on the north wall. I want at least one good archer on the battlements when the outlaws attack. They will not have the capability of erecting a lot of ladders, so they will probably use a battering ram.' He paused a moment and was not sure if he should continue. He thought of the remaining Wolves of Glory and their commander Roar. A man like Roar can be a dangerous comrade in times like this. In the past, a man with a personal vendetta never lasted long on the battlefield and he was not willing to let the hatred of one man cost his men their lives. Sir Oakheart's plan was to last in Inverwall as long as he could. He knew the longer Badrang spent in the southern capital and the more casualties the Warlord suffered, the better for the Realm. 'I want you to keep an eye on The Wolves of Glory. They have done us a great service, but I worry their search for revenge will cost us.'

Captain Guillow nodded with agreement. 'I agree, Sir, they are brave soldiers, but I do not think the older one will like taking orders.'

'He will take orders or be thrown in the cells to rot. We need to help each other, and he better get used to it.'

Down in the fields, Sir Shale led the front line of defenders against the endless horde. The young knight fought with the strength and guile of three Knightguards. Although he was the youngest of the Knights and not as strong as Sir Lenath, he was just as effective on the battlefield. Dodging the lunge of a serrated spear, he drew his hip dagger and pushed the blade deep into the chest of the attacker. With his sword-arm he parried another blow and kicked the second in the knee, causing the bone to snap. As the soldier wailed in pain, the young knight brought his own blade down through his enemy's shoulder.

There was almost silence in the minutes following. It was then, out of nowhere, there was an air piercing roar from the Dakha. Something was happening that had not yet happened during the battle.

The Inverwallians pulled back and watched as the Dakha soldiers in front of them parted and allowed their breathing weapon to come into view. The impressive figure of General Malacath stood before the defenders. Dressed head to toe in black armour with his customary red trimmings, the monster looked a frightening sight.

Although out of breath from fighting all day, Sir Shale's heart truly began to race. He swung his blade through the free air and regained his flexibility. Both lines of soldiers in the area stepped back again, allowing the two fighters enough space to start their duel.

From beneath the helmet of General Malacath a voice boomed out. 'WHERE IS THE ONE THEY CALL LENATH? I HAVE HEARD HE WOULD LIKE TO MEET ME.'

Sir Shale did not respond and instead stepped forward into the small ring of soldiers.

'You are Lenath?' asked General Malacath.

'I am not Lenath, but you will have to deal with me anyway,' replied Sir Shale with awesome courage, which drew gasps of amazement from both sides.

'Not Lenath, yet you wear the puppet colours?' replied the

monster.

Sir Shale did not respond, and instead readied himself with a stylish battle stance. He rotated his wrists quickly and twirled his longsword to the right of his Meridian shield.

The watching soldiers were transfixed on both the fighters. Not a man in attendance believed Sir Shale would go down easy, but they also all knew the power and strength of General Malacath. Less than a week ago, the monster had destroyed one of the greatest fighters in Meridian history with relative ease.

Sir Shale smiled and thanked the gods he would be getting the chance to avenge his mentor's death. He looked about his fellow defenders in attendance as he heard the war continuing further down the line. 'No one is to interfere with this!' the young Knightguard shouted.

The General let out something that resembled a chuckle and raised his heavy greatsword high in the air.

The Dakha erupted into a loud war cry and pounded their chests and shields. A chant broke out amongst the attackers. 'MALACATH, MALACATH, MALACATH!'

The air was tense as everyone waited for the first move, both fighters casting completely different shadows in the sun. Small, slender Sir Shale with his sword and shield, and tall, broad Malacath with his enormous greatsword.

Still the Dakha recited their terrifying chant. 'MALACATH, MALACATH, MALACATH!'

The Inverwallians knew Sir Shale was skilled, but they all saw him as the underdog in this fight. As the seconds passed, and there was no action, each soldier grew more and more nervous. Not one defender would have dared swap places with the brave Knightguard.

'MALACATH, MALACATH, MALACATH!' continued the Dakha, waiting for their champion to kill the smaller fighter.

It was the knight who attacked first.

Chapter 61

I
T WAS that time of day where the sunlight retreated beyond the furthest hill. The birds sang the last of their day song as dusk approached. The weather had been favourable for the travellers to make their way through the thick forests bordering Dain. As the last of the sunlight disappeared, the group reached the outskirts of the outlaw camp. Little had been said between both parties within the group. Leif, Hilvard and Bjorn had kept to themselves and did not speak much to their new outlaw comrades.

During the journey, Leif had learned the fate of Hilvard's son Idris. He learned of how the guards came two days after Leif's visit. After the beating they had suffered at the hands of Leif, they were out for revenge but there were more guards than the first visit. During their time at the Woodsman's cottage, they had found the coins Leif had left as a gift. The guards had come to one conclusion: a woodsman with that amount of money could only be one thing – a thief. The young wanderer learned about how the guards wanted to arrest Hilvard and how he had resisted. During the fight Hilvard had been knocked out with the butt of a sword and when he awoke in the cells of Dain, the guards told him his son had been killed by a loose arrow during the fray. Leif still wondered if the boy was truly dead, as it would be easy for the soldiers of Dain to lie in that situation. Hilvard, however, had been beaten beyond any sign of hope. He was adamant the guards from Dain were telling the truth and had killed his boy.

As the outlaw camp came into view, Fiora turned back to the rest of the group. 'I am going to say this once.' She looked at Leif in particular. 'You let me do the talking here. As you can imagine, these men and women are not the most trusting.'

Leif smirked. 'Who can blame them? Another day or so in these lands and I won't be trusting another soul.'

Fiora smiled. 'Something we finally agree upon.'

No more was said until Fiora turned and headed towards the noise of the centre campfire. Illuminated by the dancing flames, the group stayed close behind the she-bandit as she led them around the tents and makeshift forest houses.

As they reached the largest tent near the middle of the campsite a large crow suddenly burst out from within. It cawed loudly and circled the group until it finally perched itself on a high branch high above them. Moments later a man's figure appeared at the entrance of the tent and walked towards them. As the fire light reached him, Leif could tell it was the same man he saw Fiora speak with during his last visit to the camp. He was of a similar build to Leif, tall and lean, with pulled back shoulder length hair, tied at the back. He was clean shaven and down the left side of his face, a permanent scar crept from the corner of his eye to below his cheek.

'Fiora, what are you doing!?' said Garrow, looking at the three newcomers.

Fiora smiled back at her companion and opened her arms for an embrace. 'How is that a way to greet me after two days away?'

Garrow did not answer, and instead folded his arms, showing his disdain.

Fiora continued. 'These men are enemies of Dain and are willing to join our cause. Two are from Altnahara.'

Garrow shot an immediate glance towards Leif and saw the shining longsword strapped to the young wanderer's shoulder. The outlaw was clearly irritated and did a very poor job of hiding it.

'Fiora, may we speak in private,' he growled.

Fiora nodded before looking towards one of her men. 'Emrest, please have our new friends watered and fed. Give them one of the spare tents in the far corner.'

This clearly irritated Garrow further. He did not say anything, but his face was a picture of disapproval. He did not like Fiora already giving these new faces a place to stay, when it was yet to be agreed with him.

The two outlaws made their way inside the large tent but before Fiora closed the leather skinned entrance, she called up to the crow above. 'Come on, Trix.'

The crow gave a loud caw and dropped down, directly through the door.

The silence outside made the situation far more awkward than it was when Garrow and Fiora were there. The outlaws looked at the newcomers with contempt as they continued with their nightly chores. Some patrolling the perimeter and others prepping evening meals.

Bjorn tried to lighten the atmosphere by making a comment. 'That bird must have a valuable opinion to be invited to the meeting.'

There was no reaction from the outlaws around the group.

Hilvard gave a small smile and Leif patted the large Blacksmith on the back. 'Thankfully, you are here to give us a smile, Bjorn.'

The outlaw called Emrest eventually stepped forward and scratched the top of his messy blond hair. 'You lot will be needing some food then?'

Leif recognised the outlaw as one of Fiora's companions when he had first met the bandits. 'Yes, thank you. That would be greatly appreciated.'

They made their way through the campsite towards a makeshift hut containing a small number of stores. Although not permitted inside, Leif could just about see inside the improvised structure and was not surprised to see bare shelves and very few goods within. He thought he may be wrong, but it was highly likely the camp would not last much longer without any more supplies.

Leif, Bjorn and Hilvard, each with a bowl of heated stew, entered into their new leather skinned tent. The ground was damp, and the air was wet within, but it would not take them long to make the structure liveable.

Leif unbuckled his sword and rested it against one of the walls within the tent. He went over to one of the improvised beds. The frame of the bed was made of crude timbers and wrapped together with stingy vine ropes. He dusted off where he would rest his head and lay down on the hard surface. 'Tomorrow when the sun is up, we will make some better sleeping arrangements in here. That is, if we are allowed to stay,' he said.

'Aye, this will do us for the night. A roof over our head and food in our bellies, that's all we need for now,' said Bjorn.

Hilvard said nothing, and instead grabbed a wool blanket from a small table. He headed over to the far corner of the tent with his bowl of food. He hunched over with his back to the others and began to sob.

Chapter 62

S IR SHALE launched himself at the giant of Blackland. The monster was just as quick and swiped downward at the same. Sir Shale dodged and slashed at the heavy armour. The blade bounced off and caused no more than a small scrape on the black paint.

Instead of waiting for the giant to mount an attack of his own, Shale moved in again and cut upwards towards the heavy gauntleted hand of the General. With a clever body movement, the young knight moved to the side and wrapped his own leg around the inside of the Dakha champion's. Catching the General off-balance, Shale pushed, and the giant went tumbling to the ground, landing flat on his broad back.

The cheers from the Dakha soldiers died at the sight of seeing their General taken from his feet for the first time in their history. The surrounding Inverwallians, however, let out a deafening cheer of their own. Sir Shale wasted no time and lifted his sword high for the attack. He brought it crashing through the air towards the giant, who was now lying on his back in a vulnerable position.

In a blind panic, before the blow could land, Malacath raised his greatsword up and blocked the blow. He then sent the young knight flying with a heavy kick from the ground and with the agility of a much smaller man, jumped back to his feet.

Over the next few minutes, both the Inverwallians and the Dakha of Blackland exchanged cheers and silence as they watched each of their champions trade blows. The speed and guile of Sir Shale was proving difficult for the General to handle.

No one was expecting Sir Shale to put in such a dominant performance against the monster. The giant had never been floored in a fight and was enraged. He fumed that a young knight like Shale could have caused so much damage to his reputation in such a short period of time. However, he was not willing to let this small Knightguard have any other kind of victory against him.

Sir Shale did not allow himself to laugh, smile or even think he was going to win this. He heard the watchers continue to cheer. The audience were circling round, baying for the blood of their enemy's champion. None were brave or stupid enough to enter the fight.

Sir Shale launched another attack and dodged under a swipe from the General. With his sword he caught the blade of Malacath and went for a similar move as last time. This time the giant was ready and threw a fist in the direction of the knight. Shale took the blow of the giant heavily into his chest and felt a bone crack within him. He stepped back quickly and tried to catch his breath. Each mouthful of air sent a sharp pain into his chest. He coughed heavily, and as he did, he tasted blood at the back of his throat. He cursed his stupidity for trying the same move again and repositioned his feet.

The surrounding Inverwallians cheered even louder than before for their knight as the two fighters circled about one another. Up close it surprised every man in attendance how the General moved. They all knew he was incredibly strong, but with the immaculate footwork of a knight, the Dakha champion looked invincible.

The General sprung forward with supernatural speed and thrust his greatsword forward. Sir Shale dodged the blow to the side and sent his longsword down heavily onto the armoured hand of Malacath. The blow landed directly between the thumb and wrist of the monster. The sheer force of the counter attack caused the General to grunt with pain, and – to the amazement of everyone watching – drop his greatsword to the ground.

The Inverwallian roars dominated the air, causing the earth to shake as fighters from both sides further down the line began to fall back and watch the duel that was taking place.

Sir Shale coughed again and spat out a mouthful of blood in the direction of the Dakha observers. He turned back to his adversary who had now picked his sword up and was shaking his helmeted head, clearly infuriated.

It was then, the young knight heard a call of warning from the Inverwallian crowd. He quickly turned and saw a Dakha soldier was lunging towards him. He parried the point of a spear that was heading straight for his lower abdomen. He swiftly moved in and decapitated the Dakha soldier who had tried to attack him from behind.

By the time he turned back to General Malacath, it was already too late, and the monster was on him. The young Knightguard tried to dodge the onrushing giant but had no space to manoeuvre between the Dakha and his rival.

For the first time, Sir Shale panicked and thrust out with his longsword. The General dodged easily and slammed into the knight, body to body. This impact sent Shale tumbling to the ground with his sword dropping from his grasp. With the wind knocked out of him and blood filling the back of his throat, the Knight coughed and tried to spring to his feet but was pushed down onto his back.

The General did not give the Knight enough time to regain his feet. He dropped his greatsword and threw himself onto the smaller Knightguard. This was where he had won countless fights before. With his size, duels were usually over in seconds by this point. With heavy gauntlets, he clasped his hands together and lifted them high.

Before the blow could land hard into the face of Sir Shale, a figure appeared from behind the crouched giant. The figure was not wearing Dakha colours or a uniform from Inverwall. He wore a light chainmail cuirass beneath a brown leather waistcoat. With a quick movement, he slammed his body heavily onto the bulky General. The impact of the mystery figure sent the giant tumbling to the ground, away from Sir Shale.

The monster reached out a hand and grasped the figure on the leg. The new fighter drew back his boot and kicked the monster hard in the helmeted face.

Rolling away after the impact, Malacath quickly regained his feet. The giant took three steps back and picked up his greatsword as the Dakha shouted with hypocritical disapproval at someone interfering in the duel.

Sir Shale recognised the face immediately and grasped out the reaching hand of his saviour. He hauled himself up and regained his feet. The young knight coughed a couple of times and bent down to retrieve his own longsword.

With General Malacath standing in front of the Dakha horde and facing the two fighters, the Inverwallians readied themselves for the charge.

It seemed as though the recess in battle was about to end and both lines were ready for combat. Sir Shale turned to the man dressed in the brown leather waistcoat. 'I owe you for that one. Roar, isn't it?'

Roar frowned and looked back at the line of Dakha in front of them. Through the corner of his mouth he spoke. 'I know you said no one was to interfere, but I am not here at Inverwall to follow orders.'

General Malacath bellowed with rage and called for the Dakha to charge.

Chapter 63

SIR OAKHEART was again atop the southern battlements as the war continued between the Dakha and his own forces. Earlier in the day, he had noticed the small gap in the fighting where General Malacath and Sir Shale had fought. It had killed him to watch from afar as his Knightguard brother and the Champion of Blackland had fought. For whatever reason the fighting had stopped and there was a small stand off period. Within minutes both lines had charged into one another and the killing had resumed.

'Captain, I am going to lead a force of one hundred men out of the gate and help our forces retreat. This is the last day we will be fighting in the killing fields.'

'Understood,' replied Guillow.

Sir Oakheart approached the stone steps behind him, before turning back to the Inverwallian Captain. 'Be ready for arrows from the Dakha, they will soon be close enough to the wall.'

Captain Guillow pressed his fist against his chest and saluted his Commander. 'I will have my men target any enemy archers they see.'

'Thank you, Guillow,' replied Sir Oakheart as he walked down the first of the stone steps.

The former Knightguard Commander made his way towards the men stationed behind the south gate. 'I need a platoon of one hundred men. We are going out the gate to help our brother's retreat from the field.'

The Knightguard looked to the sky and noted sunset was quickly approaching. He knew Badrang would have his men fall back this evening. Sir Oakheart thought if he had the fighters retreat behind the wall, Badrang would rest for the night and start the final part of his siege in the morning. Better the last of the swordsmen were behind the wall ready to fight tomorrow than to die this evening.

One of the Inverwallian Captains eventually stepped forward and spoke to the Knight. 'We are ready, Sir; we await your instructions.'

'TO ME, BROTHERS!' Sir Oakheart called as he led the miniature army out of the south gate and down the hill towards the battle in the killing fields. He had the horn blower sound the retreat and could immediately see the Inverwallians infantry turn and head back. The line had grown so thin through the course of the day. Along the line the column was now only ten men deep. As he passed his retreating men, he shouted to the soldiers running with him: 'CHARGE THEM!'

Leading the line, he pierced deep into the Dakha assault line. Slashing, parrying and thrusting, the Knightguard fought. The sound of the horns echoed through his ears as Inverwallians pulled back towards the city. He knew he would only need to fight for five or ten minutes before he and his small force would retreat back with the rest of his army.

Five, ten, fifteen, and twenty minutes passed and the Knightguard continued to fight. Eventually, a battered and exhausted Sir Shale appeared by his side. The young knight coughed up more blood and spat on the stained ground. 'Think it's time we fall back ourselves?'

Sir Oakheart grabbed the head of a nearby Dakha and twisted the neck grotesquely, hearing the bones within snap. 'Yes, sound the final retreat!'

The last Inverwallian horn sounded at almost the same time as the Dakha horn. As though admitting the fighting was done for the day, both armies began to fall back in different directions.

'It seems we will have the night to rest after all,' coughed Sir Shale.

With that, the young Knight's legs gave out from within him and he rested on Sir Oakheart's shoulder. The Knightguard Commander grabbed his brother by the arm and raised him from the ground. He quickened his pace towards the city as arrows began to whiz past his head from the Dakha.

As they reached the entrance to Inverwall, Sir Oakheart dodged a well-placed arrow and it bounced off the stone wall of the Southern Capital. He was lucky another arrow just missed his head. They reached the inside of the wall and were clear of any more arrows. The broad Knightguard leaned Sir Shale against the cold stone.

The young Knight looked exhausted as he spluttered blood from his mouth. Between the coughs he spoke to his companion. 'They will be through the gate tomorrow.'

Sir Oakheart nodded in agreement. 'They are close enough to use archers. We will need to expect a Battering Ram first thing in the morning.'

As the last defender retreated behind the gate, the guardsmen pushed on the great iron-enforced doors until it closed with a loud slam. Large bolts, the width of a man, were lifted high into place by a number of men. Latches the length of a man were pulled down to secure the gate.

A silence fell over the courtyard when Sir Oakheart turned to the watching defenders. Without thinking, the former Knightguard Commander raised his bloodstained sword high into the air and bellowed a heartfelt war-cry. There was not a man in attendance that did not do the same. The shouting caused the earth to shake as the noise echoed in the ears of each soldier. Sir Shale did his best to raise his own sword and coughed out the war-cry, along with some more blood.

Although the defenders were making too much noise to speak clearly, the young Knight turned and said to Sir Oakheart, 'This is our finest hour.'

Sir Oakheart smiled at his young comrade. 'Nolan would be proud of us. We fought for him, for Lenath, for Talon and for everything our people stand for.'

Appearing next to Sir Shale was the bloodstained figure of Roar. The old Wolf almost smiled as he continued to watch the defenders bellow their cry and beat their chests. He looked around the Inverwallians and puffed out his chest. With one fluid movement, he sheathed his longsword into the scabbard by his waist. He was shoulder to shoulder with both Knightguards when he spoke. 'I have witnessed brave men before, but these men knew Sarpen was not far behind them, yet they still fought.'

Sir Shale put a hand on Roar's shoulder and spat out a large clot of blood before wiping his chin. 'Oakheart, I owe this man my life.'

'Good thing he was there,' said Sir Oakheart, as he nodded thankfully towards the old Wolf. 'I thought you had no intention of fighting in the south fields?'

There was no reaction from Roar.

'I thought it was the outlaws you were after?' asked Sir Oakheart.

Roar let out a quiet chuckle as the shouting was beginning to die around them. 'Captain Bruar will be happy to wait for me.'

Chapter 64

L EIF COULD feel the cold damp morning enter under the tent door. The leather structure had proven warm throughout most of the evening, but the young wanderer had to supress a few shivers through the night. As he lay on his coarse bed, under the cover of a woollen blanket, he continued to ponder the true fate of Idris. The young boy's body had not been seen by Hilvard, and Leif was not willing to believe he was dead until he had proof. Leif grasped the handle of his sheathed sword tighter than he had through the night. If they have killed the boy, he would make sure everyone involved paid dearly.

During his life Leif had always found trouble wherever he went. He was the type of man that would never just walk away from an unjust situation, even if it was dangerous. Although he had not seen as many winters as other men, he had seen more hardship than most. During his whole life of travel, he had never seen such corruption as Dain. The city was in a far worse state than he had thought during his first visit. When it was safe to return, he would speak with Fathad and convince the Grandmaster to help the people of the northern lands. If Leif had his way, he would imprison every nobleman or soldier that had abused their power.

As the muffled sound of forest songbirds began, both Hilvard and Bjorn stirred on the other side of the canvas tent. The big men had slept peacefully all night, both clearly exhausted by the travel to the outlaw camp.

'Well, it seems it's time for us to get up,' said Bjorn with a groan.

The other two occupants of the tent both agreed and within minutes the three men were on their feet and exiting the dark cover. The light of the sun through the trees was blinding as Leif looked about the campsite for some kind of wash area. He felt dirty, and scruffy. His hair was a mess and needed to be washed with some water.

'I don't know about you two, but I could do with some cold water on my face,' he said to his two companions and listened as they agreed.

They made their way to the centre of the camp where they could see Fiora sitting at a large table eating. She dug into a bowl of some kind of oat mixture and laughed at the sight of the three companions. 'You three look like you didn't have the best sleep. These beds aren't the most comfortable, are they?'

Bjorn laughed as he eyed up the warm oat paste. 'Ha-ha, indeed it is not, lass. Do you have an area in camp where we could wash?'

Fiora returned a cute laugh and pointed to the west. 'There is a small river just through those trees. If you listen carefully, you might just be able to hear the stream.' As she spoke, her eyes met Leif's. 'You will be able to get washed up there.'

Leif returned her gaze but quickly snapped away. 'Thanks for that.'

As Leif turned away with his two companions and made their way west, he could still feel the she-bandit's gaze upon his back. It took less than two minutes before the three friends reached the slow, narrow river. The outlaw Warin was proving the water was clearly deep enough to bathe as Leif noted the bandit's clothes on a large stone adjacent to the slow-paced river.

Bjorn took a step forward and addressed the outlaw, who had just dunked his head under the water. 'Morning. Is she cold this morning?'

'Not too cold today, you fellas coming in?' replied Warin.

'Don't see why not. I take it your friends don't like the cold water?' asked Bjorn.

'Aye, most can't handle it, but I like it. You just missed Garrow and Fiora, they were here earlier. Have you spoke with them yet?' asked Warin.

'Just spoke with Fiora,' replied Leif.

Warin perked up. 'And are you folks staying with us?'

'She didn't say anything about that,' said Leif, as he pulled his shirt over his head to reveal his lean figure. 'She must be saving that talk until after we have washed up.'

Over the course of the next twenty minutes, the three companions bathed in the cold waters of the northern river. It had felt like longer than three days since Leif had felt water, so he enjoyed every moment of the fresh stream.

'How long do you think before we can return to Altnahara?' asked Bjorn.

'It might be a couple of weeks before we can return. Fiora is certain they will not do our friends any harm as long as they don't see us with them. We still have a long-term future at the monastery, I am sure of that,' replied Leif before looking towards Hilvard. 'We ALL have a future there.'

Hilvard didn't respond, and instead scrubbed at his broad shoulders.

It was when the young wanderer had left the river and was buttoning up his brown shirt that he heard Fiora approaching. Although she had been friendly this morning, Leif still had his doubts about the she-bandit. He made a quick glance to his sheathed longsword resting on a nearby rock, well out of his reach. Hoping she wouldn't be looking to take advantage of his group's nakedness, he addressed the outlaw. 'You just missed a sight.'

Fiora did her best not to laugh but could not contain a chuckle. 'Have I now? I can imagine Bjorn would have a fine build.'

The large blacksmith of Altnahara gave a hearty roar of laughter, almost with embarrassment. 'Bit too much of me round the middle these days.'

'There is nothing wrong with that, Bjorn,' replied Fiora, before turning back to Leif. 'Can I speak with you in private?'

Leif smiled. 'Whatever you have to say, can be said to my friends also. You seem very happy this morning – why the change of attitude?'

Fiora continued to smile. 'It's just good to be home with my people.'

'You call this place home?' the young wanderer replied, as he looked around the surrounding forest.

'Yes, I call this place home,' replied Fiora, with a flirtatious smile. 'And so should you.'

Chapter 65

ROAR LOOKED out over the northern battlements as the outlaws and pirates of Brigands Bay gathered below. Like a man possessed, he scanned the lines of the fighters, looking for any sign of Captain Bruar. As a bounty-hunter, Roar was a master in the art of fighting and there was not a weapon he could not use to deadly efficiency. Although not his first choice for killing someone, he held a bow in his hands with a stack of arrows on the wall in front of him. He knew there wasn't much chance he was going to get a chance at Bruar with hand-to-hand combat.

The Brigands below yelled and screamed at the defenders atop the wall. The makeshift army was filled with the worst criminals known to the Meridian lands and seas. Murderers and thieves made up their ranks, some wearing little to no armour with coarse tattoos covering their arms. Some of the more prestigious criminals wore heavy studded armour and wielded frighteningly customised weaponry. Serrated double sided spears, curved scimitar blades from distant lands and gruesomely spiked clubs were held high in the air as the screaming continued.

Roar looked down the line of defenders to his right and then turned back to the young Captain Guillow on his left. 'This will be unlike any war our men have fought in. These men are not an organised army from an opposition lord or invader. These men kill and steal for pleasure and will relish the chance of taking the head of any man who gets in their way. For more than half my life I have hunted men like this and to see an army of them in one place sends chills up my spine.'

Captain Guillow had been born in a small village ten miles north of Inverwall. His father had worked as the personal hunter for the local Baron and at the tender age of nine Guillow had joined him in work. His skills as a bowman and hunter did not go unnoticed by the locals and at the age of thirteen he had been sent away to join the soldiers of Inverwall during a period of recruitment. Creating a great reputation for himself during archery tournaments and in small skirmishes during the eastern war campaigns, he had been raised to the rank of Captain by the time he was twenty-one. Being the youngest Captain in the history of Inverwall came with a weight of expectations and being from a humble family did not help. It had become tradition that the position of Captain was reserved for noble family members. He knew the son of a lowly hunter would not keep such a position unless he worked harder than everyone else. Every morning he would train with his men and gain their trust and respect. It was not his intention to put on a show when the Knightguards arrived at Inverwall; he only ever wanted what was best for the Meridian realms and would do anything to defend them.

Standing next to Roar, Captain Guillow knew this was a man with a similar upbringing to himself. They had only known a humble and simple life. If circumstance had been different during his youth, he himself may have joined the Wolves of Glory or one of the other mercenary groups.

'How good are you with that?' asked Roar, pointing towards the longbow in the young Captain's hand. 'I hear you are the best in the Realms?'

Guillow smiled and shrugged his soldiers. 'I've won a few tournaments, yes. But during the last tournament in Meridia, I came second to some newcomer from Dain. The man was flawless, and his technique was impeccable.'

'So, you are second best now?' asked Roar.

'You are only as good as your last arrow,' replied the young Captain.

Roar let himself give out a quiet chuckle. 'And what was your last arrow?'

'It's buried in the neck of a Dakha soldier down in the south fields.' Guillow smiled before nodding out at the army to the north. 'When do you think they will attack? I see they have some ladders over there,' he pointed out.

'I spotted the same thing,' said Roar. 'I didn't expect as many of them.'

'Surprised they haven't attacked yet,' noted Captain Guillow.

Roar gritted his teeth together with his stiff jaw. 'It seems they are trying to scare us first. They should attack soon while the adrenaline is still coursing through their veins.'

No sooner had the old Wolf finished his sentence than the screaming stopped. Through the centre of the crowd emerged the unmistakable figure of Harbour Master Neg. The fat leader sat unevenly on an equally fat horse. The greasy pirate raised his sword high into the air and called for the attack.

Roar was not looking at the Harbour Master; instead, his eyes were transfixed to the left. Sat atop an all-white horse was Captain Bruar of the Flaming Sails.

Roar notched an arrow to his bow, pulled the string taut and released within seconds. The arrow sped through the air with no back lift. Roar's ears went silent and time slowed, as he watched the arrow make its way towards the intended target. His heart sank as the arrow dropped quite a distance short of Bruar and buried deep into the ground.

Captain Guillow turned to the old Wolf and was close to slapping him about the ears. Deciding against it, he controlled himself. Instead, with the temper of a wild griffin, chastised the mercenary.

'Roar, you should have waited.' The young Captain looked out to the intended target. 'I assume that is the man who gave you the scars around your face?'

Roar spat off the battlements as the fighters from Brigands Bay to the north erupted into laughter at the short arrow. Anger filled Roar, anger mostly focused at himself. Through the years he had met countless men just as evil as Bruar, but none had ever made him this angry and full of hatred.

As Roar watched the first of the outlaws take a step forward and march towards the wall, he turned to the young Captain next to him. 'It is not because of these scars and the broken jaw I want that man dead. It is not because he humiliated me in front of my men when he beat me within an inch of my life.' Roar thought of his young comrade Torquil. 'I want this man dead because if it were not for him some good men would still be alive.'

Chapter 66

WITH NO Inverwallian soldiers stationed in the killing fields and the Brigands attacking from the north, Sir Oakheart paced the southern battlements full of thought. He could hear the beating of Dakha drums and could see the emergence of a large battering ram appear at the centre of the column. The South Wall was too tall for the enemy to use ladders, and Sir Oakheart knew the only way in for the Dakha would be the main gate.

As a knight, Sir Oakheart had never liked the use of fire in any war. However, he had no choice in this situation.

'Now!' the Knightguard commanded, as he raised his sword high above his head and then pointed the blade out towards the Dakha.

Two dozen fire-arrows were sent into the air in the direction of the giant battering ram. These arrows sounded crueller than the normal kind. The noises they made through the sky were like hissing thunder.

The first set of arrows hit the structure hard, and within seconds, a second volley landed. In the moments to follow, the wooden structure began to smoke, and the flames grew. Screams of pain from the Dakha soldiers pushing the ram followed the growing heat.

Cheers of joy and pride rang from the Inverwallian defenders stationed on the wall. The cheers were short lived, however, as no sooner had the flames began to grow than they were extinguished by Dakha soldiers carrying buckets of water. Passed from soldier to soldier a conveyor of water was thrown onto a smouldering battering ram.

Sir Oakheart cursed under his breath and should have known Badrang would anticipate the use of fire arrows. With the line of water buckets, fire would not destroy the structure and would barely slow it down. Still he ordered more arrows but with the wooden ram now soaked with water, they did almost nothing. The knight was running out of ideas quickly and knew it would not be long before the ram would reach the gate.

The Inverwallian arrows continued to hail down on the advancing Dakha horde as they made their way up the steady slope towards the south gate of Inverwall. The arrow supply had lasted the duration of the siege and it was unfortunate there was not enough men to fire the ammunition. The Inverwallian soldiers, who did not have a bow and were stationed atop the battlements, were given slings to hurl rounded pebbles down at the invaders.

Still the endless horde marched with destructive intent.

The massive battering ram eventually reached the high gate of Inverwall. The cheers and war-cries of the southern tribes echoed and droned through the city.

The Inverwallian men stationed behind the gate breached the door in anticipation for the first knock. It came less than a minute after and shook the very foundations of the south wall. The Inverwallians pressing against the door were repelled back half a yard as the vibrations shook them to the bone.

'BRACE THE GATES!' bellowed Sir Oakheart as the ram was swung again into the steel door. 'We must buy our archers some more time!'

Still the relentless cheering of the Dakha cut deep into the Inverwallians. Each man knew today was their last, but none were willing to lay down under such pressure. They knew with men like Sir Oakheart atop the wall, Sir Shale still coughing blood among them and Sir Lenath lying in his bed, they would never see a greater day.

The large soldier nicknamed Stonesword, who was stationed at the back of the inner column, dropped his sword and shield.

'You there, back in line!' shouted his Captain.

Stonesword ignored his Captain's command and ran through his comrades towards the southern gate, where he joined those on the front line embracing every impact.

The Captain was furious. 'I said back in line!'

Stonesword again ignored him and rammed his own broad shoulder hard into the gate, making a loud thud of his own. 'I am with you, brothers, let's see how long we can hold this monster.'

Sir Oakheart never appreciated dissent in the ranks, but with the valour shown by Stonesword he admired the young soldier who had duelled with Sir Nolan immensely. He scanned around his soldiers and respected every one of them. 'All here are worthy of knighthood,' Sir Oakheart muttered under his breath.

It would not be long before the gate would bend under the impact and Sir Oakheart wanted to be there to meet the forces of Badrang when it happened. He called to a nearby archer general. 'You are to lead the wall. I am going to the courtyard.'

The archer general returned a nod. 'May Amundsen watch over you, Sir, it has been an honour fighting with you.'

'You too, brother,' replied Sir Oakheart as he unsheathed his longsword and unclipped the long white cape of the Meridian Knightguards. The perfectly white cloth dropped to the stone floor of the battlements. The broad knight turned and made his way down the carved steps.

The sight of seeing their commander enter the courtyard, weapon in hand, had an instant reaction in the hearts of the brave defenders. Those not bracing the gates from the never-ending thuds, raised their weapons high and roared with confidence as the former

Knightguard Commander took up position at the head of the first column.

In the distance, Sir Oakheart could hear the screams on the northern battlements. He gave a quick glance and could see the invaders from Brigands Bay were now on the wall. Chills ran up his spine and sweat dripped from his forehead. He thought of all the great men who would die today. When he was in Meridia he knew there was no chance of winning this war. With the vast forces of Badrang to the south and the Brigands from the north, the Southern Warlord had bettered him. He thought of young Captain Guillow, and of the Wolves of Glory. 'Good luck, friends,' he muttered.

He could feel the eyes of his brave companions on his back as the booms continued on the south gate. 'Men, today we fight our final battle. Badrang seeks to take what does not belong to him and today we die stopping him. We all have friends, family, companions, who live north of here and we owe them our lives.'

A deafening roar followed the man they called Sir Oakheart. He felt pride he had never felt before. In all his campaigns, and throughout all his years of service, this was his toughest challenge. He thought of his time with the Queen and their forbidden love. He thought of his time in the east campaigning with his brothers. He looked back on his time joking with Sir Shale and Sir Lenath. He thought of training with Sir Nolan and Sir Talon in his younger years. In all his life, he had never been happier.

The Former Knightguard Commander turned back to the gate as another loud smash landed and a blinding beam of daylight pierced through the open gate.

Chapter 67

LOOD COVERED his eyes and screams filled his ears. The world was still, yet time moved faster. He was tired, yet fresh, and death had never been closer to him. He felt like a man half his age as he swung his longsword left, right, up and down, with malicious intent. Sweat ran down his cheeks as outlaws exhaled their last breaths by his hands. He had not fought with such passion in years. With every kill he knew he did these lands a service, a service he would never be paid for, but Roar did not care about money anymore.

All kinds of foreign weaponry were used by the pirates of Brigands Bay, weapons that were not mentioned in any book on swordplay. Serrated spears, spiked clubs, curved scimitars from distant lands, ripped at the defending soldiers' armour. The Brigand's blades were barbed with potent poisons to ensure death to the defenders within days.

Roar continued to fight alongside his fellow Wolves of Glory. Mallard and Willem were also coated in blood, some of it their own. Though largely uninjured, they had sustained a couple of minor wounds to their legs and arms. They were on the front line against the invading Brigands. More and more outlaws climbed the tall ladders and flooded amongst the defenders.

Roar allowed himself a quick glance out into the northern fields – still Bruar and Harbour Master Neg sat atop their horses, watching the carnage unfold from a distance. The old Wolf dodged a swipe from a particularly ugly pirate and countered. He then went on to kill three more corsairs with two swipes of his own.

Captain Guillow still lived and although his skills as an archer were now useless, he fought bravely with a sword and shield. He knew his time was coming but he fought on defiantly. Blocking a spiked mace with his shield, he drove his shortsword deep into the belly of an attacker and spat.

'Fall back towards the stairs!' he commanded as he looked over to the old Wolf. 'Roar, get out of there. We will hold them where the wall is narrowest!'

Roar and the Wolves of Glory could not hear the Captain of Inverwall call to them. Instead, they continued to kill anyone who got in their way. They were oblivious to the Inverwallians falling back and were about to be surrounded by outlaws from all angles.

Captain Guillow had a choice to make: fall back and leave the Wolves to their fate, or rush in and help them. The Captain took less than half a second to make his decision. He gritted his teeth together and dropped his shield. He approached the first corsair he saw, parried the blow and grasped the sword-arm of his enemy. At the same time, he drove his own short blade through the gut of the pirate and wrestled the blade from his hand. Now armed with two weapons, the Grandcaptain of Inverwall cut a path of death through the invaders. He kept his eyes on Roar and the rest of the stranded group as he dodged, parried and carved. Catching one slash on his arm, he almost dropped a sword but soon regained his composure and countered with an attack of his own. He fought and spat until he finally reached his surrounded companions.

'Roar, we are going to make a final stand to the east. The wall is narrow there.'

Through blood stained eyes Roar nodded before giving a quick glance out to Bruar and Neg – they were no longer to be seen. A rush of blood went to the old Wolf's head, but he quickly thought better of it. Although a skilled fighter, he thought Bruar would not risk his own life on the walls.

'Lead the way,' said Roar.

Captain Guillow nodded in return and looked at the survivors around him. He then looked past them and could see a line of fresh invaders marching towards them atop the battlements.

'If we make it to the steps, we have a chance of holding them longer there,' barked the young Captain.

At the same time, Mallard and Willem killed a stray corsair who was about to attack Guillow from behind. The remaining Wolves of Glory, and the surrounding defenders, began to fight their way east towards the stone steps of the northern wall. Roar fought shoulder to shoulder with the Captain, who was swinging his two blades freely. The smell of death lingered in the air as blood flew high after each kill.

'We are almost at the steps; it will be difficult for them to get through us there,' said Captain Guillow. After he spoke, he stopped dead in his tracks and looked at Roar. His eyes were still, and he could feel the cold steel bury deep into his back. He felt the warm blood trickle down his spine as he fell to his knees and died.

Taken aback with shock, Roar looked past the young Captain. He could not believe what he saw. Quickly, he looked down at the dagger protruding from the young Captain's back. He recognised the dagger immediately – it was the same blade Rommel had once tried to kill Bruar with. Roar looked back to the Captain of the Flaming Sails, standing a dozen yards from the man he had just killed.

Captain Bruar wore the same smile he had worn countless times in the past. He knew how angry the old Wolf would now be. He thought of what Torquil had said to him weeks past which had stuck with him. "*How about putting a sword in his hands and see what the outcome would be in a REAL fight?*" Bruar had always been a proud man, and ever since that comment, he had felt he needed to prove himself.

Now at the narrowest point in the wall, both sides faced off. If the corsairs of Brigands Bay were to get to the steps, they would have a clear run at the backs of the Inverwallian defenders in the south courtyard.

Rage coursed through Roar's veins, as he grasped the handle of Rommel's dagger and dragged it out of Guillow's lifeless body. Longsword in one hand, and the dagger in the other, he took a step towards his nemesis.

Bruar, with a smirk painted on his face, opened his arms. 'You are surprised to see me here, Roar!?'

Roar said nothing and took another step forward.

'How many friends of yours have I killed now? Let me see, there has been a couple, hasn't there? Was this another one?' He nodded past Roar to the youngest Captain in Inverwall's history. 'Oh yes, and I almost forgot about the Innkeeper at Balderstone.'

There was no sign of a reaction on the face of Roar as he walked amongst the dead men on his way to the Captain of the Flaming Sails.

'I have killed your friends, beaten you to within an inch of your life and I have no doubt you want to kill me,' continued Captain Bruar.

Still Roar did not speak and continued his march along the battlements.

'So, it comes to this, Roar,' said Bruar, as he unsheathed his sword and pointed it in the direction of the old Wolf. 'Me and you, in a REAL fight!'

Roar finally smiled. 'This won't be a fight, Bruar. This is going to be an execution.'

Chapter 68

I T H A D not taken the three companions long to settle into living at the camp. Their tent was now properly furnished and had an almost cosy atmosphere to it. Hilvard had put his skills as a woodsman to good use and had built up a nice supply of wood and timber for the outlaws to use.

Bjorn had set about reinforcing the foundations of the main structures within the camp. With the high winds of autumn on their way, he was sure the tents would now hold against the bad weather.

Leif had set about training some of the outlaws. With the use of wooden swords, he taught them proper footwork when one-on-one with a trained soldier. He was surprised by the lack of woodland knowledge within the camp. He was not so clever on survival himself, but some of the inhabitants did not even know what they could eat and what they couldn't.

It was coming close to evening and scouts had reported a caravan carrying two prisoners from a nearby village would be heading to Dain. This would be the perfect first target in their war against the tyranny of the Grandcaptain and his men.

In the past few days, Fiora and Leif had grown a little closer. They were similar people, and both knew it. They were both ambitious and clearly had the same opinions on the world. Fiora had never discussed her past with the young wanderer, something that intrigued Leif. However, it would never be something he would push to find out. With the time they spent planning, they were developing what was close to a friendship, much to the disdain of Garrow.

Garrow and Fiora had led the group together for months and through that, had developed a romantic relationship. They ate together, they slept together, and they fought together. Garrow did not like the outspoken voice Leif possessed.

Leif had never been a jealous man, and even now he still knew what was his and what wasn't. However, he still possessed a strange feeling for the red-headed outlaw.

'Warin, Marek and Emrest, you three will be coming with me and Leif on this evening. We have all had enough time to plan this, and I will not tolerate any slip ups,' called out Fiora as she addressed the campsite. 'We all know our jobs and together we can strike a serious blow at Duke Delgath's troops.' She smiled as the campsite applauded with agreement. 'Tonight marks the beginning of our revolution.'

The applause rang louder as Leif leaned over and whispered in Fiora's ear. 'See, just a little planning and look, I've turned this campsite around.' He then smiled mischievously and gave her a wink.

Fiora responded with a discreet elbow into his ribs and returned his wink with one of her own.

The evening had come, and the five companions had made their way to the spot of the ambush. Each outlaw waited beside the road for the horse-drawn prison carriage to approach. They saw two riders ahead of the carriage, where another two soldiers sat.

'I count four,' whispered Leif from the darkness of the trees.

'No, five – there is always one in the carriage with the prisoners,' replied Fiora.

'Ok, five soliders. The last one will be difficult. He knows we cannot hit him with arrows.' Leif turned back to the other outlaws. 'You three are to stay here until we give the signal.'

Each man nodded and loaded an arrow to their bows.

Before he and Fiora moved from their cover, Leif finally added, 'Remember, these men do not know we are here OR how many of us there are.'

Leaving the group, the two outlaws emerged from the cover of the trees and stepped in front of the approaching cart.

In the light of the moon, Leif spoke. 'In the name of the northern people, halt this wagon and release the prisoners.'

'BANDITS! Unsheathe your swords, men!' shouted the head soldier at the front of the column.

Leif let out a loud whistle and an arrow sped past the head of the soldier. The young wanderer raised his hand and smiled. 'No one needs to be hurt here. You have people who do not belong to you and we would like you to release them.'

'Stay your blades, men! We are surrounded!' called the soldier, who had panic written across his face. He returned his gaze back to Leif. 'This is a bold move, bandit. One my Grandcaptain will not take lightly.'

Leif continued to smile and unsheathed his own sword. 'I would not expect him to take this lightly. Now are you going to release the prisoners? Please instruct your comrade to come out of the carriage. I have the area surrounded with archers – one false move and we turn you all into pin cushions.'

The solider almost knew for sure they were not surrounded but he did not possess the courage necessary to question the bold outlaw. 'You heard him, men, bring out the prisoners.'

When the captives had been brought out and unshackled, they were sent over to Leif and Fiora. Upon seeing their rescuers, both prisoners held back tears. One a man, the other a woman, they made their way to behind the two outlaws. Leif held his nerve and turned back to the five guards of Dain. 'You all know following us is not an option. Even with two prisoners, you will not catch us. We know the forests better than you.' Leif allowed himself a pause, and the soldiers to think about what he said before continuing. 'I ask for only one thing.'

'Have you not already asked enough?' replied the soldier.

'I think a man in my position can ask for whatever he wants,' said Leif, with smug confidence. He whistled again, and another arrow shot out from the darkness and narrowly missed the soldier.

'You have some nerve, boy. You know our Grandcaptain will tear this forest apart to find you. So, what is it you ask?'

'I ask that you convey a message to your leader. You are to tell him the people of these lands will no longer stand for tyranny or injustice. This land is for everyone, not just the corrupt. The people are tired of living from the scraps of his table. Tonight, he has suffered a blow, but it is a grain of dust compared to what the common people have suffered in recent times. Tell your leader–' Leif looked at Fiora and gained further courage before turning back– 'we are coming for him.'

'And may I ask,' said the soldier, with explicit sarcasm, 'who is coming for him?'

Leif laughed. 'Never was big on names but tell him, Leif is coming for him.'

There was a small lapse of silence before another voice added. 'And so is Fiora Delgath.'

Chapter 69

CARNAGE FOLLOWED the opening of the South Gate. The Dakha flooded the courtyards of Inverwall like water into a leaky vessel. Invaders spilled out into the defenders as steel, iron and flesh clashed. Screams and roars were heard throughout the mass of fighters on both sides. Blood stained the stone floor as lifeless bodies fell to the ground.

Sir Oakheart fought like nothing anyone had ever seen. Killing and maiming invaders to his left, right and front, he didn't stop. Fighting with the strength of five men, he drenched his sword in enemy blood. Dodging, cutting and thrusting, he found himself fighting next to his Knightguard companion Sir Shale.

Still spitting blood, the young knight Sir Shale held his feet as he countered attacks from all angles. Before an attack could land at Sir Oakheart's back, Shale leapt forward and gripped the spear. He then drove his longsword deep into the chest of the Dakha soldier.

Sir Oakheart turned in time to see the spear that would have killed him had Shale not intervened. He nodded with thanks towards his companion. The former Knightguard Commander then froze with shock as a thrown javelin landed hard through Sir Shale's throat. He watched as his fearless knight-brother gargled his last breath through his blood-filled mouth and fell to the floor.

Rage, pain and mist filled Sir Oakheart's mind. Through the mist he could see Queen Orellia call him. In this daze, he felt his enemies close in around him. Having lost everything that meant something to him in this world, he was going to die trying to avenge it all. Before a spear could pierce his chest, he cleared his head and rolled the point of the blade. Side stepping, he brought his gold-hilted longsword down through the air and split his enemy's head in two. Blood burst from the neck up like an erupting volcano and coated all those standing in the vicinity.

The experienced knight wheeled about again and growled like a wild animal. Before a low attack from a sword could catch him in the thigh, he stepped back and counterstruck down through the air. As he looked about the area, he could see fewer and fewer Inverwallian uniforms. It would not be long before he was encircled by enemy soldiers. Looking at the floor near an enemy, he saw the dead body of Stonesword, three spears protruding from the young soldier's abdomen.

Sir Oakheart was now past feeling any loss and beat away another two strikes. Still he fought like a madman and killed all those who dared approach him. For a moment he thought of Sir Lenath in the infirmary at the Main Keep but he did not allow himself to get distracted and swiftly snapped away.

There was a loud booming of drums in the lines behind the Dakha soldiers, signalling General Malacath was about to join the fray. Through the crowd the giant marched, greatsword in hand.

Sir Oakheart spilled further Dakha blood before turning towards the General, and within a split second, charged the monster. The sudden attack caught the undefeated Malacath off guard and Sir Oakheart crashed into his black-armoured foe. Sparks and emotions flew from the blow, as blood, sweat and tears ran down the face of the knight. The impact of going chest to chest with the monster of Blackland sent both fighters crashing to the ground.

Watching their Commander charge in the face of adversity inspired the remaining defenders of Inverwall to fight even harder. They watched as both fighters regained their feet, before both armies collided again, ensuring there was no interference in the final champion duel of Inverwall.

Circling about one another both fighters swung their weapons through the air in preparation for the fight.

'YOU WILL DIE!' called out the heavy voice of General Malacath.

'All men die!' replied Sir Oakheart.

'YOU ARE NOT THE FIRST TO TELL ME THIS. BUT I AM NO MAN!' bellowed the Champion of Badrang, before he attacked.

The heavy greatsword came crashing down towards the former Knightguard Commander. A simple attack that would have killed a lesser man, the blow was dodged with ease by the seasoned Oakheart. Returning with his own attack, he hit hard into the black armour that was guarding the chest of the monster. Sparks flew where blood should have as the General stepped back away from another attack. The duel continued for what seemed like an eternity for both fighters.

The Inverwallians and Dakha also continued their fight to the death. The number of defenders was quickly decreasing and Sir Oakheart knew it would not be long before the Dakha would finish the last of them off, along with himself.

Still locked in battle with the monster of Blackland, he fought with the strength of all the fallen Knightguard before him. A stray javelin sped through the air towards the Knightguard as gaps appeared in the Inverwallian defenders. The Knight dodged the javelin in one moment, and in another, blocked the swing of Malacath's greatsword. This was his chance; he moved forward and swung his sword with both hands from his right side. The General blocked the blow but with lightning-fast speed, the Knight attacked again, this time from the left. Staggered by the second attack, the General was off-balance. Sir Oakheart took a small step back before lunging forward and driving the point of his sword through the chainmail between the General's torso and hips.

The monster staggered back and gave a heavy grunt. The General then reached down with a heavily gauntleted fist and dragged the knight's blade out of his gut. He swiped and caught the Knightguard hard across the face with the hilt of the greatsword. Blood began to fall from the darkness of his helmet as he grunted again.

Sir Oakheart took a step back after the blow to his face. He watched as General Malacath fell to one knee and dropped the greatsword that had killed Sir Nolan.

'You bleed like a man,' growled Sir Oakheart.

Before the Knightguard could finish the job, he felt the sting of cold steel hit the left side of his ribs. He cursed and killed the attacker as he felt the warm blood pour down his side. Another sharp pain hit him from behind, and then another from the right. All around him the Dakha closed in, spears in hand keeping their distance from the Knight. He could see through his closing eyes, the Champion of Badrang fall from his knees and was now lying face down in the earth.

As the southern invaders closed in, the knight fell to one knee and let his sword slide from his right hand. Raising his left hand to wipe away the blood from his forehead he welcomed the peace of death. He felt his eyes begin to drop as he heard the last of the Inverwallian defenders die, and the Dakha hordes cheer their gruesome victory. Through red mist he looked ahead, and in the distance, could see the womanly figure of Queen Orellia, his one true love. He made no attempt to stand and instead reached out an open palm for her to take. He knew he could now tell her how he truly felt. He could now be with her.

No Dakha soldier dared be the one to have the final blow; they all watched as the Knightguard released a heavy sigh and fell onto his back.

Sir Oakheart, former Commander of the Knightguards of Meridia, was dead.

Chapter 70

ROAR WAS not surprised when he saw how well Captain Bruar handled a sword. He knew men like the Captain do not become the leader of a group like The Flaming Sails without being able to spill blood when necessary. It did not matter – Roar knew he was going to kill the seasoned corsair.

The opening exchange of swordplay was masterful and all in attendance could not help but marvel at both fighters' skills. The Commander of The Wolves of Glory and the Captain Flaming Sails duelled without interruption for a full ten minutes, before a mistake was made. As Roar took a side step to his right he was hit with a sudden cramp in his left calf. He staggered slightly, but quickly regained his composure and blocked the swing of Captain Bruar's cutlass. He cursed his aging muscles and took a step back.

Captain Bruar smirked at his adversary. 'Two seasoned fighters battling it out. Guess I'm not the pushover you thought I would be?' He spat towards the old Wolf and launched another quick assault.

Parrying with the longsword in his right hand, Roar took a swipe with the dagger in his left, and almost caught the Captain in the gut.

Bruar took a step to his left and let out a chuckle. 'Almost got me there.'

Both fighters circled about one another on the narrow battlements. Matching each other's footwork step for step, they continued their battle dance.

'There isn't a man in my business who hasn't heard of your skill with a blade. You put all other bounty-hunters to shame, apparently. I see now the stories are true,' said Captain Bruar.

More clashing of steel was exchanged and again, neither fighter landed a telling attack. Still Roar said nothing as he thought of all the innocent people his enemy had killed. During a brief interval and before the next exchange began, he sheathed Rommel's dagger in his belt and grasped his longsword with both hands.

With the tip of his sword pointing high into the air, Roar stared at his reflection in the blade. He had never been a religious man and was not about to start asking the gods for any favours. He gripped the handle tighter and awaited his enemy's next move.

'Still doubting yourself, Roar?' asked Bruar from across the stoned battlements. The Captain took a step forward and sliced his blade through the air with both hands. Meeting only the steel of Roar, the Captain cursed and attacked twice more before again stepping back.

The corsair smirked at his foe. 'This is a bit of a stalemate. You seem to have the ability to block all my moves, and I yours. How long have those tired old arms of yours got left in them, Roar?'

Again, the Captain launched forward and found nothing but more swordplay as Roar dodged and parried all swings coming from the corsair. As both fighters circled about one another again, they could hear the Dakha cheers ring out from the south courtyard. Roar knew this meant the last of the Inverwallian defenders stationed there had been killed.

Knowing it no longer mattered if they held the steps, Roar knew his final act would be to kill the leader of The Flaming Sails and avenge all his fallen comrades. He was finally ready to speak. 'You do realise this has all been a game to me, Bruar? Now I feel it is time to kill you. But not before I humiliate you in front of your men.'

The old Wolf took a new battle stance and stepped forward onto his left foot and brought his sword through the air, hitting it hard against Bruar's cutlass. In a flash, Roar slammed his body forward and was now shoulder to shoulder with the Captain. He lifted up his elbow and drove it into Bruar's face. He then forced the Captain to let go of his cutlass by slamming his own sword down onto the pirate's blade. The cutlass fell to the floor with a clatter and the Captain quickly scrambled back out of reach.

Roar stood out in the open. He looked down at the Captain's blade between himself and his enemy. He allowed himself a smile of his own. 'Pick it up, Bruar, you wanted a REAL fight.'

Bruar was no longer smiling as he moved forward and picked up his weapon. He quickly scurried a couple of steps back. He tested his sword through the air before launching another venomous attack on the Commander of the Wolves of Glory.

Roar went to meet the steel, blade on blade, but faked at the last moment. Bruar had swung and hit nothing but air, taking him by shock. He had been ready to absorb the blow of metal colliding with metal and without that coming he lost his balance. He stumbled forward and was then tripped by the outstretched leg of Roar.

Now lying on his back, the Captain made a move to retrieve his blade that was now on the floor just to his left hand. As he went to lift the weapon, Roar's foot stepped on the flat of the blade and the point of the Wolf's longsword was now at Bruar's throat.

'I would say you are about as good as I thought you would be,' said Roar, before he stepped back again and allowed the Captain to rise to his feet, cutlass again in hand.

Panic was beginning to appear on Bruar's face. He looked about to his men on the west part of the wall. About to call for help, the Captain instead shook his head and launched a quick attack towards Roar.

The Old Wolf parried two of the swings and returned one of his own, before landing a hard, straight punch with his left fist, that caught Captain Bruar hard in the mouth.

Bruar went tumbling to the ground, again releasing his sword from his grasp, as blood began to trickle down his chin.

'I've owed you that punch for a long time, Bruar, but there is still so much I need to give you!' said Roar, before looking down at the fallen weapon of the Captain. 'You have one more chance to pick up that sword and kill me. A wolf always grows tired of playing with its food!'

Bruar again looked to his men behind him for assistance; none of them moved. 'Help me! Give me another sword!'

Still none of them moved.

'You cowards! You traitors! I order you to give me your swords!'

One corsair stepped forward and immediately turned back to face the rest of his ground. 'None of you are to help him. By the orders of Harbour Master Neg.' The corsair turned back and smiled at Bruar. 'You should not have killed my man back at Balderstone.'

Sheer panic painted itself across the face of Bruar. He looked back at all the Inverwallian soldiers standing behind Roar. Each one had an arrow pointed at the outlaws of Brigands Bay; the Captain knew they were waiting for the first one to interfere in his duel with Roar.

'Roar, I will leave here and never return. You will have seen the last of my face if you let me live here today!' begged the Captain.

'Pick up the sword, Bruar,' replied Roar, with calmness in his voice.

The Captain took three steps to his right, bent a knee and retrieved his weapon. 'Please, Roar,' he begged again.

Roar looked into the eyes of his enemy, with a still peace. 'You are to leave here and never return to these lands.'

'You have my word, Roar. I promise you, I never lie. You remember that about me, I never lie, Roar,' said the Captain of the Flaming Sails.

Roar nodded and took a second to sheath his own longsword back into its scabbard. He turned his back on the Captain and began to make his way towards his comrades stationed at the top of the steps.

The Captain smirked through his thin mouth and launched

himself towards the exposed back of Roar. He brought his cold steel through the air as he cackled with maniacal laughter.

Before the blade could land, Roar spun round, dagger in hand. He caught the sword-hand of the Captain and at the same time, drove the point of Rommel's knife deep into the heart of Bruar. He said nothing as the lifeless leader of The Flaming Sails fell to the floor.

The outlaws across the wall all unsheathed their weapons. Roar turned back towards his companions at the steps. He was ready to end it all, he was ready to die. Howling the war-cry of the Wolves of Glory, Roar and the last surviving defenders of Inverwall charged their enemies on the northern battlements.

After five days of siege, Badrang had taken Inverwall.

Epilogue

A HEAVY SUN beat down on the travellers as they reached the beautiful city of Meridia. They had been travelling for two full days before they arrived at the capital of the Meridian Realms. At the head of the marching column, Rommel and Sir Talon rode side by side.

Rommel had enjoyed his conversations with the new Knightguard Commander and had a lot of respect for the man who had sworn his life to serve the Queen and her people. Sir Talon had told him of his campaigns in the East with Sir Oakheart, Sir Lenath and Sir Nolan. Rommel knew it had been difficult to leave his brothers to die in Inverwall.

'He has faith in you, Sir Talon. He gave you his position because he knows you are capable of greatness,' said Rommel, before his mind wandered back to the fate of his own friend Roar. He had a frightening image of his friend lying dead, covered in blood, before he snapped his mind away. He shook his head and shuddered. 'Our friends have sacrificed so much, so we can live. We owe them greatness.'

Sir Talon nodded as he steered his horse past a large stone in the middle of the road. 'You are right, Rommel. I have come north to do the best I can for my brothers. There is much to be done before Badrang arrives.'

'When do you expect him to attack?' asked Rommel.

'I do not know. He may wait until winter, or he may wait until next spring. I must speak with the council and get their opinions, but first there is some urgent business I must attend to. When we arrive in the city, there is something I must do. When I am finished, I will send for you and Hunter. You can wait at The Laughing Prince Inn – we will make sure you have a room and food there,' said Sir Talon.

Rommel, who was still unsure if he and Hunter were going to stay long in the capital city, agreed and as they entered through the south gates shook hands with his new companion from atop their horses.

'We will wait for you at the Inn,' said Rommel as he shook the knight's hand. He took a quick glance and looked down at the scroll in Sir Talon's left hand. 'Good luck Sir Talon, whatever it is you are doing.'

After parting ways, Sir Talon and the soldiers from Inverwall turned left towards White Castle. Atop his horse, he rode through the cobbled streets as the common people gazed in amazement at the returning Knightguard. He could not help but notice the amount of homeless people he passed. He knew most of them would be refugees from Inverwall.

Better to be homeless than to be dead, thought the Knightguard Commander.

He turned up through a different street and could see the high tower of Whitecastle, the home of Queen Orellia Kinlay and her Knightguard council. Upon reaching the stone steps he turned back to the Captain of the troops he had taken north. 'Please have the men assigned to squadrons stationed in the south quarters. Pass on my thanks to each of them.'

'It will be done, Sir,' replied the Captain, before saluting and turning his horse in the opposite direction.

Sir Talon dismounted his own horse and tied the reins to a nearby post. He then turned back to the steps and began to ascend towards the high oak doors of White Castle. He reached out and pulled open one side of the doors and entered. The corridors of the castle were dark and gloomy. The tapestries looked unwashed and the candles remained unlit. The air was cold and damp, so different from when he was last here.

He made his way toward the west wing but before he could reach the first step came face to face with another member of the Knightguard.

'Talon!? It is great to see you, brother! We received your raven this morning and were expecting you about now,' said the Knightguard as he pressed a clenched fist to his chest in the customary salute.

'Thank you, Locke. It is good to be back,' replied Sir Talon.

'Where are you heading? I believe our Queen is in the East Wing, in her study,' said Sir Locke, who wore the same clean white Meridian robes.

'I am on my way to the council room; I must speak with Blake,' said Sir Talon. First things first, he thought.

'Blake? I believe he is in the council room, yes. When you are done with him and the Queen, pay us a visit down at the Griffin Quarters. We would like to know how our brothers are faring. We heard about Nolan. We had the ceremony yesterday.'

Sir Talon showed little reaction. 'Thank you, Locke. I will see you all later today. I have some news from Oakheart.'

Both Knightguards saluted and parted ways. Sir Talon walked the spiral, stone-steps towards the council room of White Castle. He eventually reached the heavy-set door, but before he entered he looked down either side of the corridors. No one was watching, so he unsheathed his sword and entered the large room.

Sat in a chair near the window, looking down on the city, was Sir Blake, the man Sir Oakheart had been positive was a traitor to the Meridian Realms. Sir Blake sat cross-legged looking out into the daylight, longsword spread across his lap. His bald head shone in the sun, as he caught Sir Talon's eye.

Neither Knight said a word as moments passed. Sir Blake

eventually stood and was now holding his longsword in his right hand. He nodded towards the new Knightguard Commander.

Sir Talon, who also had his bare sword grasped in his fingers, returned the nod. Both knights made their way around the large circular council chamber until they were face to face. Silence continued, as both knights studied each other up and down, almost sizing one another up.

The new Knightguard Commander moved forward and reached out his right hand. His open palm was then met by Sir Blake's, and Sir Talon finally spoke. 'It is good to see you, brother, what news from our Lord Badrang?'

Printed in Great Britain
by Amazon

61380419R00201